I0687201

TIMELESS ESCAPES

A Collection of Summer Stories

Ruth A. Casie
Lita Harris
Emma Kaye
Nicole S. Patrick
Julie Rowe

Timeless Scribes
Publishing

Timeless Scribes Publishing LLC

Print   ISBN-10: 0-9910520-3-X
         ISBN-13: 978-0-9910520-3-5

Digital ISBN-10: 0-9910520-2-1
         ISBN-13: 978-0-9910520-2-8

Cover created by Julie Schroeder Designs
Edited by Mallory Braus
Copy Edited by Michael Mandarano

This edition published by arrangement with Timeless Scribes Publishing LLC.

www.TimelessScribes.com

Contents

Introduction
by Roxanne St. Claire

There's a reason we call the perfect romance novel "a beach read." There's something insanely pleasurable about turning the pages of a love story while kissed by sunshine and caressed by a warm sea breeze, the steady splash of ocean waves as nature's background music. The only thing as delightful as a trip to the beach to get lost in a book is the book that does the traveling for you.

On the fast-turning pages of this engaging anthology, you can take five unforgettable trips to a fictional island to fall in love over and over again. It's only a short boat ride from St. Thomas to Star Island—made all the more enjoyable if handsome Capt. Jack is your escort—a jewel in the turquoise waters of the Caribbean. There, you can escape to the Celestial Harbor resort, grab a sun-washed recliner by the sea, and meet heroes who'll take your breath away and heroines who will make you root for their happy ever after.

Each novella in this anthology gives a romance reader that something special that we love in our beach reads. You'll get a second chance at love when a couple on the brink of heartbreak uncovers a surprising secret about their marriage that forces them down a path of rediscovery. Opposites attract when a young woman trying to heal from a break up falls into the arms of that sexy boat captain and takes a ride she'll never forget...or want to end.

When a novelist seeking inspiration finds herself on the shores of Star Island, an unexpected trip to the past crashes through her writer's block and takes her on a shocking and enlightening journey to Regency England. And, finally, two stories in which friction between old friends fades when they're forced into a situation that brings out the best of each, along with the chance to finally become lovers for life.

If you have the opportunity to enjoy this beach read with your toes in the sand and an umbrella drink at your side, that will just make the experience even more pleasurable. But if you're landlocked this summer, *Timeless Escapes* is your ticket to the tropics, no sunscreen needed. But you might want a tissue to wipe a tear or two and an uninterrupted afternoon to get lost in love.

xoxo

Roxanne St. Claire

New York Times & USA Today bestselling author of The Barefoot Bay Books: The Barefoot Bay Quartet, The Barefoot Billionaires Trilogy, and The Barefoot Brides Trilogy.

www.roxannestclaire.com

Second Chance by the Sea

Ruth A. Casie

❧

Alan and Eloise Stuart are a power couple. Alan's company, Stuart Associates, is on the brink of releasing new software that will make his company the pre-eminent financial software provider.

Eloise has worked hard for the North Star Project, the not-for-profit agency focused on human trafficking awareness and prevention. In her position as North Star's executive director she is responsible for the agency's outstanding growth in both public recognition and financial contributions.

Over the course of their ten year marriage, Alan and Eloise have been focused on their careers and have grown apart.

Life takes a drastic turn when they travel to the U.S. Virgin Islands, the venue of their destination wedding, for Aunt Lil's funeral. While going through Aunt Lil's papers they find that their marriage was never registered. Will an impending natural disaster be the final straw that breaks them up or will it rekindle their love and send them back to the altar for a second chance?

❧

Dedicated to ~

My sister Scribes – you are my writing heart. I could never do this without you.

My brother and sister-in-law, Alan and Eloise. Yes, it's true their marriage wasn't registered and they had to re-marry after ten years but everything else about the story is pure fantasy. They are truly only for each other. They have a true romance.

My very understanding family for their patience and good sense to never roll their eyes when I bounce a plot idea off them.

My editor, Mallory Braus, who pushes me and helps me make the next book better than the last.

Second Chance by the Sea
by Ruth A. Casie

Eloise Alexander-Stuart stared out the window and watched their flight skim over the clear blue water on its final approach to Cyril E. King Airport in St. Thomas, U.S. Virgin Islands. A finger of runway reached out into the channel beckoning the plane to land. The sleek plane's back wheels glided over the runway's threshold and touched down with a slight bounce. The nose wheel followed. The reverse thrust of the engines and raised flaps slowed the speeding aircraft to a gentle roll. Within minutes the jet lumbered off the runway and taxied to the gate.

Alan Stuart powered up his cell phone. "Jeez, four and a half hours and already over a hundred emails."

"Alan, we should have been with her. She didn't have to die alone." Eloise let out a desolate sigh and dabbed her eyes with the last of her tissues. Two packages of spent paper hankies littered her handbag.

"I feel bad, too, but don't beat yourself up. If we knew she was sick we would have been here." He kissed her forehead.

She closed her eyes to make the pain—or was it guilt?—go away. "I know you're right but I can't believe she's gone. I spoke to her last week. She's always been there for me."

He placed his arm around her shoulder and squeezed her close. His shirt pocket vibrated with an incoming call. He peered at the display. "It's Ed."

"I'm glad we won't have to wait." Eloise looked out the window at the sun-filled sky but between the ache in her heart and the tears in her eyes she couldn't see any of its beauty.

Alan answered his phone. "Hello, Ed... Yes... By the baggage claim... Sure..." He ended the call and stashed his phone back in his pocket.

The crackling over the intercom was ignored by the passengers who were gathering the things around their seats. "Welcome to Cyril E. King Airport, St. Thomas, U.S. Virgin Islands, where the time is approximately 2:00 p.m., plenty of time for sun and rum. Please remain seated until the captain has brought the plane to a complete stop at the gate and has turned off the seat belt sign."

The jet rolled to a stop and the engines wound down. Passengers took off their seat belts and filed into the aisle queuing up to leave. Finally, the cabin door opened. The weather in New York was warm, but the ninety-five-degree heat was hot even for St. Thomas in May. They left the comfort of their first-class seats and made their way to the baggage area. The carousel lurched into action with their suitcases, high priority tags dangling, leading the march. A testament to their arriving late to JFK and barely making the flight.

"There's Ed." Alan motioned to a middle-aged man standing by the railing. The attorney looked comfortable in casual pastel clothes. They would never work on New York's Park Avenue but seemed perfect business attire for the St. Thomas climate.

"Alan. Let the porter help you with those." The man next to Ed loaded their bags on a trolley and brought them to the waiting topless jeep. Eloise opted for a seat in the back. Ed sat behind the wheel. Alan slid into the seat next to him.

"I've gotten a boat to take us directly to Lil's place rather than wait for the water taxi to the island." Ed started up the jeep and pulled it into the traffic.

Eloise bent forward over the seat backs to make certain Ed could hear her over the din of the wind and cars whizzing around them. "Can you give us a little more information about how Aunt Lil passed away?" She knotted and twisted the shredded tissue in her hand afraid but needing to hear the details.

Ed pushed against the seat and stretched his head back. He kept his eyes on the road and yelled over the wind and noise. "Wednesday afternoon Lil had trouble breathing. Her housekeeper called Captain Jack. He ferried them across to the hospital here on St. Thomas."

She could imagine the panicked housekeeper

and how Aunt Lil would have been more concerned with comforting her companion than worrying about herself. She let out a heavy sigh.

"The minute they arrived at the emergency room Dr. Baker took care of her. He told me he gave her a clean bill of health when she came in for her semiannual checkup about six—eight weeks ago."

"There weren't any warning signs?" she asked.

"No, nothing. She passed peacefully in her sleep. The death certificate says congestive heart failure."

"Thank you," she whispered glad Aunt Lil's passing had been easy. She closed her eyes and stifled a sob. She didn't think there were any tears left. But the ache grew deeper the closer she got to Aunt Lil's home.

"Ah, here we are," Ed said. He pulled the jeep onto the public dock. With the help of the boat captain, they stowed the baggage. At its narrowest point, Star Island was a quick five miles off shore, at least the way Captain Jack maneuvered his boat. He had them across the water within minutes.

Eloise's mind traveled to an earlier time. She and her parents spent the summers with Aunt Lil. Her sophomore summer wasn't any different. The lazy days without her college friends drove her to become inventive. A long-distance swimming team from California and their training schedule filled the local paper.

For years she'd been swimming in the

channel. Granted, she hadn't done any long-distance swims but the thought appealed to her. She needed a challenge. With preparation she could do this. The news articles provided details about the team's training and exercises. It was all the information she needed. She set her goal to swim the channel between Star Island and St. Thomas before she returned to New York.

Her mom—a pool paddler, not a swimmer—was not happy with her plan. Aunt Lil thought it was a great idea. She bought her a diving watch and fashionable pink goggles then sent her off to conquer the channel. The challenge suited her, not only quelling the anxiety of deep-water swimming or the endurance and ability to deal with the natural elements. It was all about goal setting and attainment.

She spent her days training and preparing. Between the wind and the current, the navigation would be tricky. She decided to stay clear of the jetty that led out to the ocean and swim the narrowest portion. The wider sections were out of the question. She knew her limits.

Two weeks before she and her parents packed up to return to New York she paced the shore. The width of the narrow channel looked more like five hundred miles than five miles. Her adrenaline pumped but still she hesitated. Although she was a strong swimmer she was no superstar. The voice in her head, the one that told her she could do this, kept nagging her to get in the water. She glanced at the path back to the house. It would be easy to call it a day but the voice mocked her. This was a defining moment. When faced with challenges would she fight or flee?

She put on her bathing cap, her goggles perched on her head, and waded into the shallows. The familiar gentle lapping eased her mind. She pulled the bright pink goggles down from her forehead and put them in place. She dove into the water. Her arms reached out and she settled into her pace. The strong current and consistent rhythm of her stroke propelled her across the water. The buoy, the halfway marker and the point of no return, loomed in front of her. She glanced at her watch. Fifteen minutes ahead of schedule—but time wasn't a factor. Completing the challenge was her goal.

She estimated another ninety minutes, give or take, to get to the other side. She filled her lungs, pushed off the buoy, and kept on swimming.

After an hour her pace began to slow. Her kicks got sloppy and her arms were like lead weights. The shore must be close. A time check indicated she'd be on the beach in ten minutes but a glance toward land told her a different story. The shore was not as close as she'd expected. She checked off her options. There weren't many. She could stop and float but her muscles would tighten and she'd be in bigger trouble. She treaded water to get her bearings. Her anxiety built to a full-blown panic but she swapped it for determination. She focused her energy and continued swimming.

"Stroke," someone yelled alongside her. "Stroke. You're close. Keep up the tempo and you'll be home free." Doing the back stroke, the swimmer stayed next to her, maintaining the cadence until they reached the shore.

She stood in the shallows, the water up to her knees. The muscles in her arms and legs screamed from overexertion. Her adrenaline plummeted and left her exhausted. Through her large gulps of air she smiled the type of smile that would last a week. She swam the channel. She met the challenge.

"That was quite impressive." He stood next to her and sluiced the water off his body.

She leaned over, her hands on her thighs, and held up one hand. One gulp of air, then another.

"Has anyone ever told you that you have a terrific smile?"

Still bent over, she turned her head and squinted at the lean, muscular physique planted next to her. Her eyes traveled from his powerful legs, up to his ripped abs and came to a screeching halt at his Paul Newman–blue eyes.

Her breath under control—well, at least from the swim—she straightened.

"My name is Alan Stuart." He held out his hand.

"Hi. I'm Eloise Alexander." She took his hand. His grip was strong and firm. Her senses ran riot from the exertion, or was it the hunk standing next to her?

"I meant it. Your swim was impressive." The broad smile that played across his face was almost as radiant as his eyes.

"Thanks for calling the cadence."

"I'd been watching you train from this side of the channel. Your pace was too fast today. Slow and steady wins the race." They ambled up to the beach together.

"Are you a lifeguard?" Visions of mouth-to-mouth resuscitation flittered through her mind.

"No, I was on the long-distance swim team at the University of Southern California and, well, I knew what to look for."

The sound of the boat horn coming into port brought Eloise back to the moment.

"Got everything?" Ed asked.

Alan gave her his hand and helped her onto the dock.

"El, you okay? You seem to be someplace else." He didn't let her hand go.

She glanced at his eyes. The ones that made every woman who met him melt. "I was thinking about the day we met."

He put his arm around her and drew her close. "Ah, you mean the day I gallantly saved your life."

She laughed and snuggled closer. "You did not. I was tired, that's all."

"Please, let me think you needed me. There are so few instances." He kissed her forehead and went over to the captain to help with their luggage.

The smile slid off her face. For a moment she felt…alone. Need him? If there was ever a time she needed him it was now, but they were set on a collision course and she had no idea of the outcome. She shook off the uneasy sensation and grabbed some of the small bags. Alan was on his cell phone.

"Anita, yeah, they have their assignments… All right… I'll check in and let you know what's going on when I have a better idea… No, I'm not certain how soon I'll be back." He punched End and slipped the phone into his pocket.

"Problems?" Eloise asked.

"No. I'll have to call the office later." He grabbed the suitcases and got them into the taxi.

Anita. The woman inserted herself into every aspect of Alan's office. As his company grew, Alan relied on Anita more and on her less, a causality of both their high-powered jobs. At first she thought his secretary was a blessing. Anita did remove some of the burden from her giving her the time she needed to spend on her own career but now her messages went unanswered. And whatever time they did have together Alan spent on the phone with Anita or the office. She looked at his retreating back and wanted him to make time for her like he did when they were first married.

"Okay, all set." Ed herded everyone into the taxi. They pulled away from the dock and headed toward the highest point on the island.

"You haven't been here in a while." Ed, in the front seat, turned to them.

"No, not for the last five years. Star Island doesn't look much different," Eloise said.

"No, nothing was here five years ago and there still isn't. Oh wait, I'm wrong. Now cell towers dot the landscape," Alan teased.

"That should make you happy." She didn't try to hide the sarcasm.

"Ouch," he said, covering his heart with his hand. "I'm deeply wounded." His cell phone rang. He gave her a pleading glance.

She shook her head turning away from him. The taxi climbed the hill and gave them a full view of the channel. With the wind in her face, her eyes slid closed and she was back on the beach.

They came out of the water where he'd left his things. She stretched out on the sand and gathered her strength.

"I have a friend's launch. I can take you back if you like?" He handed her a thermos of cold water.

She smiled. "I hadn't thought about the return. I'm certainly not going to swim." She took a long drink. "I'm lucky you were here."

He smiled at her and she was lost. No one should have eyes and a smile like that. It started a tingling in the pit of her stomach. They strolled over to the nearby pier. She took the line off the cleats and he pulled the boat away.

"Do you live here?" she asked, enjoying the wind and spray.

"No, I live in New York. I'm on vacation helping my old swim coach."

"Long-distance swimming in New York?"

He laughed and her heart beat a little faster. "No. I'm in technology for one of the large banks. I'm an active USC alum. Coach wanted to bring the seniors here for training. I got a group of my old fraternity brothers to sponsor them. I got to go along and train with them. Do you live on Star Island?" He nodded across the channel.

"No, I live in New York, too. I'm here with my parents visiting my aunt."

They saw each other every day. They swam, windsurfed, took out Jet Skis, and visited the zoo.

He taught her how to snorkel and she fell in love with the coral reefs and with Alan Stuart. Back in New York they became inseparable—best friends.

After she finished college her parents made them a dream destination wedding on Aunt Lil's beach. That was ten years ago.

She opened her handbag and touched swimming goggles and smiled. She'd grabbed them from her gym bag as an afterthought. Every year since her wedding, Aunt Lil sent her pink goggles. Her chin quivered as she choked back a sob.

They drove up the incline. "What the hell is this?" Ed said, staring at the open gate. "I locked it myself."

The taxi stopped in the circular drive alongside a Cadillac Escalade.

"Jeez." Ed slammed the taxi door. His neck corded and his nostrils flared.

"What's happening?" Alan asked as he paid the driver.

"You'll find out soon enough," Ed said. He marched to the house and got to the front door as it opened.

"Ah, finally I get to meet the power couple." A middle-aged man wearing a clichéd Caribbean linen suit and T-shirt sauntered out the front door as if he owned the place.

"Blake, you're trespassing. Gates are locked for a reason. What are you doing here?" Ed demanded.

Blake held up his hands, swaggered past Ed, and made a beeline for Alan. "You must be Alan Stuart. I'm Blake Donovan of Donovan Real

Estate. I didn't think you'd be here so soon. I left some information inside for you. We'll be leaving." He gave Alan his card.

"We? Who is we?" Alan gave the man an icy stare. "Are you for real? Scouting out the property?"

"The property is well situated. I'm glad you finally got someone to let me see the place. The views are everything you told me they would be." A man came out the door and stopped when he saw the small group. "Didn't you tell me you had an exclusive on this property?" he said, his voice clipped and ruthless.

Alan turned to see who had the audacity to come with this real estate agent. "Who the hell are you?"

"Mr. Molinetti. What are you doing here?" Ed's cool, disapproving voice matched his intimidating stance.

Blake stepped forward. "Now wait, Ed. We talked—"

"No, we didn't. *You* talked. You always talk and never seem to listen." He turned away from the man. "Mr. Molinetti, I don't know what Blake has been feeding you but Second Chance by the Sea is not for sale."

"Lillian told me she wanted to sell. It was too much for her," Blake interjected as beads of sweat dripped down the sides of his face.

Alan glanced at Eloise. "Ed, get them out of here."

Eloise got out of the car and marched up to the group. "Gentlemen, I'm Eloise Alexander."

"My condolences, Ms. Alexander." Mr. Molinetti was gracious enough to look sincere.

"Thank you but more than your condolences, I would rather you both leave," Eloise said.

"Do you understand who you're talking to?" Blake shifted uncomfortably from one foot to the other.

"Actually, at this moment I don't care." Eloise sailed into the house.

Alan stared after her. That wasn't how his social-worker wife usually handled situations but it was effective if out of character.

Mr. Molinetti gave Blake a scathing stare and turned to Ed. "I'm sorry about this."

Ed held up his hand. "Lillian's answer was final. There isn't anything else to discuss."

"When Ms. Alexander is ready to discuss selling the property please contact me. We can handle this between us." Mr. Molinetti dealt out his card to Ed and Alan. "Blake, let's leave these people alone."

The two men got into the Escalade and drove off. Ed and Alan stared after them.

"I was going to tell you once the memorial service was over. Molinetti has been waving cash all over the island, talking about buying up land. He approached Lil. She spoke to the locals in town and quickly figured him out. If she sold, the locals would be put out of business. Molinetti wants the entire area in order to build an exclusive hotel complex. From the plans he showed Lil and me this property is the linchpin for his resort." They stepped through the front door into a large open room.

"Really? Why?" Alan went to the bar and took two cold beers out of the fridge.

"Location. Over the years, as people on the

hill sold out, Lil bought their property. She owns it all. The views here are magnificent. Lil told him no last week. Perhaps he thinks the new owners will have a different answer." Ed took the offered can and popped the top.

"Mr. Molinetti is the type of man who doesn't take no for an answer." Alan took a long pull of beer. He had taken an immediate dislike to the man.

"No, he won't. Several of your neighbors approached Lil. It appears Mr. Donovan is telling them Lil changed her mind and decided to sell. She had a hell of a time convincing them she had no intention of leaving the place. It came to a tense face-off between her and Donovan. The neighbors stood behind her."

"And he has the balls to come here now?" He shook his head in disbelief.

"Donovan is not your brightest star as far as working large deals." Ed walked over to the window and looked out over the pool.

"I guess not. A top-notch resort could be good for the island." Ed's jaw tensed. Alan knew where Ed stood on the question. "So you're against a large resort on Star Island."

"One underwritten by Molinetti and his group, yes."

∞ℂ℞

"No, Morgan, I haven't told him. There's been a lot to organize over the last two days. We came back from Aunt Lil's memorial service a few minutes ago." Eloise rolled her eyes glad her BFF, Morgan who was on the other end of the phone, couldn't see her.

"I hope you know what you're doing," Morgan said.

"I spoke with the developer. I rejected his offer. We aren't interested in selling the property," Eloise said.

"So you and Alan decided."

Her mouth dropped open. "I…I didn't speak to Alan about the offer," she stammered, trying to decide what to say.

"Do you think it was wise not to discuss the deal with him? He's the whiz kid with finance and business. Why didn't you talk it over with Alan and let him take care of it?"

"I always handle our personal accounts," she said, biting her lip. Now she wasn't so certain.

"I don't think this is a personal issue. This isn't like you, El. What's going on?"

"Nothing. I may have jumped the gun with this but Alan will understand. He's been difficult to speak to about almost everything. He's deep into this National Bank project."

"Why haven't you told him yet?" Morgan's voice was saturated with exasperation.

"You don't simply blurt this out over the morning paper or afternoon cocktails." Her bravado returned.

"That's not acceptable." Morgan bit out each word.

She winced at the command in Morgan's voice. This conversation wasn't going to get any better.

"I need to go back inside." She searched for a reason to end the call amicably.

"Oh no, you don't. You've got to tell him

sooner or later."

Couldn't Morgan drop it? They'd gone over this for weeks. "We're going over Aunt Lil's papers. Not my favorite thing."

"Of course, but don't think I'm letting you off easy. We're not done."

"I love you, too." She headed toward the house.

"I know," Morgan relented. "You'll be fine. Call if you need to talk and, El, tell Alan."

She knew she was running out of time but she couldn't find the right moment. She absently rubbed her arm. Maybe there wasn't a right hour or minute for this news. Maybe the entire idea was crazy.

"I will. Bye." She ended the call and held the side of the phone close to her lips. For a moment she was an apprehensive teen standing at the edge of the shore trying to decide what to do. If only it was as simple as stepping into the water. She joined Alan inside.

"I don't like going through Aunt Lil's things." Eloise, her arms crossed tightly in front of her, peered over Alan's shoulders. Organized stacks of papers and folders covered the table, not at all Aunt Lil's style. Organized chaos described her desk and filing system.

"There's no one else," Alan said, his head buried in Aunt Lil's financial papers.

"Sometimes it's hard to comprehend. I expect her to parade through the door any minute." Eloise dropped her arms and reluctantly took a seat next to him.

"I knew she was never well organized. I'd be laughing if this mess wasn't so bad. She has bills for work done on the place three years ago. She paid this one twice and here is the check for the overpayment, never deposited." He waved the outdated check in the air and tossed it back onto the pile.

"She had enough money, didn't she?" Eloise leaned forward.

"Yes, yes, more than she needed. This has nothing to do with her finances but everything to do with her organizational skills. This will take some time to straighten out. Time I haven't got."

No, she knew he had a lot on his plate at the company. The engagement with National Bank was huge. If this program was successful he could write his own ticket with any other financial firm. The last thing he needed was this mess.

Alan looked up from the papers in his hand. His mouth dropped open. "El, have you seen this? When Molinetti was here with Donovan he left us an outstanding bid for this property and he wants an answer immediately."

"Yes. I declined his offer." She picked at something on her shorts. She didn't look at Alan.

Alan's hand fell to the table with a thump that made her jump.

"You told him what? Why would you make such a huge decision without discussing the offer with me?" She was startled by the challenge in his tone.

Morgan had warned her. What were her choices? Selling off the property would destroy hundreds of people. After several moments of staring at him blankly she found her tongue.

"Well, I thought you'd agree with me. How can we let the house be torn down and turned into a resort?"

"Are you saying we keep the house and property? Where would either one of us find the time to oversee this place?" He got up. His hands fisted at his sides.

"We don't need the money," she argued, her chin lifted high.

"I don't care if you gave every penny to your damn agency. That's not the point. How can you make this decision without discussing it with me? God forbid you ask for advice, an expert opinion, or even a sounding board."

She stood up and faced him. "So you don't want the property because it would be a burden to you?"

"No, that's not it at all. I may have come up with the same decision you did—but I wasn't given the opportunity." He spit out the last words. "This is like our ski trip to Denver." His brows pulled together in a frown. His blue eyes turned as dark as a storm-tossed sea.

"The Denver trip was nothing like this. I couldn't reach you and the hotel needed an immediate answer," she argued.

"Do you have any idea how I rearranged meetings and deliverables to go on the trip with you, only to find out the day before our flight that you canceled the reservations so you could extend your stay at your conference? Where were you? Oh, yes, Miami."

"Ask your girl Friday, Anita. I couldn't reach you so I got a hold of her and asked her to confirm your schedule. She kept telling me your calendar changed frequently and she couldn't give me an answer. I waited as long as I could. I was looking forward to the trip, too. I couldn't wait to go. And I didn't cancel those plans the day before. I canceled them the week before. I called you repeatedly from Miami to talk to you. You never returned my calls. I extended my stay at the conference because we weren't going to Denver and you wouldn't be home anyway. Besides, Denver has nothing to do with this. Molinetti pressed me for an answer. I said no."

"I have no idea why I'm even here." He threw down the paper he held and went to the bar. He splashed two fingers of bourbon into a glass and took a large swallow.

"Would you have decided to sell the property?" she asked after she gave the bourbon some time to take effect.

"I don't know. And right now my input doesn't matter, does it? You already made the decision." His voice rose with each word.

She had never seen him this angry.

"This is not the type of decision you make lightly," he said through clenched teeth.

"I didn't make the decision lightly." She struggled to keep her voice from giving away her frustration.

"I can't deal with this right now." He gulped down the last of the bourbon.

"It could be an income property or we can use it as a getaway for ourselves. This house is a great place to come for the holidays. I'd like to keep the tradition for our family."

He ran his hand through his hair. "That's not in the stars for a long time."

She dropped into the chair as if she had taken a body punch. Well, so much for a family.

He set the glass on the table and picked up the flyer on top of the mail. "The clambake is tonight. You still want to go? Everyone will understand with the memorial service and all." His tone cooled.

"No, Aunt Lil loved the clambake. I'd like to go." Her stomach clenched. Now what? She blocked out everything and tried to think what to do next.

"El? I said what time do we have to be there? I don't see the time on this." He turned the paper over.

"I…I think about five." She needed to move, to get away from him.

"Good, that will give me the entire day. I can get through a good portion of these papers before we leave."

She stood by the veranda doors and stared out across the water. "I think I'll go for a swim." She looked over her shoulder. He was already lost in his work. She doubted he even heard her.

She grabbed her towel from the railing on the veranda and headed to the beach. Rather than take the winding road she decided on the shortcut through the woods.

The wide path was well used by the locals. She slowed down to enjoy the lush, vibrant rain forest. The canopy of tall trees was covered with dense blossoming vines. She couldn't keep the smile from her face. When she was a child she relished traipsing through the dappled green tunnels. She compared it to gliding down the aisle of a flowered cathedral. The delicate hibiscus, open during the day and closed at night, painted the hillside with splashes of color. The intoxicating sweet aroma of white oleander growing on tall bushes filled the air. The chirping of the birds and the crunch of the leaves under her feet made her feel at home. Why had she been away so long?

What was she going to do? Years ago they decided to put off having a family and wait until they were ready. Well, she was ready. She let out a deep sigh. But he didn't want a family. Tears raced down her cheeks.

At the bottom of the hill the path ended at Aunt Lil's beach. She wiped away the tears, put her towel on a lone chair, and walked into the lapping water. She cupped her hand and splashed the water over her arms and chest. The channel didn't look as daunting today as it did all those years ago. With some practice, she could swim the channel and repeat her earlier accomplishment. She waded out farther and lost herself in the swim.

ℹℂℂ

"Hello, Anita. What's up?" Alan hoped the call would be short. He continued reading the paper in front of him.

"Alan, the plans are coming along. National Bank wants to schedule a meeting. When should I tell them you'll be back?" Anita asked.

"You wouldn't believe the disaster. Getting through these papers will take me much longer than I originally thought. Frank can handle the meeting. They don't need me in New York…"

Alan's voice trailed off. He reread the document in his hand and slowly got out of his chair.

"They asked for you specifically, Alan. I got the impression this was not a request but more of a demand. You should come back."

He didn't hear what she said. Stunned into silence, he glared at the document in disbelief.

"Alan, are you there?" she said impatiently.

"Shit." He blurted out and tossed the papers onto the desk.

"Alan?"

"Damn you, Aunt Lil. Couldn't you keep anything straight? How could you do this? Not registered our marriage?" Alan said to himself. Exasperated, he sat down heavily in the chair.

"Alan?" Anita asked.

"What?" His confusion at hearing a voice on the other end was momentary. The last thing he wanted was to deal with the office. "Anita. Tell Frank to handle the meeting with National Bank. If he has any questions have him call me directly. Is. That. All?" he asked, spacing the last three words evenly.

"Yes, I'll take care of things here. Bye."

He hung up and redialed the phone. "Hello, Ed." He sat hunched over, his finger tapping on the desk.

"Alan, how are you and Eloise doing?"

"She's having a bit of a hard time going through Aunt Lil's things, but she'll be fine. Thanks for asking." He tossed out the words. Eloise was emotional right now but she would get over it. "Maybe you can help me." He took a deep breath.

"Sure."

Alan let himself relax. He knew he could count on Ed. "I found the paperwork from our wedding. It's ridiculous." He laughed nervously. "I don't think it was ever registered."

For a moment Alan thought the line had gone dead, the silence was so complete. Finally, Ed found his voice. "Are you sure?"

Alan picked up the paper. "Aunt Lil was pretty disorganized. I remember the minister rushed out to catch the ferry. He was officiating at a christening on St John. We were cleaning up after everyone left. Aunt Lil found the license. The minister overlooked the papers when he left. I offered to take them to the courthouse the following Monday. She refused and said she would take care of everything. I'm going through her desk and found the signed license, the addressed envelope, and a large note, *Take to Courthouse*. The note pretty much says it all." He set the clipped paper and envelope down.

"Hold on. Let me call over to Marie. She works at the courthouse. I'll see what she can find." Ed put him on hold for several minutes.

This can't be happening. He took a deep, quieting breath. If Aunt Lil was here he'd… He calmed himself. He should have handled it himself instead of leaving it to her. Her intentions were always good but her follow-through left much to be desired. He should have known better.

"Well, Alan. You're right. You and Eloise are not married."

ഇരു

"You have a good swim?" Alan asked, entering

their room. Eloise came out of the bathroom wrapped in a towel.

"I forgot how I enjoy ocean swimming. I'm going to start a daily routine. The more I swam the more things started to come back, breathing, stroking. Even the exercises." She was eager to begin. She held a second towel in her hand ready to dry her hair.

Alan took the towel from her. "Here, let me do that. You're not going to believe what I found in the file in Aunt Lil's desk." Her head was propped against his chest while he rubbed her hair dry.

The rumble of his chest made her already tingling skin tingle even more, in a different way. "Oh, additional unpaid bills." She slipped her arms around his waist.

His hands on either side of her head, he raised her face up to look at him. He kissed her on the nose and handed her the towel. "My turn," he announced and headed into the bathroom.

"Are you going to tell me what you found?" She sat on the bed and dried her feet.

"I left the papers on the dresser." He turned on the shower.

Eloise picked up the papers and read them. She reread them and rushed into the bathroom.

Alan's six-foot frame rose above the shower curtain. He peered over it at her. "You want to join me?" His eyes twinkled but she barely noticed.

"We're not married." Her voice was a whisper. She searched his face for an explanation.

"Is that why you won't join me in the shower?" he teased and kept scrubbing his hair.

"Alan, be serious. We're not married." How could he joke at a time like this? She glared again at the documents. This must be a mistake. "Are you certain?"

"Yes, I called Ed and he checked the records at the courthouse. Our marriage was never recorded." He rinsed his hair and wiped the water from his face. Droplets clung to his long lashes and made them glisten. His thick black hair sprang into soft waves that, when dry, he spent an excessive amount of time trying to tame. "Ah, we've been living in sin these last ten years." He pulled back the curtain and stood in front of her in all his glory. "Come to me, my pretty," he said in a husky voice, his arms reaching for her.

She loved his body. From the first day she'd met him, when they'd spent the day on the beach, she'd thought he was, well, magnificent. Now he wasn't the same man she married—correction, thought she married. He had been caring and tender, but now he had no time for her and didn't want a family. She closed her eyes. "What are we going to do?"

"Do? I don't think we need to *do* anything. Things have been fine for ten years. Why change them now?" He reached for her again. She easily avoided him. "You're serious," he said, a wounded tone to his voice. He wrapped a towel around his waist.

"I'll get dressed. We should be leaving soon." She left the bathroom. She couldn't believe her ears. She sat on the edge of the bed, the papers scattered next to her. She tried to put the pieces of their relationship in perspective but she couldn't. She didn't know where to begin.

"Is the clambake at Celestial Harbor again? What's the charity this year?" He walked out of the bathroom looking and smelling wonderful.

"Yes, it's the Storm Relief Fund this year. A tropical depression passed through here a few months ago and did serious damage. Families in the east district are still making repairs. With hurricane season starting next month they want the repairs completed. Alan, we have our own repair work to do." She pointed to the papers. When he said nothing she got up and dressed.

"I can't believe you're so upset." He slipped into his clothes, stood in front of the full-length mirror, and battled with his hair.

A soft buzzing sound disturbed the quiet of the room.

"Your cell phone's ringing." She picked it up from the dresser and glanced at the display. "Your office, surprise, surprise," she said, her voiced dripping with sarcasm.

"My office. It better be important." He stared at the device with an exasperated expression. He took the phone from her. "Yes, Anita... What do you mean National Bank is on the line? I told you, Frank's handling things while I'm gone... All right, put them through." He sat on the edge of the bed. "Hello, Dave. What's the problem?" He opened his briefcase and pulled out the airline flight schedule.

"You'd think of leaving here? Now?" she asked, horrified.

He waved her off. "Dave, I'm not in New York... There's a flight—"

She rushed out of the room and onto the veranda. Tears dampened her cheeks. She shuddered inwardly at the thought that he could leave her now. Her chest ached as much for their marriage as it did for the loss of Aunt Lil. They were both dead. She took out her phone and texted Morgan. *Not married. Aunt Lil never filed papers. Alan doesn't want to commit.* Within three minutes her phone rang.

"What the hell is this?" Morgan asked.

"Alan found the license and paperwork from our wedding in Aunt Lil's things. Ed got a confirmation from the courthouse. Our marriage was never registered." She paced the veranda and wiped her nose with a cocktail napkin from the table.

"And?" The frustration on the other side of the phone came in heavy puffs of air.

"He said it wasn't important now."

"You didn't tell him yet, did you?"

"I mentioned babies and he said no time soon. What was I supposed to say? Guess what, too late. I'm already two months gone."

"Eloise, I've humored you long enough. Tell him, because if you don't I'll fly down and I will." Morgan's voice held a note of authority.

"You stay where you are. I have plenty to deal with. Besides, he's making plans to go home. Something is up with the National Bank job. I left him pulling out the flight schedule."

"Before he leaves, El. You need to tell him before he leaves or I'll camp out in his office when he gets back. Do you understand?" Morgan wasn't giving her any sympathy.

"Alan's coming. I'll speak to you later.

We're off to the charity clambake. Bye." She ended the call. She didn't want to listen to Morgan's threats.

"Ready?" Alan popped his head out the veranda door.

"Sure." She smoothed out her skirt, grabbed her shawl and handbag, and met him at the car.

How was she going to tell him she was pregnant? How was she going to tell him she wanted the baby? It took her several weeks to get used to the idea, but once she examined her life she realized how much she wanted a family. She never thought Alan would—no, she had to be honest with herself. If she had any idea Alan wanted a baby she'd have told him as soon as she found out, before she told Morgan.

She glanced at him driving the car. He was silent. His mind was elsewhere, probably thinking about the office. He never did tell her when his flight left.

"I don't want to stay too late tonight. I have an early day tomorrow," he said.

"That's fine. I'd like to get to the beach early."

They were driving past Aunt Lil's beach. How idyllic their wedding had been. Then, they'd wanted each other. When he launched his technology company they talked about the long hours and strain. They made a pact to keep close. But over time his firm took on a life of its own. The more prosperous his business became the more their time together diminished.

Her career accelerated, too. He was

supportive. But they grew farther apart. If she had a dollar for every time one of them was available but the other was not she would be a millionaire. She couldn't remember the last time she and Alan ate more than a quick meal together or sat and watched television. Maybe she should stay here and he could go back to New York. Alan pulled into a spot in Celestial Harbor's parking lot. They both got out of the car.

He grabbed his phone. "Be right with you." He went onto the beach to talk quietly.

"Ah, Ms. Alexander. How good to see you," Mr. Molinetti said, swaggering up to her and shaking her hand. "I hope you will reconsider my offer. I assure you I am quite serious about the property and I'm determined." She didn't miss the thread of warning in his voice. "I always get what I want. Why don't we cut to the chase. How much will it take for you to sell me Second Chance by the Sea?"

"Mr. Molinetti—" She gave him a hostile stare. She didn't like his threat or where this conversation was going.

"Vince. My friends call me Vince." He patted her hand with his other calloused paw.

"Mr. Molinetti, I don't think you realize what a close-knit community this is." She pulled her hand away and put on her agency voice. The one she used in negotiations.

"That's the way of progress." A flash of heat ran across her skin at the sound of his brittle, ruthless voice.

"A large enterprise like yours would leave no room for them." Her eyes narrowed. Her opinion of him, which wasn't terrific, plummeted even further. Weasels were higher on her list.

"My enterprise, as you call it, will provide jobs for one thousand islanders. True, the smaller businesses may have to relocate on other islands nearby. Eloise, the income and lifestyle of the islanders who work for me and those whose property I buy will be greatly enhanced." Mr. Molinetti had on his game face, too.

"What about the environment?"

"Well, you have to break a few eggs to make an omelet. We'll clear some of the land but the grounds will be landscaped. They'll be better than ever."

"Mr. Molinetti." Alan returned from his call. He put a protective arm around her and boldly met Molinetti's stare. Their statures were different but if silent signals could be evaluated it was clearly a draw.

"It's Vince. He likes to be called Vince," Eloise said, her voice heavy with sarcasm.

"I was asking your wife to give me a second chance. Get it? A second chance to buy Second Chance by the Sea." The man chuckled at his own joke. "Well, we can talk about my offer in a day or two. I have to admit the more I investigate the island the more I'm convinced this is the perfect place for my *enterprise*, as Eloise calls it."

"You'll excuse us, Vince. I'm certain we'll bump into each other during the evening," Alan said, leading Eloise toward the fundraiser table at the entrance to the beach.

She didn't ask him about his call. He would tell her soon enough when he planned to leave.

"Hi, we're Alan and Eloise Stuart," he said to the two people sitting at the registration table.

"Hi. I'm Jenna Reagan and this is my brother, Ryan Masterson. I'm the new owner of Celestial Harbor." Jenna turned to Eloise. "I've heard a lot about you. I understand you're the executive director of The North Star Project, the agency against human trafficking." The pretty woman rummaged through the envelopes searching for their reserved tickets.

"Yes, I am," Eloise said.

"Lil spoke of you both often. I was so sorry to learn about her passing," Jenna said.

"Are you Ryan Masterson, CEO of RMT-Designs?" Alan asked.

"Yes," Ryan said, clearly surprised someone knew about his company.

"Eric Feder over at Celion told me about you. He didn't want you to leave," Alan said, shaking his head.

"You're Alan Stuart of Stuart Associates. I recognize you from your picture in *Financial Technology*. I've been following your company. You've created some innovative software for the financial services industry."

Eloise glimpsed at Jenna and nodded toward the men. "We've lost them. Business—technology business, in particular—is Alan's favorite subject. How are you feeling? The baby must be due soon." Eloise didn't miss Jenna's baby bump.

"Not for another month. As an administrator of the Storm Relief Fund I would like to thank you for your generous donation." Jenna's smile slowly morphed into a mild grimace.

"You're welcome. We couldn't think of better people to help. Are you all right?" Eloise asked, bending over the small table, her hand reaching out to cover Jenna's.

"I've got this. It's nothing but practice contractions," Ryan said. He looked for confirmation from his sister and relaxed when she nodded.

"Here are your wristbands. They'll get you all you can eat. Nice meeting you." Jenna clipped a paper bracelet on Alan then on Eloise. "Enjoy the evening."

Tiki torches scattered around the beach painted everything with a soft glow. The distinct hollow metallic sound of steel drums playing calypso and reggae music set the mood. Weathered hatch cover tables, decorated with small glasses filled with oleander blossoms, were scattered on a section of the beach. The buffet was laid out near the fire pits. The aroma of roast pig, jerk chicken, and spicy fish gumbo caught the breeze and made her mouth water. The temperatures hadn't moderated much since they'd landed. It was still hot, but a gentle wind made it comfortable.

"It's a shame about Sam," Eloise said with sadness in her voice.

"Who?" Alan asked.

"Ed told me about Jenna's husband, Sam. He was killed in Afghanistan. I'm not certain if he even knew she was pregnant." She glanced over her shoulder at Jenna sitting at the table laughing with other guests. Which loss was worse, death or indifference? Her heart pounded in her chest. She wasn't certain. Both were devastating.

They ambled over to their first stop, the bar. "Something with rum?"

"None for me. Club soda with a bit of lime

will be fine," Eloise replied.

He gave her a quizzical stare. "You okay? You don't drink club soda."

She pursed her lips and nodded. "I'd prefer club soda today."

Club soda in her hand, a rum something in his, and they were ready for the buffet table. "The food smells wonderful. Where should I start? You want some fried dumplings or the gumbo?" Eloise asked.

She passed the gumbo and picked up some johnnycakes. The fragrance of the curry with ginger, tamarind, and other spices wafted through the air. She followed her nose to the jerk chicken, put a small piece on her plate, and took a side of rice and beans.

Eloise left Alan grazing the buffet and found an empty table. Ed Riley and his wife sat not too far away. Mr. Molinetti was with some people on the other side. The tables were beginning to fill quickly. She set out their place setting.

"Not normally my kind of food," Alan said, putting down his overloaded plate and drink.

"Really? You'd never know from your plate. Your trainer would pass out looking at that."

"I didn't want to hurt anyone's feelings. It's okay to indulge sometimes." He grinned from ear to ear.

"Yeah, you always hurt the one you love." She stared at her food and slowly raised her face.

He tilted his head and stared at her deeply. "El—" His pocket buzzed. He tossed down his napkin. "Jeez." He pulled out his cell phone. "I should have left this thing back at the house. Hello? Yes, Frank… One minute." He went out onto the beach to talk.

She watched him. He used to call her during the day. To hear her voice, he told her. There were times he would surprise her with lunch. He traveled from his office in Manhattan to hers in Westchester to spend thirty minutes before he made the return trip. And the movies. He used to take her to "chick flicks" armed with tissues, popcorn, and a shoulder to cry on. Now, he barely made time for her. How would he make time for a baby? He didn't want a family and he didn't want to be married. Her heart ached at the thought.

With a purposeful stride he came across the sand and back to their table. He put his napkin on his lap then ate the warm johnnycake. "I'm going back to the house after dinner. I have to get some things together for tomorrow. I'll be leaving the house early. Do you want to come back with me or should I see if Ed and his wife will give you a ride back?"

Interruptions from the office happened so many times he'd stopped apologizing for shortening their time together. But tonight it cut deep. She hoped maybe there was some way to repair things. "I've been thinking about the marriage license issue." Eloise pushed her food around her plate and couldn't take a bite.

Alan nodded, eating the jerk chicken.

"You're right. There isn't any need to get married. Yes, I'm certain. Not being married will give you the freedom you need."

His fork hung in midair. "What freedom?" He put his utensil down and finished chewing. His elbows on the table and his hands clasped. He gave her his full attention. "What are you talking about?"

"Oh please, Alan." She threw her napkin on the table. "Obviously you don't feel a need to be married to me. We're not. You're free to go your own way." Her hand flew up into the air.

She forced herself not to shrink back from the penetrating stare he leveled at her. "If I remember correctly, ten years ago neither of us thought a piece of paper defined our relationship. We laughed at the idea. Am I correct?"

She said nothing.

"Answer me, El," he demanded a bit loudly. People around them quieted.

"Yes, we did. We got married to please our parents," she said, her chin sticking out. She wouldn't let him intimidate her. People were beginning to stare.

"Listen, El, if getting married is important to you, tell me."

Wasn't being married important to *him*? The thought of begging him made her even more irate.

"Important to me? Since when did what's important to me matter?" Her body tensed and her heartbeat pounded in her ears.

"I could say the same thing to you. How many times have we made plans and canceled them because of something at the agency? Even this year's vacation. I won't mention Molinetti. And forget phone calls to Morgan. So, when will what's important to me matter to you?"

"Is everything all right?" Ed stood next to their table, his napkin in his hand.

Startled by the interruption, they stared at Ed.

"You were a bit loud," was all he said.

El glanced around. The people near them

turned away and refocused their attention on their dinner.

"Oh, thanks, Ed." Alan turned to El. "Get your things. We're going."

She started to object, but she didn't want to stay, either. She picked up her things and headed for the car.

౫◌ଔ

She sat in her nightgown on the veranda, hugging her knees, staring at the channel in the distance. She didn't want to be near him while he packed. She closed her eyes and thought about the comfort of drifting in the water and about the elation she'd felt when she conquered it.

She woke with a start at the sound of a car door closing. She must have fallen asleep. The dawning sky brightened. She heard more than saw the car going down the gravel driveway, kicking up stones. He hadn't said good-bye.

The final thump was the sound of her heart sinking.

She stood and tried to work out the stiffness in her back and legs. The sun would be up soon. She could lose herself in her swim.

A smile played across her lips. Yeah, a swim would be good.

The taxi pulled up in front of the airport. He paid the driver. He found a seat in the terminal near an outlet and cranked up his computer. The taxi driver mentioned the incoming storm. He hoped Dave could land. This shouldn't take long. Now he needed the results from last night's tests and he could get back to the island. With his earpiece in, he dialed the office.

"Anita, let me speak to Frank." The computer connected to his office without too much problem. He browsed the list of reports for any mention of the test results.

"He's on the phone, I think with one of Dave's people. You want me to have him call you back or do you want to wait?"

"I'll wait," he said absently and continued to scan through the material on his computer.

"Is it true you and Eloise aren't married?" Anita whispered conspiratorially.

"What?" The question was personal and the topic none of her business. Alan gave Anita his full attention.

"When we spoke you said the license was never filed," she purred like a kitten.

Who would believe anything this strange? He chuckled to himself thinking the situation would be funny if it was anyone but them.

"Is Eloise coming back with you?"

His antenna went up. A quick vision of Anita ready to pounce on an unsuspecting mouse ran through his mind and he had Mickey written all over him.

"If you need to talk to anyone… I'm sure things are strained between you two. Have you thought this may be a blessing?" Her voice was smooth and intimate.

He couldn't believe his ears. Sure she was flirtatious. Women flirted with him all the time. He didn't notice her teasing anymore. But when did Anita target him? He certainly hadn't given her any encouragement. He drummed his fingers on the edge of the computer. He didn't have time for this. "Anita, Dave is landing in about an hour. Interrupt Frank and get him on the phone."

"Sure, I'll get him for you. Any idea when you'll be returning?" There was a hopeful ring to her voice.

"Not yet." Perhaps he should reconsider those warnings Frank gave him about his secretary. While he listened to the mindless music, he thought about Anita's invitations for drinks after work and offers to stay late to help him with reports. Frank mentioned something about his calls not being returned. He told her to let Frank's calls through no matter when he called but now he wondered. He heard static on the line. His computer connection dropped. Jeez, he hoped he didn't lose the call.

"Alan? Can you hear me?"

"Frank, yeah. We have a bad line but I can hear you. What the hell is going on in New York? Which one of Dave's staff were you speaking to? He's landing in about an hour. Anything I should be aware of before he gets here?"

"Speaking to? I've been sitting here having my morning coffee and reading over last night's test results for the last hour. Why? Did your high-fashion secretary tell you I was on the phone with Dave's office?"

Alan forgot about Dave for the moment. "Let's start at the beginning. What exactly has Anita been doing?"

"I'm glad you asked." Alan couldn't miss the relief in Frank's voice.

"For one, she's been controlling everyone's

contact with you, and I mean everyone's, even Eloise's."

"What? Eloise's calls?" Alan said, his computer sliding on his lap as he half stood. He dropped back onto the chair. What had this woman been up to?

"Things can be strained when you're working on deadlines like we are but I thought you and El were solid." Frank's brusque tone switched to concern.

"Things are fine with us. We've been busy with our own jobs. You know how work can be." The cool defensiveness in his own tone caught him by surprise. He stopped. "Go ahead, Frank. I'm listening." He took a deep breath. "I'm ready to hear what you have to say."

"Alan, I was your big brother at the fraternity and I've never relinquished my responsibility. Anita is making it appear, and I say *appear*, that you and El are on the rocks and she's waiting in the wings to swoop down and save you. Her talons are drawn and you're her target."

Alan raked his hand through his hair. "Thanks." The line crackled. "Frank?"

"I'm here. I'm not going anyplace."

"I appreciate your candor. Let me chew on this a bit. Before we lose the connection, I have two things for you. One, check out some real estate guy named Molinetti. He's been waving lots of money around here trying to buy up property."

"Sure, and the other item?" Frank asked.

"Dave's stopping here on his way to the Argentina conference and wants to hand me a signed agreement for the next phase. He should be here within the hour…"

"What airline flies this early?"

"He's on his own jet. I hope he gets in soon. The wind is beginning to pick up and the newscast mentioned something about a tropical depression. Anyway, I'd like to give him the status of the project. How do the results of last night's test look?"

Eloise put on her bathing suit and grabbed her beach bag. Her argument with Alan stuck in her mind, and sleeping on the veranda hadn't helped. The swim would tire her enough to relax. The breeze picked up on her way down the hill, the brightening sky tinged red. She stared out at the channel. The water was stirred up but she didn't see any small whitecaps. She checked the beach— no warning flags. She put on her pink goggles, dunked herself in the water, and set out.

She stretched her body until she was as sleek and trim as a seal. She timed her strokes to the roll of her hips and shoulders to get the most out of her pull. She got about two miles out, nearing the middle of the channel, when she realized something was wrong. The gentle waves turned rough. The swells were three feet and were getting larger. She tamped down her growing concern. She didn't need to panic. Calm and steady. She'd been distracted, thinking about everything but the water around her. She pulled toward land but a swift current caught her. A rip current.

She changed her strategy and swam at a forty-five-degree angle toward shore. She would have a long walk back. But the current wasn't cooperating. She couldn't get out of its grasp. Every instinct told her to head for the safety of shore. But no matter how hard she swam she was pulled farther away. She needed to think clearly. Conserve her energy. She treaded water and let the water take her. Helplessness was not a feeling she embraced. The shore flashed by as the riptide pushed her along. She realized she was being carried out of the channel toward the sea. Surely she would get out of the current before she reached the final jetty. She forced her body to relax. She couldn't afford her muscles to tighten on her now. She needed to keep her wits about her. She swam and maneuvered to the edge of the riptide and tried repeatedly to break free. Once she did she would have to swim for her life. Right now she had some protection from the land on both sides but once she was out in the open sea...

She didn't want to think of that right now. Now she needed to stay calm and wait for her opportunity.

"Thanks for the status, Alan. Sounds like you have everything under control. I'm glad to get one more project off my plate." Dave and Alan sat in the comfortable main cabin of Dave's company jet. Alan glanced at the pilot outside as he watched the crew refuel the plane.

Alan sat back and luxuriated in the comfortable leather chair. They both signed the contract. Each of them took their copies. "I appreciate you delivering these yourself, Dave."

"Our agreement said the signed documents were due today. Since I was passing the island I thought I would deliver them personally and give Eloise my condolences. But this weather is turning quickly. My pilot filed a new flight plan. We'll have to leave as soon as we've fueled up. I'm sorry I won't be able to see her." Dave glanced out the window then checked his watch while Alan checked to make certain they both signed every page.

"I'm sure she'll understand."

"We're ready to leave, sir," the pilot said, entering the cabin on his way to the cockpit.

Alan gathered the papers and put them into his briefcase. "Safe trip, Dave. I'll tell the office I have an executed agreement. I'll speak to you when I get back to New York."

The men shook hands and Alan deplaned. He clutched his briefcase tightly to avoid the wind ripping it out of his hand. By the time Alan got into the terminal, Dave's plane stood on the runway, the next one to take off.

He glanced at the sky. Storm clouds were gathering. He needed to get back to the island.

He hailed a taxi and headed toward the dock.

He kept watching the gulls. There were much fewer than usual. They must have flown out ahead of the storm. That was not a good sign. The taxi drove along Veterans Drive and he noticed the choppy water touched with whitecaps. He didn't like what he saw. People were putting their storm shades over their windows, scurrying to bring things indoors or tie them down.

The taxi finally pulled up to the dock. He paid the driver and rushed to the pier.

"What do you mean the ferry is closed?"

"Sorry, sir. Harbor patrol posted a small craft

warning." The ferryman pointed to the signal flag on the dock halyard. The single red triangle whipped about in the growing wind.

"Captain Jack may be able to help you. You can find him across the dock. His boat is *Jack's Craft*."

Alan crossed the dock to the modest craft. Jack stood on the boat's deck getting ready to leave.

"Jack? I need to get back to Star Island." Alan pointed across the channel and shouted over the wind.

"Sure, I'll take you. I'm headed to the island myself. Get on board. If we don't leave now we won't be able to leave at all. They may change the warning. This blow may reach gale force." Jack had the ropes off the cleats.

"Thanks." Alan boarded the bobbing boat. Eloise was alone. They'd given the housekeeper some much-needed time off. He dialed the house number—no answer. He called her cell but instead got her voice mail. What was he thinking last night? Rubbing the back of his neck, he thought she needed some alone time and decided he'd talk to her when she came to bed. But he fell asleep. When he woke and realized she never came to bed he searched the house for her. They never went to sleep angry. He should have woken her but she was curled up in the overstuffed chaise and looked so peaceful. She needed her sleep. To be honest, he didn't want to argue.

She must be up by now. The house was too large for one person to batten down for a storm. He didn't like the idea of her being alone in this. No, he had to get back now. He hoped she knew where the storm supplies were kept. His phone rang.

"Hello," he shouted above the steady wind. "El?"

"Alan, is Eloise with you?" Ed asked.

"Ed? No. I left her at the house this morning. Why?" He covered his free ear with his hand. Jack pulled the boat away from the dock and maneuvered through the rough water.

"They were setting the storm warning flags on the beach and found her things. I know she goes for a morning swim—"

"Did you check the house?" A shiver of apprehension ran up his spine, forcing his shoulders back.

"Yes. No sign of her. We've already checked in town and she didn't go into St. Thomas. I checked with the ferryman."

Gusts of wind ran across the surface, raising sprays of water. Eloise wasn't getting any closer to land. She was caught tight in the current. She glimpsed back, startled at the angry black sky. She was coming up to the last jetty. No, this wasn't good. Again she tried to get out of the current but it was still no use.

She swam past a protective jetty and the full force of the wind hit her—probably twenty-five miles per hour. On this side of the rocks debris floated past her. She briefly thought of heading for the jetty but knew the danger of getting caught between the angry current and the rocks.

Think, she commanded herself. One by one she ticked off the options. In the end she realized she had none. Her shoulders tightened and her chin trembled. The sour taste of fear filled her mouth. Her body as well as her mind was bruised and battered from the rough waves tossing her around. Little by little paralyzing fear knotted her insides. She closed her eyes and slid beneath the water. The panic subsided but somewhere deep inside someone called the cadence. *Stroke.* A wave caught her and shot her to the surface. She shook her head to clear her thinking. One arm after the other pulled her through the water to the beat of the cadence in her mind. She kept her efforts focused on swimming toward shore but even with the amount of energy she exerted she made little headway. But she kept on going.

Large drops of rain spattered the deck of the boat. Alan raced to the rail.

"Give me the binoculars." Alan held out his hand.

Jack grabbed the binoculars off the peg next to the wheel and handed them to Alan. "Something wrong?"

Alan brought the binoculars to his eyes and searched the water. He knew she was in the water. He felt her nearby. More than anything he wanted her safe in his arms. The water turned ugly. The rip current was bad. None of this was good news. In desperation he scanned the St. Thomas shoreline. How long had she been out? She'd been away from this kind of swim too long to be strong enough to manage in these conditions. His anxiety level ratcheted up.

The evening hadn't ended well for either of

them. Did she fall asleep on the veranda or purposefully avoid him last night? How had this whole thing started? Not being married. If being married was important to her of course they would get married, but why didn't she tell him? Anita! His mind raced along with the boat. She blocked El's calls—not only the ones about Denver but other times, too. He didn't want to go his own way. There was no way without her.

Stroke, Eloise. Keep a nice, easy, steady stroke. He needed to be next to her and talk her through this like he did the last time. He gave the glasses back to Jack and took off his shoes and shirt.

"What are you doing?" Jack grabbed his arm. The rain came down harder.

"My wife is out there." Fear swept through him. He pulled his arm free. "She went for a swim before they got the flags up."

Jack and Alan stood at the wheel searching the water on the starboard side. "This is a small channel. She's too far ahead of you. You'll never reach her starting from here. You'll get caught up in the rocks." Jack pointed to the rock jetty.

"Thanks, but I can't stand by and do nothing." Alan unbuckled his belt.

"I have a wet suit below. Put it on. I'll take you as close as I can. We'll follow the current to the far end of the channel." Alan disappeared quickly into the hatch. Jack turned the wheel and raced into the stormy water.

Alan came onto the deck holding on to anything he could. The boat rocked and bounced like a rubber duck in a bathtub with the plug pulled. Jack stood at the wheel, peered through his binoculars and searched the water.

"She's a strong swimmer but she's been out too long. She's not used to rough water. I need to find her now." They passed the jetty, the boat rocking from the blast of wind.

Jack brought the boat around and took a call from the harbor.

"There's a sand bar ahead. I can't go any farther this way. Besides, they have an emergency on the island. This will probably be a short blow. We can make the dock and come back out when the storm calms down."

Alan glared at him then grabbed a coiled rope and slung it over his shoulder. The rain pelting the wet suit made a loud plopping noise. "Go back, Jack. The storm is going to get worse before it gets better."

"I thought we could outrace the weather. I can't leave you here. All you'll do is get yourself killed. We'll go back and call for more help." Jack, drenched to the skin, stood struggling to control the wheel.

"I have a better idea. You go back and call for more help while I go find my wife. No offense, Jack. I can't leave her. That's not a choice." The men stared at each other. Both understood what needed to be done.

"Wait." Jack patted down his shirt and pants and finally took a lighter out of his pocket. "Take this. A lighter may come in handy."

Alan stared at the lighter, then at Jack.

"Light, heat, I don't know. I can't let you go with nothing." Jack fumbled with the lighter and handed it to Alan. The anxious expression on Jack's face said it all.

"Thanks." Alan nodded and tucked the lighter into the makeshift pocket glued onto the leg of the wet suit. He acknowledged the concern etched in Jack's face. It matched his own. Time was running out. If she got pulled into the ocean there was no telling where she would wind up or how long it would take to find her. He pushed the thought out of his mind. He needed to stay focused. He clapped his hand on Jack's back. With nothing left to say, he sat on the gunwale and flung his legs over the side.

Jack grabbed his shoulder and shouted above the wind. "The rip current this far down the channel isn't wide. Use that to your advantage. Your best bet is to follow the current and head for Sagamore Cay. It's not inhabited but caves dot the hills and you can use them for shelter." Jack pointed to a small island in the distance.

Alan nodded then dropped into the water. He used the boat's side as a springboard and swam toward the cay. The boat's horn blasted and he watched as Jack headed back toward the dock. He quickly got the feel of the current. It gathered momentum as it narrowed toward the channel and the ocean beyond. He strained to get a glimpse of Sagamore Cay but he was in a trough surrounded by walls of water. He needed a higher vantage point. He swam into the next swell. It lifted him high enough to get his bearings. From his perch on the crest he could see land in the distance. If he kept going straight he couldn't miss it.

He agreed with Jack. If Eloise was caught in the current the best way for him to find her was to swim at its edge. The current tried to grab him but he managed to stay out of its grasp. Debris was everywhere. From his vantage point the channel was huge. How would he ever find her out there? He pushed the doubt aside. He was determined to find her. He had to find her.

Somewhere in the distance—she couldn't tell which direction—a boat horn blasted. Instinctively she knew the boat was too far away to be of any help. Her arms were lead. She couldn't keep the cadence of the stroke. Every time she raised her arm she cringed in pain. Perhaps if she rested for a minute… She didn't even need to tread water. She kept bobbing along with the other debris.

    Debris.

    She needed something to grab on to. She took off her goggles and tossed them away. Now she could see more clearly. A good-size tree trunk floated into view. She swam for it and grabbed on for dear life.

Alan swam alongside the current. The wind and spray picked up and made it difficult to see. The howling of the wind, the crashing of the water, was deafening. Debris floated everywhere. He pushed pieces of tree trunks and garbage out of his way. Clumps of seaweed tangled around his hands but he shook off the slimy clumps and kept swimming. Another stroke and something caught his hand. He pulled the debris out of the water. His heart pounded. He held Eloise's pink goggles.

    He continued on the outskirts of the current and kept his course. Up ahead more debris floated at the edge of the current. He came up to a big tree trunk and was about to push it out of his way when he thought he saw a hand. His heart raced. He maneuvered around the log. He prayed it was Eloise. The log caught the current and sped up. He couldn't hang on much longer. Hand over hand he traveled down the log and finally reached the other side. Someone clung to it halfway down its length. He knew it was Eloise. His heart raced with relief. In slow motion he watched her hand begin to slip free. *No*, he silently screamed and lunged for her. They both sank into the churning water. She floated lifeless toward the bottom. He kicked hard and grabbed her outstretched hand. He kicked even harder and brought them both back to the surface.

He watched the log catch in the current, upend, and slowly sink. He held her close with one arm. "Eloise," he yelled above the deafening sound of the wind and the water. "Eloise." He jiggled her face until her eyes opened.

"Alan?"

"El. I need you to work with me." Her limp body begged to go with the current. He wouldn't let it take her. He managed to grab the rope and lash her to a piece of debris. He secured the rope around himself and angled off from the current.

Each stroke was torture. He pulled his arms through the water for her life and his.

Finally free of the current, he slowed his stroke and glanced at her face. She was awake. "El, can you swim?"

She nodded.

He helped untie her from her float but kept the line between them. She followed next to him stroke for stroke until they found themselves in shallow water. Exhausted but alive, they stumbled out of the surf and onto the sand on Sagamore Cay.

The wind picked up. The palm trees were bent over, their torn fronds dancing in the wind. "We've got to get to some shelter," he yelled over the squall. He untied the rope from around her and dropped it in the sand. A strong blast barreled down the beach, kicking up sand and slamming into them. Eloise lost her footing. He wrapped his arm around her shoulder and blocked the wind. Together they staggered into the forest. A few hundred yards up the incline they found an opening.

"Wait here." He leaned her against the entrance and checked out the cave.

"Nothing inside. We can wait out the storm here." Her face was pale. She shivered from the strain and cold. He wouldn't pretend he was a Boy Scout. He fumbled in his pocket and pulled out the lighter. *Thank you, Jack.* He gathered some rocks and dry wood in the cave and made a small fire. He held her in his arms to warm her and to feel her next to him. He'd almost lost her. She nodded off as soon as they sat down. He tilted her face to his and pushed away the strands of wet hair. He held her close and kissed her forehead. *You scared me, El. I've never been so scared in my life.* He watched the rhythmic rise and fall of her chest and relaxed.

She snuggled closer.

He got as comfortable as he could. They both slept to the sound of the wind and the crash of the water around them.

They woke in the morning to the call of birds and bright sun.

Alan, the top of his wet suit unzipped to his waist, put his hand on her forehead.

"I'm all right," she croaked. "Although my arms and legs may never move again. How did you find me? I thought you left for New York." She picked her head up off his shoulder but stayed close.

"Back to New York?" He tilted his head back and gazed into her eyes, baffled by her question. He brushed the sand from her face and pulled her closer. Letting her go was not an option.

"I wasn't going to New York. Dave stopped here on his way to the Argentina conference. I met him at the airport to sign the contract for the next phase. I was on my way back to the island when Ed called and told me they couldn't find you." For a brief moment the fear and anxiety of losing her resurfaced.

"Captain Jack took me out as far as he could and pointed me in your direction." He stopped and took a breath. "Why would you think I was going back to New York?"

"You were talking to Dave and reading flight schedules. I put two and two together."

"And got five." He tried to laugh but it came out more like a croak.

"Dave thought he'd send his assistant. When we couldn't find a convenient flight he decided to change his flight plan. Besides, I wouldn't leave without talking to you."

"Oh." Her voice was a whisper but her sound of despair concerned him.

"What is it, El? What's wrong?" He gently turned her face up to his.

"We used to make time for each other, even if we spoke for a few minutes. Now, you're never available. I find I'm eating dinner alone and talking to Morgan more and more."

"You're not the only one with that complaint. I was beginning to think you preferred Morgan's company to mine."

"What?" His statement startled her into silence.

"Things will change when we get back." If only he knew how prophetic that was. Her heart ached for them, for what they once had.

"I fought for us, for our relationship, but you pushed me aside. You had more important things to do." She tried to pull away from him but he wouldn't let her go. Too tired to fight she quickly gave up and let him hold her.

"You are my heart, you are my soul. You belong there and you will never leave," he whispered with her head on his shoulder.

Eloise's breath caught. She sat up. "Our vows. You remember our vows."

"Of course I remember. What would make you think I wouldn't? I love you. Do you understand?" He held her by her shoulders and stared deeply into her eyes. Something was terribly wrong. He recognized the doubt in her eyes. He hesitated, blinking in confusion.

In the next heartbeat he pulled her to his chest and held her close. "Forever, El." He closed his eyes, willing her to say something to take away the nagging feeling.

"Forever," she murmured.

He felt her tears run down his bare chest. He tipped up her head and kissed her eyes. She relaxed. He kissed her nose. She smiled. He kissed her lips, lingering, savoring every moment. She sighed and held him close.

In the distance a boat horn sounded. He raised his head. "It must be Jack. We need to get to the beach. Do you think you can walk?"

"Yes," she said. She stood on wobbly legs. He helped her to the beach. Jack and Ed were pulling a rubber raft out of the surf. The boat secure, Jack and Ed rushed to help Alan and Eloise.

"How'd you know we were here?" Eloise asked.

Jack pointed to the rope on the beach. "I'm glad Alan picked up the orange rope. It was easy to spot."

"Let's get the two of you over to a doctor," Ed said.

"I don't need a doctor," Eloise said.

"Sorry, not your choice," Ed said as he and Jack helped them into the raft.

∞♥

"Alan."

Hearing his name, Alan looked up. Dr. Baker walked toward him across the emergency waiting room.

"Dr. Baker. How is Eloise?" He stood slowly.

"She's fine. So is the baby."

Alan's mouth opened and closed like a beached fish. "You must be speaking about someone else. El isn't pregnant."

"Alan, trust me. Eloise has passed every test. I suspect she's about eight weeks along."

Alan slid back into the chair. How could he not know? A baby? He was going to be a father. Eloise. He got to his feet. "Is she all right? The swim. She was exhausted. Are they both—"

"They're both fine. See for yourself." Dr. Baker showed him a frame from the ultrasound. "And I heard a nice, strong heartbeat, too."

Alan held the picture, unable to tear his eyes away. "We're going to have a baby."

"Yes, you are." The doctor, a broad smile on his face, clapped him on the shoulder.

"Is there anything I should know?" Alan asked.

"I'm glad you asked." His voice rang with a gentle authority. "We need to talk."

Alan gave the man his attention. "It sounds serious."

"I've had a long talk with her. I'm speaking to you not as a doctor, but as someone who's known the family, and you, a long time. She's healthy and strong but please, be aware she has been under a great deal of strain between Aunt Lil's death and now this. If you two need to discuss something I would, well, be considerate." Dr. Baker sat next to him. He took off his glasses. "She doesn't think you want a child." He spoke with a gentle softness.

The shock of the doctor's statement hit him full force. "Why would she think that?"

"She said you don't want a family."

Now things were making sense. He hung his head and laughed. "I may not have thought to start a family but that doesn't mean I wouldn't welcome it. Of course I want a family. That's why I've worked hard to build my company. I want a baby. More than one. I didn't think she wanted a family." He glanced at Dr. Baker.

"She needs to know you want the baby. She needs to believe it." He stood. "I've signed her out. You can take her home. And, Alan, I'm here to listen." Dr. Baker led Alan to Eloise's room.

Alan peeked inside the room. "El?"

She turned to him with red eyes and a running nose. "Are you all right?" She sniffed.

"Yeah. A little bruised and my arms feel like they're ten feet long. Other than that I'm fine. The doctor said we can leave."

"Has the storm caused much damage?" she asked as she stared out the nearby window.

He knew that ploy. Small talk. She didn't want to talk to him about the important subject, the baby.

"No, a few trees down and lots of debris scattered around. The islands were lucky. The winds never reached gale force." He came up behind her and held her close.

"I was crazy with worry when I couldn't find you. I didn't know where to search first. I don't know what I would do if I lost you, El." He spoke softly, his chin resting on her head.

"I thought I had already lost you," she whispered.

"You can't ever lose me. You are in my heart forever. I made that vow ten years ago and nothing has changed. I don't want anything to change. " He kissed the top of her head. "We have a lot to celebrate."

"I suppose."

"It's not every day my beautiful wife makes me the happiest man in the world. Not only is she safe and sound but so is our baby. Definitely something to celebrate."

She picked her head up slowly.

He wiped the tears on her cheek. "Why didn't you tell me?"

"I…I didn't think you wanted a baby and when you said not in the near future I didn't know what to do."

"Have I been that preoccupied with work that you would doubt I love you? No, don't say anything. I know the answer. That will change, El. I'm serious. You and our baby are more important to me than anything else."

She took his face in her hands and drew it to hers. "I love you and I will forever." She buried her head in the crook of his neck.

"Mrs. Stuart, the doctor has signed you out." The nurse came into her room with a wheelchair.

"Your chariot, m'lady." He took the chair from the nurse and wheeled it to her.

"I don't—" she protested.

He held up his hand. "I know, but they won't let you walk out on your own. Let's humor them. Captain Jack's waiting for us at the dock."

Eloise sat in the shade on the veranda. She wore a soft jersey tank dress with a high hemline in front and a low hemline in back. The color, sherbet orange, set off her tan skin. She wore a white hibiscus in her long auburn hair. Alan sat next to her in a soft tan linen suit and white dress shirt, an orange hibiscus pinned to his lapel.

"Dave called while you were napping. He sends his regrets that he can't be here. He told me three weeks in Argentina and he was dying to get home to the family."

"I spoke with North Star earlier. I tried to give them my resignation. They wouldn't accept it. They made me an offer that's hard to refuse. I can work part time, from home, and they'll give me an assistant. The arrangement can be permanent if I like. But I'm thinking if I choose the right person I can groom them to take over. What do you think?"

"It's a great offer. You should take it." He stretched his arm across the back of her chair.

"Well, you two appear to be comfortable, not killing each other." Morgan walked onto the veranda.

"What are you doing here?" Eloise started to get up.

"You stay right where you are." Morgan gently pushed her back onto the chair. "For your wedding, of course. I was his best man at the last one and refuse to relinquish the job to anyone else." Morgan Stuart, Alan's older brother and silent partner, went to the bar and poured two glasses of bourbon and one glass of sparkling water.

Alan looked at the glass with a raised eyebrow when Morgan handed the sparkling water to Eloise. "El told me you were her confidant."

"She needed to tell someone. I'm glad she came to me. When Mom was pregnant with you I told her I wanted a sister but you came along. I'm glad you at least came through for me." He held up his glass in salute.

"What have you two been up to?" Morgan asked.

"Your brother saved my life." She squeezed Alan's hand.

"You mean you weren't simply tired?" Alan teased.

"No, I wasn't tired. I was ready to give up but your voice calling the cadence kept me going. When I thought I couldn't pull another stroke I heard you beside me this time and ten years ago."

"I will always be beside you." He brushed his lips against hers.

Morgan took a sip of his drink. "You missed all the excitement at the airport this morning. Your instincts were right, Alan. Your Mr. Molinetti was working a money-laundering scheme. Frank sent the report to Ed while you two were recovering. They caught him when he tried to leave the island."

"That's a relief. Did you take care of the other things we discussed?" Alan asked Morgan.

"Your wish was my command." Morgan gave Alan an elegant, if not overdone, bow. He winked at Eloise.

"What is this about?" she asked.

Morgan sat next to them. "The first order of business—I fired Anita. When I spoke to her she was under the illusion Alan wouldn't stand for it. She'd convinced herself she was, let's just say, better for him. I made her see the light. Anyway, when I finished relieving the company of your secretary, I promoted Frank to head of the New York division."

"New York division? The company only has one division," Eloise said, taking another sip of her club soda.

"Not anymore," Alan said. "We now have a Virgin Islands division. I can do my business here as easily as in New York." He watched her over the rim of his glass of bourbon.

"Alan, you would do that?" she whispered.

The sheen in her eyes told Alan she was excited. He took her hand. "Of course. It's a great place to raise a family." He sat back in his chair.

Eloise didn't let go of his hand. "I always thought calling this place Second Chance by the Sea was wrong." She stared at Alan and melted when she saw the full heat of his Paul Newman–blue eyes. That look that he saved only for her. "No, it's the perfect name."

About…

Ruth started reading romance books while traveling the world for business. Traveling alone can be daunting but she found a book in hand could see her through long waits at the airport as well as good company at dinner for one. For some of her longer treks, she pared down her wardrobe to make room for books. Her favorite genres are romance and adventure.

A seasoned professional with more than twenty-five years of writing experience in communications and marketing for a large financial institution, she gave way to her inner muse and began writing a series of historical fantasy romance novels. Ruth is published by Carina Press and Harlequin Books.

When not writing you can find her home in Teaneck, New Jersey, reading, cooking, doing Sudoku and counted cross-stitch. Together with her husband, Paul, they enjoy ballroom dancing and going to the theater. Ruth and Paul have three grown children and two grandchildren. They all thrive on spending time together. It's certainly a lively dinner table and they wouldn't change it for the world.

❧

You can read more about Ruth online at www.RuthACasie.com, on Twitter at twitter.com/RuthACasie, or on Facebook at www.facebook.com/RuthACasie.

Time travel is more than a Wellsian fantasy for Rebeka Tyler. Tossed into the 17th century she must fight for her life against the dark druid and protect her heart from the druid knight Lord Arik before she can discover who she is and where she belongs. Check out **Knight of Runes,** available now! www.RuthACasie.com/books.html

Knight of Runes

England, 1605

When Lord Arik, a druid knight, finds Rebeka Tyler wandering his lands without protection, he swears to keep her safe. But Rebeka can take care of herself. When Arik sees her clash with a group of attackers using a strange fighting style, he's intrigued.

Rebeka is no ordinary seventeenth-century woman— she's traveled back from the year 2011, and she desperately wants to return to her own time. She poses as a scholar sent by the king to find out what's killing Arik's land. But as she works to decode the ancient runes that are the key to solving this mystery and sending her home, she finds herself drawn to the charismatic and powerful Arik.

As Arik and Rebeka fall in love, someone in Arik's household schemes to keep them apart, and a dark druid with a grudge prepares his revenge. Soon Rebeka will have to decide whether to return to the future or trust Arik with the secret of her time travel and her heart.

Want to read about Max and Ellyn, Rebeka's parents as well as Fendrel and Dimia, Arik's parents, read **Mistletoe and Magick,** a short story in **Timeless Keepsakes** available now! www.RuthACasie.com/books.html

In the mood for more paranormal romance by Ruth A. Casie? In order to save the man she loves from execution as a traitor, dare Lisbeth rely on her knight to find a way to save them both or does she trust her magic and risk exposure and persecution as a witch? Check out, *The Guardian's Witch*, available now! www.RuthACasie.com/books.html

The Guardian's Witch

England, 1290

Lord Alex Stelton can't resist a challenge, especially one with a prize like this: protect a castle on the Scottish border for a year, and it's his. Desperate for land of his own, he'll do anything to win the estate—even enter a proxy marriage to Lady Lisbeth Reynolds, the rumored witch who lives there.

Feared and scorned for her second sight, Lisbeth swore she'd never marry, but she is drawn to the handsome, confident Alex. She sees great love with him but fears what he would think of her gift and her visions of a traitor in their midst.

Despite his own vow never to fall in love, Alex can't get the alluring Lisbeth out of his mind and is driven to protect her when attacks begin on the border. But as her visions of danger intensify, Lisbeth knows it is she who must protect him. Realizing they'll secure their future only by facing the threat together, she must choose between keeping her magic a secret and losing the man she loves.

Chasing Fireflies

Lita Harris

≈

Marnie Shaw is a travel agent whose fear of flying has kept her safe within the confines of New York City. As the top agent for her firm, she wins an all-expenses paid trip for two to the U.S. Virgin Islands. She decides to confront her fear and take the trip alone when she is dumped by her live-in boyfriend.

Her plans of losing herself while relaxing in the beauty of the island is disrupted when Captain Jack, a handsome, scraggly bearded, boat captain, shows up at her bungalow unannounced and refuses to leave.

Will a night on the beach with Jack open her eyes to realize there's more to life than what she has, if only she would let go of her expectations and take a risk? Or when her ex shows up begging for forgiveness, will she settle for the safety of her quiet, risk-free life?

≈

Dedicated to ~

The Scribes, what can I say that hasn't already been said? You ladies ROCK!

Jo, the best friend anyone could have. Thanks for being there. Our friendship truly is timeless.

My editor, Mallory Braus, working with you is a pleasure. You get the best out of me with each story. Thank you for believing in me.

Chasing Fireflies
by Lita Harris

Marnie Shaw wiped away tears as the plane touched down in St. Thomas and she replayed the voice mail on her phone. "Sorry, kid, but I'm just not feeling it. Have a safe trip." What a fool she had been, caught up in his charm. She knew she had rushed into the relationship with him and they had moved in together too quickly, but he made her laugh. She overlooked his selfish ways, in the beginning at least when he used to carry the groceries up the stairs and put them away. Now he didn't even lift an empty beer can or throw it away until there wasn't any more room on the coffee table.

Maybe she had seen the end coming but didn't want to believe it. Love isn't easy to find— if it even exists. She remembered what her grandmother told her. "Finding the perfect love is like chasing fireflies in the city. Possible but not likely."

Her heart lightened as she readied herself to embrace the island that was a nice change from the urban environment of New York City, where you could rarely find a tree. She was eager to step out onto the beach and soak up some sun and kick around in the surf—anything to help her forget Nick. She waited until the last person disembarked the plane. No need to get caught up in the rush of people; she got enough of that in the city. This trip would be one of relaxation and discovery.

Nick hadn't called her since he'd left and she was coming to terms with that. She wouldn't know what to say to him. Did she miss him? Want him back? To leave her alone?

In hindsight, she saw he was self-centered, selfish, and superficial—everything she wasn't. How could she have ever thought it would work?

If she hadn't won the Top Travel Agent vacation to the U.S. Virgin Islands she wouldn't even be on the plane, but it gave her time to think during the five-hour flight. She hated flying. This vacation was all about her. The first thing on her agenda was to check into the bungalow. Time alone was warranted so she opted not to stay at the main hotel in favor of solitude. The last thing she wanted was to be bothered by strangers on the other side of a wall. She turned off her cell phone.

Even the airport calmed her, so much quieter and much smaller than Newark Liberty Airport. Baggage handlers greeted each passenger with a smile and a willingness to help. No pushing and shoving. Her shoulders relaxed as she made her way to the baggage carousel. The trade winds filled the airport with fresh air instead of manufactured air-conditioning. Each moment awakened her senses.

"Excuse me, miss, can I get that for you?" A skycap extended his hand to take her bag.

"Thank you. Sure."

He gently took the luggage from her grip and guided her to the sliding doors. "Where are you going, miss?"

"Um, let me see." Marnie pulled out her itinerary and scanned it. "Celestial Harbor on Star Island."

"Ah, very nice place. Not much storm damage so your stay will be very relaxing." The skycap stood curbside and flagged a taxi.

She wasn't used to pleasantries. Her life back home was filled with rushing around and barely acknowledging another person. Not that she meant to be impolite. It was just that way. "Yes, I've heard good things about that place. Is it far?"

A taxi pulled up and the skycap placed the luggage in the trunk. "Not as long as the water is calm." He smiled.

"Water? Isn't the bungalow on the mainland?"

"No, miss. Just a short boat ride across the harbor. It's such a small island that it's not even on most maps." He held the door open for her and she took a seat inside. "To Celestial Harbor, Jon."

Her knee-jerk reaction was to body block someone from stealing her cab. This was the first time she didn't have to fight to protect her ride. She could get used to it here. Marnie handed the skycap a five-dollar bill. "Thank you and have a wonderful day." And for once she meant it.

Palm trees lined the roadway as the taxi driver made his way closer to the water's edge. *Does everyone smile here?* She closed her eyes and took in the calypso music that had only briefly been introduced to her on the streets of the city in the summer. She would stop and Nick would grab her arm and pull her away, claiming they didn't have time for that.

What an ass he was.

What an ass she had been.

The distance was good for her. She gently swayed to the music as she sat in the seat. She *wanted* to dance.

The taxi came to a halt. "We're here, ma'am. Thirty dollars please." He jumped out of the taxi and opened the door for her and then placed her luggage on the curb next to the dock.

She quickly counted out the fare plus tip. "Thank you. Jon, is it?"

He nodded and his face broadcast the largest smile she had ever witnessed. "Wait for the boat. Captain Jack will take care of you."

"Have a wonderful day, Jon." She shielded her eyes with her hand as she looked out over the clear blue water. Her hair whipped about as a half bottle of defrizzer defied the island's humidity. With any luck she would make it a day or two without having to waste time keeping her unmanageable mane under control. She had the curse of the Shaw women.

A dingy forty-foot cabin cruiser sputtered up to the end of the dock. *No way I'm getting on that dilapidated fish boat.* She picked up her suitcase and spit her hair out of her mouth.

No, that can't be what's taking me to the

island.

And yet it had to be—the words *Jack's Craft* were spray-painted along the side of the boat and the operator looked like he could be a Jack.

The boat banged against the pilings and came to a sudden stop.

She had never been on a boat and this one didn't seem promising—neither did the heels she wore because she didn't take the time to shop for island wear. Marnie carefully maneuvered her way to the boat since Captain Jack didn't offer to help her and he seemed to lack the hospitable skills she had grown accustomed to in the past hour. Her heel caught in the splintered and weathered decking. *Shoes, no shoes? Splinters, no splinters?* She opted for shoes, no splinters and continued on her way.

The boat bounced against the dock, nearly knocking her off her feet. A suitcase saved her from falling over the side of the boat. She momentarily thought about leaving her luggage behind, fearing it would sink them. No, she would hold on to it. She had seen *Titanic*—the suitcase could come in handy.

"Captain Jack?"

No answer.

"Hello. Is Captain Jack here?" she called out louder.

He stepped out of the cabin and with one hand skillfully tossed a rope up onto the dock to secure the boat. His face was covered with a scruffy day-old beard and his scraggly hair, sun-kissed at the tips, briefly covered his eyes. From the side she could see that too much sun contributed to crow's-feet. He tossed his head back and she gasped. His eyes! A gorgeous blue she'd never seen. She sucked in a breath and dropped her luggage. She reminded herself to breathe as he came closer.

"You going to Celestial Harbor?" He wiped a screwdriver with a tattered, oily rag then brushed his hair out of his eyes with the back of his forearm. His clothes were rumpled and old. He didn't look much like a boat captain to her. Where was his uniform like she had seen in movies? He looked like a car mechanic after tearing apart an engine.

She nodded. The sunlight bouncing off the ocean made her squint but she held his gaze. If he was her means to get to the island, so be it. She shoved her luggage to the edge of the dock with her foot and waited for him to help.

And waited.

Nothing.

She reached over to the rope draped between two pilings and steadied herself as she swung her bag onto the boat. He was nice enough to catch it for her.

"Thanks."

"No problem." He slid the suitcase against the wall of the watercraft.

His searing blue eyes blinded her. *Stop looking at me.* She didn't like attention, it made her nervous. He turned his back to her and moved a box to the side.

She stretched her right leg down onto the edge of the boat. It bobbed and she tightened her grip on the rope. Her stomach churned as she feared she was going to fall into the water. She dug her free heel into the beat-up wooden planks.

Composed and steady, she tried to step onto the boat again. With her leg a few inches short of a full reach, the boat kicked against the dock and she let go. She fell onto the deck face-first, sunglasses smushed into her nose.

Jack ran over to her. "Did I tell you to get on yet?" He stood over her and put his hands through her arms and pulled her up in front of him.

"I didn't think I needed an invitation." She adjusted her sunglasses and stared him down. Maybe she was wrong and not all islanders were nice. He certainly wasn't, but she had no choice—he was her only way to Celestial Harbor.

This was going to be a long ride no matter how short the trip.

"You saw I was securing your bag," he said as he returned from the cabin. "You can sit in that seat at the back. And don't touch anything." He untied and cast off the lines from the boat.

Marnie pulled her hair back into a sloppy ponytail. No use fighting the wind. She held on to the makeshift rope handrail and maneuvered through boxes, bottles, and newspapers. Definitely not how she pictured a water taxi.

Captain Jack slowly backed the boat away from its temporary home. The heel of her shoe caught in a rope strewn haphazardly on the deck and she fell onto a pile of boxes, her face flush with embarrassment. She wanted to disappear into the deck and hide. "Damn. Why is there so much stuff in the way? What kind of boat business are you running here?" She pulled herself up and gathered her composure as best she could.

He looked over at her. "Are you okay? I can't stop the boat right now."

"Great." Her ankle throbbed. "This is not how I wanted to spend my vacation." She tried to reach her shoe to get it off her swelling foot. *Damn.* She sat back against the stack of boxes waiting for Jack to come over. She didn't like being helpless but she had never been in this situation, either.

She thought of Nick. He would have jumped to help her. It would be the perfect opportunity for him to do his caveman thing, but that wasn't going to ever happen again. *Bastard.*

It finally came to her—she didn't want to be alone. That's why she had stayed with him.

Jack swung the boat out of the channel and threw out the anchor. He walked toward her with a half smile. "It's those stupid shoes. You're from a city, right?"

"What does that matter?" She shifted her hips to make it easier to get up as he extended his hand to her.

"Because it's only those types that would wear shoes like that on a boat. New York or L.A. and I know you're not from L.A.—no tan." He pulled her up gently and helped her to the seat he'd pointed out but a few minutes before she fell.

She was taken aback by his momentary kind gesture. "Isn't that a generalization?"

"Maybe, but I find it to be true. I've noticed that city girls are more concerned with their appearance than being practical for the conditions they're in." His slight sarcastic tone bit at her. He laughed and left her alone.

She watched him walk into the cabin and return with an elastic bandage and a pair of dirty, cracked rubber thong shoes.

"Here, put these on. You'll find you won't even need these once you're settled in."

Her first instinct was to refrain from accepting the shoes—they were disgusting and she cringed at the thought of walking in footwear that was obviously worn by someone else. She considered tossing them overboard but she didn't want to be disrespectful. Plus, she didn't know what his reaction would be.

She reluctantly held out her hands and he plopped the dirty footwear into her open palms. "Thank you." She didn't mean it but wasn't in any position to offend.

He pulled up the anchor, the rope sliding through his weathered hands with ease, like he had done it a thousand times. His back muscles rippled through his threadbare T-shirt, his jeans— well, they fit perfectly. He carried himself with an assuredness she'd seen many times by men on Wall Street. She doubted his confidence and bombastic nature came from life on the high seas. Her interest was piqued and she tried to ignore the pain gyrating through her ankle.

"You're not from this area, are you? I mean, it's not like you grew up on a boat on the ocean." She wrapped her ankle since he'd left her to fend for herself. She was soothed somewhat by the rocking of the boat so she relaxed into the motion of the ride.

"No," he yelled over the roar of the engine.

"Unbelievable," she whispered under her breath. He couldn't be from here—he wasn't nice, not at all. "So are you going to tell me?" she yelled louder than he did.

The engine quieted in the open water.

"How's your foot?"

"Hurts." The swelling had stabilized, though, and the skeevy rubber thongs did feel much better than her three-inch heels. She didn't even own a pair of sneakers. That was the first thing on her shopping list. They must have sneakers on the island.

He leaned out farther and cupped his hand over his ear. "Can't hear you." He waved his hand and motioned for her to come inside the cabin.

"Are you serious?" She looked at her ankle, which was not getting any sympathy from the ship's captain. She shrugged. It wasn't like it was broken and she was going to nurse it in her bungalow for the duration of her vacation anyway.

She grabbed the handrail along the side of the boat and cautiously made her way to the cabin, taking care not to slip or—even worse—fall overboard. Each painful step took her closer to the cabin where she would be safer and out of the open sea. Her stomach tightened as the boat pitched and she braced herself from falling. She cringed at the thought of the ocean beneath her as a bottomless pit capable of swallowing them whole. No one would know she was there and she would surely die if something happened and they had to swim to shore. A wave of nausea overcame her. *No, no, no. He knows what he's doing.* She put her trust in Captain Jack to get her safely to Celestial Harbor.

She grabbed the cabin doorway and braced herself as the boat lurched forward.

He spun the chair around for her to sit. "You looking for company?" He watched her make her way to the seat next to him.

"I'd rather be inside, that's all. It's filthy out there. Why can't the rest of your boat be this clean?" She looked straight ahead and took in the beauty of the sea, trying not to think of the vast ocean floor beneath them. She wasn't about to let him know she was scared to death of drowning.

"What do you mean? The boat serves its purpose." He glanced at her.

She didn't take her eyes off the front of the boat. Her steady gaze quelled her fear of sinking to the bottom like a brick. "Your passengers might prefer a cleaner boat. That's all."

"You're the first to complain. I do more than transport people to their lodgings."

"Such as?"

"I run mail and medical supplies. Take people on fishing trips. Whatever's needed."

She threw him a sideways glance and caught him looking at her. *He's really cute.* Her hands were sweaty and her breathing grew shallow. Why couldn't she think of something witty to say? Because she was too focused on surviving the boat ride to the island. What if this was her only chance to make an impression with him? She spun her chair around. "People like me?" She smiled, proud that she made the gesture and leaned back comfortably in her seat.

"We're here." He throttled back the engine and slowed the boat as it closed in on the dock. A woman stood there in a flowing floral dress holding an armful of garlands made from yellow-and-pink plumeria flowers. "So how's your foot?"

The boat came to a rest against the dock.

"It hurts." She winced from the pain as she slid out of the chair.

"Wait here a minute." He left her in the cabin.

Never one to take direction very well, she hobbled onto the deck and watched him as he tossed a line of rope on the dock then wrapped the rope around a metal hook to secure the craft.

She steadied herself against the rails and boxes, careful not to take another tumble.

"Didn't I tell you to stay put?" That slight arrogance crept into his voice.

She ignored him and continued walking to the rear of the vessel. He wasn't going to tell her what to do. She respected the fact that it was his boat but it wasn't like she was a child that had to be monitored. She wanted to get off the boat and onto land as fast as she could.

Captain Jack jumped onto the dock and reached out to help Marnie out of the boat. She took his hand and nearly melted in place. He gave a gentle, warm, and comforting squeeze. She led with her good foot and carefully pulled herself up each step. One hand in his, the other holding her heels and grabbing the short rail against the dock.

"Hello. You are Marnie Shaw?" the flower lady asked.

"Yes, I am." She looked at Jack, seeking confirmation that he got her name—her complete name. She wanted to make sure he knew who she was in case he came looking for her—for any reason.

The greeter extended her hand and offered a flower to Marnie. "Enjoy your stay. My name is

Cecelia and I am available to handle any requests or concerns you encounter during your stay. Thank you, Captain Jack. Any mail today?"

He brought Marnie's luggage from the boat and placed it next to her. "Not yet. The plane was late and the mail wasn't ready when I left." He jumped back onto the craft and removed the rope from the metal hook. "I'll have it on my night run. I think you have more guests arriving later." He went into the cabin then cranked the engine.

The sunlight momentarily blinded her as she watched him motor away.

"Does he come out here often?" Marnie turned to Cecelia.

"Just about every day. If he's not bringing guests, he's bringing supplies and mail. He's always just a phone call away." Cecelia picked up Marnie's bag and tossed it in back of the golf cart at the end of the dock.

The wind kicked up and carried the scent of oleander with it. She could get used to it here— but of course that would never happen. Living on an island with the beach a few feet from her front door? It was a nice thought, but it couldn't be her reality—or could it? It wasn't like she had anything to go back to. She barely tolerated her job. Her apartment might not even be hers for much longer if the condo rumors were true. She'd ignored the gossip in her building and didn't have a plan for what she would do if she was forced to make a decision. She liked things the way they were.

The golf cart chugged up the crushed-shell driveway and came to a stop in front of the main building. "We'll get you checked in and then I'll take you to your bungalow." Cecelia put the gearshift in Park and then escorted Marnie to the front desk.

A mounted swordfish hung on the wall not two inches from her head as she passed through the doorway. Heavily used fish nets filled with the occasional red or blue glass ball were draped from the ceiling. A starfish holding a pen was perched on the counter next to the guest book. Calypso music streamed from an old CD player behind the lobby desk.

"Good afternoon. Checking in?" A young woman, about twenty years old, turned the guest book to Marnie so she could sign in. "Right here please."

Marnie couldn't resist plucking the pen from the starfish and entered her name into the book. A familiar signature stood out a few lines up the page.

Nick!

It couldn't be *her* Nick…

Maybe she was wrong—but how many Nick Corsentinos could be staying here? Hell, he couldn't even afford the trip, never mind know about the place. She had made all the arrangements. She had to be wrong. She carefully slid the pen into the arm of the starfish and spun the guest book around so it faced the clerk.

"Thank you, Ms. Shaw. Your bungalow is ready and Cecelia will take you there. You are the first bungalow on the beach. Enjoy." The clerk handed Marnie a key attached to a silver-dipped sand-dollar key ring. She joined Cecelia in the golf cart, which was already running.

They puttered along the neatly landscaped

trail, just wide enough to accommodate the cart or two people walking side by side. The grounds were laid out to stimulate the senses. Yellow, white, and pink hibiscus dominated the edges of the shell-filled path. Sea grass softened the hard lines of the palm tree trunks. The scent of gardenia wafted through the air, inviting you to grab hold of it. Occasional clumps of storm debris appeared in random spots best hidden from the guests so as not to detract from the beauty of the island.

The golf cart came to an abrupt stop in front of a mildly damaged bungalow as Cecelia stepped on the brake, nearly causing Marnie's luggage to fall off the back. "This is your home for the rest of your stay. Feel free to treat it as such. We apologize for the broken shutters but the contractor is doing the best he can to fix the storm damage."

Marnie stepped out of the unfamiliar vehicle, taking care not to put her weight on her swollen ankle. The blood rushed to her foot and the fluid felt like it would burst her ankle wide open. "The first thing I'm going to do is prop my leg up on that coffee table on the porch."

Cecelia yanked the luggage from the cart, dragged it up the front stairs, and plopped it inside the bungalow. "It's a nice day to relax on the veranda. I'll send a beverage pitcher over to you. Any preference? Alcohol or not?"

Marnie thought about Nick. She kind of missed having him around. Sort of like dust bunnies—you can get used to them but you're glad when they're gone. She shrugged away the thought. "Alcohol, please. An island drink with rum." She walked into the bungalow and could see from a quick glance that the interior was simple yet true to the island. Shells, nets, ship wheels, and sand dominated the decor. The bedroom was in the back.

She could manage her bag the rest of the way. If nothing else to prove she could.

"Use the phone if you need anything. The instructions are next to it. One pitcher of piña colada coming up in about half an hour." Cecelia pushed the luggage farther into the common room and quietly closed the door.

Marnie limped to the bedroom, using the wicker furniture to help her along. She pushed open the curtains on the picture window facing the ocean. The quiet after the storm. Waves gently lapped the edge of the shore. Palm fronds dipped and swayed with the breeze. She closed her eyes and drifted away, taking in the—

A sudden rap on the door startled her.

Her throbbing foot reminded her she couldn't run to the door. But she could take off the skeevy rubber things from her feet. "Who's there?" she yelled out the window and waited a moment. No answer. "Again, who's there?"

A young man with a flowered shirt, which told her he was from the resort, walked around to the bedroom window and raised the tray he carried. "Your drink, miss."

"Oh, that. Wow, that was quicker than Cecelia said it would be." She steadied herself but hesitated before making her way to the front door. "Would you put it on the table on the veranda please?"

He nodded. "Yes, ma'am."

The tip. "Wait, what's your name?"

"Theo."

"Theo, thank you. Will you be here later?"

"Yes, ma'am. Tonight is the clambake so I will be working until eleven tonight." Condensation frosted the glass pitcher.

"Great. I'll make good on your tip later. I'm just a little inconvenienced at the moment." She put some weight on her foot but the pain was still too fresh to carry the full load of her body. Well, Captain Jack said she wouldn't need shoes while she was here and he might be right.

Theo walked to the front of the bungalow. She loved the way it was situated—on the shore with a panoramic ocean view from three sides of the building. She found a bamboo stick resting in a corner and grabbed it. "Hmm, this'll work. You are now my new best friend." She stepped using the stick as a cane and maneuvered easier through the tight quarters. Maybe she could have some of the furniture pushed aside just for the time she'd be there.

She opened all the windows and embraced the fresh sea air as it swept through the bungalow. Sand dust twinkled on the glass tabletops. Maybe inviting the outside into the house wasn't a smart move. Oh, well, it would all be blown the other way once the wind changed direction. She picked up her trusty makeshift cane and made her way to the front door.

A pitcher of piña colada waited for her on the porch table.

She stopped and rifled through her carry-on

bag for a book. Something that was quick to read. She wasn't in any mood for anything too intense.

No drama today.

The thought of Nick possibly being on the same island as her was enough for her to deal with.

But could it be him?

She cleared her head and settled on a tourist guide of St. Thomas. She hadn't planned to go there but she could if she wanted to. It wouldn't hurt to know something about the place. It would give her the perfect excuse to hop on Jack's boat. She didn't have to stay on Star Island the entire time she was there. Right? She smiled as she thought of his blue eyes.

The door slammed against her but she quickly jammed the bamboo stick to stop it as she made her way onto the veranda. The pain in her ankle had reached maximum intensity and she needed to elevate it—that much she knew. The camping skills she learned as a child had helped her a few times in her adult years. She closed the door, making sure it latched this time to cut down on the sand dust littering her temporary quarters.

She turned around and nearly dropped her book.

"What are you doing here?" She fought to suppress a smile, not wanting to seem too excited that he was there. After all, they had met less than an hour ago. "You scared me. I didn't hear you coming. Do you usually sneak up on guests like this?"

"Don't you know you can't leave a pitcher of piña colada out here in the heat like this? Such a waste, so I helped myself." Captain Jack downed a tall glass of the sweet coconut-rum delight like it was water.

She sat in the chair across from him and took in his long, tan legs, resting on the rail. His rubber shoes weren't skeevy—he must save the disgusting footwear for his paying passengers. "You make yourself very comfortable here." She propped the bamboo stick against the rail then leaned over the table to pour herself a drink. His feet were inches from her head. *Ill-mannered yet intriguing. Hmm.* "Yes, very comfortable. Do you mind?"

"What do you mean?"

"Your feet. Would you at least move them away from my face? That's repulsive." She waited.

He slid lower in his chair and moved his feet about two inches away from her. "Better?" He closed his eyes and pulled his sun-bleached, sea-worn cap down over his eyes.

"If that's the best you can do," she responded sarcastically and finished pouring her drink. "You haven't answered my question."

He tipped the peak of his hat with his glass. "If the question was, would I move my feet, I answered it. I moved my feet."

"Why are you here?" She stared him down, ready to battle wits—she was from the city and could take on an islander with a few words and the flick of her little finger. Her head swayed as the rum started to hit her. She'd miscalculated the effect of the cool, sweet nectar as it caressed her throat as smoothly as coconut milk. She drank so little and rarely that she was a lightweight when she did.

She sat back in the chair and balanced her empty glass on her lap. Her good foot was planted firmly on the floor. It took a high school drunkfest for her to learn that one—not two, but one—foot on the floor keeps the room from spinning.

It seemed to be working.

"So again, why are you here?" She put her glass on the table, next to the near-empty pitcher. It seemed a shame to waste what was left and she wasn't going anywhere so she wanted the rest of the drink. *Why not? I'm on vacation and getting over a breakup.*

He pushed his hat back farther on his head. "I had to run some food here for the clambake tonight and there's some people who need to head back to St. Thomas."

"So?"

"I'm hanging out until I have to leave."

She struggled to keep from wavering. She didn't want Jack to think she was drunk. "And this porch is the official waiting area?" She leaned closer to the melted beverage.

He bent forward and pushed it toward her. "No, but it is the temporary residence of the person who stole my beach shoes."

Her hand missed the pitcher handle when she reached for it. "I stole nothing. Hell, I should do you a favor and toss them in the ocean. They're disgusting. How do you even have the nerve to give them to someone to wear?" She rested her elbows on the wide chair arms to steady herself.

Jack stood and leaned over her, placing both of his hands on the arms of her chair. "Maybe, but they're mine and I'm here to claim them. Where are they please?" he whispered like it was an invitation for her to come closer.

She sank deeper into the chair. "I'll get them later." She slid down lower as she grew nervous. She never planned on meeting someone and he interested her but she was still coming to terms with her breakup. "I want to read my book and finish my drink." She pressed her palm to his hard yet inviting chest. With the sun in her eyes she could only feel him and smell the sweet scent of pineapple, coconut, and a slight hint of rum that told her he was close. His chest pressed against her hand and she didn't resist.

He leaned in closer and gently cupped her face. His skin was surprisingly soft—not weathered like she'd imagined. He lingered.

Damn sun. She couldn't see him.

She closed her eyes and relied on the image of his magnificent eyes burned into her memory. She leaned back and welcomed his lips as he kissed her—softly, tenderly. It wasn't the kiss of a craggy seafaring captain. No, it was the kiss of a man who knew what he wanted but who had been hurt. Confident, but enough reluctance to be wary. "I'll be back later to collect my shoes. I'd prefer you didn't toss them in the ocean." He backed away as she sank into the chair and dropped her book.

The sun hovered over the ocean as it rested on the horizon. Tiki torches lined the pathway to the clambake. Cecelia was nice enough to pick up Marnie and drive her over to the festivities. She had spent most of the afternoon nursing her ankle with an ice pack and the stroll along the shore made her feel better as the saltwater bathed her foot. She was growing fond of her cane and planned to bring it home as a souvenir. It would be perfect for a limbo contest if she ever decided to have one. Not that there were many of those in the city, but she could be the first to have one at a party.

The golf cart came to a halt and she stabbed her bamboo cane in the sand to steady herself as she exited the vehicle. Dusk was near and the torches added an authentic feel to the event. She stopped short of a pig roasting in the ground on hot coals. A table full of corn on the cob, cucumber salad, and other items she couldn't identify waited to be eaten. After this afternoon, she would make it a point to eat something before she touched another drop of liquor. Especially since she knew Jack would be there.

He had kissed her so quickly that she kept trying to recapture the moment but the alcohol had gotten in the way.

Then there was the matter of Nick. She caught herself missing him and sighed. Maybe it was the rejection making her think about him. He was familiar to her and Jack wasn't—it scared her to venture into a new relationship. Maybe she was reading more into the kiss than there was. She picked up a plate shaped like a clam shell and filled it with corn, salad, coleslaw, and a roll. That should be enough to stave off any effects of the alcohol, at least for a little while. It wasn't like she'd planned to get drunk—she hardly drank, which is why she got buzzed earlier. The line behind her filled up with people and she wasn't in a mood to chat. She moved out of the way and found an empty chair next to the fire pit. The sun was nearly gone. She scanned the crowd for Jack and was disappointed that he wasn't there. She had forgotten his shoes anyway. Oh well, she could use some alone time.

"Hey there." A familiar voice came from behind her and she immediately recognized the large hand resting on her shoulder. It couldn't be. She spun her head around. "Surprised?"

Her eyes opened wide. "What the hell are you doing here?" Her plate of half-eaten food fell to the ground at the shock of seeing him.

"Come here, sweetheart." Nick opened his arms wide as if he expected her to run into them.

She grabbed her stick and stabbed it into the ground—practically through his bare foot. "Are you here to ruin my vacation?" She threw the chair back because he blocked her way.

"It's simple. I missed you. I made a mistake." He stepped aside to allow her to pass. "What happened to your foot?"

"Nothing that concerns you. The last thing I need is you here." She limped away. Maybe it was her, but it seemed like the pain had intensified the minute she saw him. All the nights she'd mentally spent forgetting about him and now he was in her face. She'd finally realized he was an ass and now she had to find a way to ditch him on an island smaller than her grandmother's farm.

Her shoulders clenched as she felt him following her. *Why?* She had finally come to terms with her decision to forget about him and now she could smell him he was so close to her, like a dog that wouldn't go away. Annoyed, she drove the bamboo deeper into the sand with each step. The last one sent her to the ground as she overcompensated her reach.

Nick knelt down beside her. "Are you okay?"

"Go away." She swung her arm out at him.

"Will you listen to me?" He reached out to her.

His familiar touch would be handy right now but she had to stay strong. "No, you have nothing to say that I want to hear." She positioned her good leg under her to support herself, dug the stick into the ground, and pulled herself up. She placed her weight on her strong leg and steadied herself. "I'm telling you right now. Leave!" She waved the stick at him, securing the distance between them.

Nick held out his hand and laughed. "What's the matter with you? I'm not going to hurt you."

She jabbed the stick like a javelin into the sand beside him. "You're right. You're not. Want to know why?"

He pulled the stick from the ground and tucked it under his arm. "Shoot."

"Because you already have. You couldn't possibly do any more damage than you already have." She stood firm even though her ankle throbbed worse now than it had earlier in the day. "Do you realize what kind of crap you pulled? You couldn't even tell me face-to-face. A *message* on my voice mail? What was that? Two years meant nothing to you and I realize that. Unfortunately, I realized too late that we aren't meant to be together and I'm done with you." She leaned forward and poked him in the chest. "Nothing. It meant nothing." She attempted to pass him but he grabbed her arm then quickly released his grip. She looked down at his hand. "Don't you ever touch me like that again. Any feelings I had for you left when you did. We're so done."

"That sounds like Jen talking." He lowered his face to her neck.

Her best friend, Jen had been right about him from the start. Nick was an ass. Why hadn't Marnie seen it sooner?

She could feel his breath against her skin. For a moment his familiar scent was inviting and it confused her. "Stop. Don't think that's going to change anything."

That was his way—he used sex and intimacy to diffuse anger. *Not this time.* Nick reached out to her. She was firm and yanked away her arm. "Just one thing I'm curious about. How the hell did you afford this trip?"

He stepped back. "Grandma Alice died and she left me a few bucks."

Her shoulders softened. Marnie had liked his grandmother. "When did she die?"

"Yesterday. Got my cut from the money she kept in the kitchen cabinet." He grinned.

"Are you kidding me? She's not even buried and you took your cut?"

"Well, I figured I could bring you back for the funeral." He smiled and folded his arms across his chest, full of himself.

"You are such an ass." Marnie shook her head. "No, correction. I've been the ass. Enjoy the rest of your trip and stay away from me."

She ripped the makeshift cane from under his arm and pounded the sand with each step that took her closer to her bungalow and another step away from him. Her stomach growled. She should have at least taken a roll back to her room. She needed a drink. Cecelia must have known she'd be back because a pitcher of piña colada was waiting for her on the veranda.

"I was wondering where you were." Jack sat in the chair as if he'd never left, only this time his hat was spun around with the peak at the back of his head. Wait, there was something different—he was wearing clean shorts and a loose buttoned-down Hawaiian shirt. Not the tight T-shirt and jeans that captured her interest earlier that day.

She lurched up the short flight of stairs. "At the clambake."

"And back so soon? It just started." He leaned forward and filled two tall glasses with piña colada. "That's the highlight of the resort." He waited for her to take a seat and handed her a glass but pulled it back slightly.

"Nice surprise. I couldn't see you from the ground. Did you bring the drink?"

"No, Cecelia did. Have you eaten?" He laughed.

He knew? "A little bit. Nothing was very appealing." She took a sip, leaned back, and propped her foot on the table with her trusty cane. "I couldn't get past the roast pig."

He laughed. "Yeah, that gets some of the guests. What's commonplace here can be off-putting to some." Jack removed his feet from the railing and moved his chair closer to her. "The surf gets louder at night."

She peered at him over the rim of her glass. A bush rustled—Nick was hiding behind it. She subtly shooed him away, but he stood firm. She knew how stubborn he could be, a quality that came in handy at times. But not right now. "Is there a police force on this island?" she asked louder than warranted. Nick sidestepped.

"Why would you ask that?" Jack took off his cap, uncovering dark, sun-streaked hair.

Momentarily distracted by her attraction to him, she sat back and answered loudly. "Oh, you never know. I mean if someone were harassing you it's just good to know the police are available." That Nick understood. As a former bouncer he knew what happened when the cops got involved. He waved his hand and took off.

Jack emptied his glass then reached across to pour another drink. "Is he gone?"

Startled, her shoulders pitched back and she sat up straight. "Who?"

He sat on the edge of his chair. "Your boyfriend."

"Ex-boyfriend. How did you know?" She sucked down half the drink and relaxed into herself as her shoulders softened. The pain was tolerable as long as she had her foot raised. The air was warm but comfortable and the drink refreshing. She'd be careful not to get tipsy again.

Now that she knew for certain that Nick was around, she needed her wits about her.

And then there was Jack.

This vacation was turning into an adventure and one that she was glad she took. The roar of the sea was a reminder of how much she ignored life around her while living in the city. Always running around, oblivious to the beauty of the world. She leaned on the arm of the chair and tipped back her head.

"He told me." Jack leaned in closer.

She turned her head to him. "What do you mean, told you?"

Jack refilled his glass. "How do you think he got to the island? Swam? I brought him over and he asked me if I knew where you were." He took a swig. "I didn't know then but I ran into him later…"

"And you told him?" She narrowed her eyes.

"I told him you were here but not where you were staying. How was I supposed to know you didn't want him to know? It's not that difficult to find someone once they're here anyway." He kicked off his sandals. "He's not very bright, that ex of yours."

She cleared her throat and kicked back her drink. "He has some good qualities." Though at the moment she was at a loss for finding any. The time away had given her clarity and she realized the relationship had been all her. Other than brute strength and keeping her refrigerator in constant need of replenishment, he hadn't brought much to their union. But was she ready for another relationship? Doubtful.

"I guess everyone does. What are some of yours?" He leaned back and put his cap back on.

That's an odd question. She sat back and lifted her nearly numb foot from the rail and attempted to cross her legs. That wasn't happening so she opted to rest them on the accompanying ottoman. "I'm organized."

He laughed. "Okay, that comes in handy, I

guess, but not what I was getting to. Just trying to make conversation. I don't get to talk to many people since I spend most of my time on the boat."

What exactly was he getting at?

She found him mysterious, a loner, yet he'd been waiting for her when she got back. Neither mentioned the kiss—she blamed the liquor and knew better than to make it more than it was. But why was he here? Whatever the reason she wanted him to stay a bit longer. "I can ice skate."

"I can surf. What else you got?"

That intrigued her, riding the waves, wind in her face. Her fears had held her back from doing much of what she wanted in life. This vacation was to prove to herself that she could conquer her fear of flying and the water.

"That depends on what you're looking for." She shifted in her seat, not sure what to make of the conversation.

Jack stood and held out his hand to her. "How about a swim?"

Her stomach curled into a knot. She tightened her sweaty hands around the cool glass.

"Well?" he challenged her.

"Um, I can't swim." She dropped her head to hide her face, waiting to hear him laugh at her.

Instead he placed his hand under her chin. "So, this is the perfect place to learn how." He took her glass and placed it on the table.

"What about my ankle?"

She looked into his eyes as he draped his arm around her shoulder and pulled her up, his other arm around her waist. "Let's just take a walk down to the break and see how you manage that.

I'm not going to throw you into the surf but you can't waste your time on the veranda."

She trusted him. He was offering something to her and she didn't know how to react—it felt honest. Her stomach fluttered as he walked her down to the edge of the shore. It wasn't the alcohol; she'd hardly drunk any. He was kinder than she expected him to be and it was nice to have company.

Streams of moonlight bathed the whitecaps as they broke against the sand. Jack held on to her and clutched her waist a little tighter as each wave crashed into them.

"How's your foot?"

She kept her head down so he couldn't see the joy in her face. Things were happening so fast. She couldn't keep up. "The water washing over it is making it feel better. Maybe it's wishful thinking."

"Or maybe it's not as bad as you thought and you've been babying it," he said jokingly.

There it is. The ass factor. "I'm not babying it. And it's rude of you to insinuate that." She pulled away from him. She wasn't helpless and he hadn't struck her as the protector type. She had enough of that and wasn't buying into it again. The sand gave way from under her as the tide pulled out. Her arms flew out to her side and she wobbled to steady herself. "See, still standing and no help from you."

No sooner did she defend her stance than a wave knocked her to the ground and sent her tumbling like a fish caught in the undertow. She dug her good heel into the cold, compact sand and pushed herself up. "Are you just going to stand there? Do you have any emotion in that sea-crusty heart of yours?"

"I'd help but I don't want to be rude and impose on your independence." Jack smirked.

She scratched her way to dry sand and sat, not even caring that she was soaked and would have to spend most of tomorrow morning fighting with her hair to combat the frizz. She didn't care if it curled but she couldn't come to terms with her hair being bigger than she was. The sand stuck to her and had even gotten into her teeth. A piña colada would be prefect to cleanse her palate.

Jack sat next to her. He didn't say anything—just sat and looked out into the sea.

She felt like an idiot. There were people worse off than she was and she'd been bitching about a stupid sprained ankle. It wasn't like this was going to change her life. She glanced at him.

"Thank you." She ran her fingers through her hair and cleared away knots and seaweed.

"For what?" He picked up a broken shell and tossed it into the water.

"For making me realize I had been feeling sorry for myself." She ran her tongue against her teeth in an attempt to dislodge the offending sand particles.

He propped himself up on the sand and turned to her. "No credit due. I was just tired of sitting on the porch. That's almost as bad as working in a high-rise all day."

As goose bumps ran up her arms, she wondered how his arms would feel around her keeping her warm. "Have you ever?"

"What? Worked in a high-rise?" He sat up and wrapped his arms around his knees. "Yes, once. Right out of college. Majored in finance and took a job on Wall Street with a securities firm. Lasted for about three years and I had to get out. It was like I was being strangled. I had to get back to the sea."

She stretched her legs in front of her and leaned back to match his position. "How did you learn about the sea if you're from New York? Did you have a boat there?"

He threw another shell into the surf. "I never said I was from New York. I said I worked there. Grew up in the Keys."

"Florida?" She leaned in closer.

"That would be correct. I have family up north, so since I majored in finance my parents thought Wall Street was the place to be. Isn't that where every finance major ends up?" He stared into her eyes. "So what do you do for a living?"

She thought about the many times she'd tried to have a conversation like this with Nick. Unless they talked about football or the newest beer to hit the market, there wasn't much of a discussion. Nick's way of communicating with her was in the bedroom. It was nice to sit in the moment and have intelligent dialogue with a guy who listened to her and was interested in what she had to say. She smiled and couldn't hide it from him if she tried—she liked him.

"Travel agent." She shifted to get more comfortable. Her clothes were drying but she still felt like she was covered in sand and couldn't wait to get back to her bungalow and shower. But he intrigued her and, well, she had the time, even if

Nick was lurking somewhere in the background.

"Do you like it?"

"For the most part," she lied. She took the job only because she was desperate for money at the time but she didn't want to tell him that she settled for something easy. She was good with comfortable and not taking chances on something more exciting.

"So you travel a lot?"

She threw her head back and laughed. "Hardly. I'm afraid of flying."

His eyes didn't leave hers. "You had to fly to get here." He looked at her with compassion and understanding and didn't make fun of her.

Her heart softened. It was like she could tell him anything and he would listen without judgment—well, except for her choice in footwear. She smiled. It was nice being with someone who seemed genuine. Why was he so interested? She never thought of herself as anything special but he made her feel that she was. Whatever the reason, she was enjoying herself and was relaxed with him and found him easy to talk to. "I'm trying to conquer my fears. At least that's what my best friend, Jen, told me I have to do."

He edged closer to her. "Does she tell you how to do everything?" he asked softly.

Marnie lowered her face to within inches of his. "No, just when I'm being unreasonable," she whispered back.

"What do you think Jen would have to say at this minute?"

She inched closer and parted her lips—

"Captain Jack. Captain Jack!" a man's voice

bellowed from nearby.

Damn! She pulled back and straightened herself.

She could tell something was wrong and stood up and brushed herself off.

"Captain Jack. Whew. I found you." Theo stopped short and bent over to catch his breath.

"What's the matter?" Jack asked.

Theo held his stomach as he composed himself. "We need you to transport a guest to the hospital."

Marnie stepped forward. "What happened?"

"He had too much to drink and he insisted on participating in the limbo contest and broke his leg. Snapped it just like a toothpick. Crack." Theo twisted his hands imitating a break.

"You're sure?" Jack asked.

"Most definitely, sir. We wouldn't ask you to run at night if we weren't. The lifeguard stabilized the gentleman so he's ready to be transported." Theo started back to the clambake.

Jack slid his arm around Marnie's waist to help her. "I'm not babying you—just so you're clear on that."

"Well, a little help is nice. It's a long walk and you do seem to be in demand for medical transportation." She smiled and tugged at his waist as they followed Theo.

The circle of people made way for Captain Jack as he neared the limbo area. Marnie realized how hungry she was as the smell of roast pork wafted through the air. No way would she eat it but it smelled good.

"Here, move aside please." Theo waved his hand, commanding the crowd to disperse even further. "So sorry to make you go out at night, Captain Jack, but you can see he needs help."

"Ow, oh, God this hurts." Nick was strapped onto a body board to hold him steady. Alcohol permeated the air around him.

"Jeez, how much did you drink?" Marnie yelled at him and waved her hand in front of her face to clear away the stench.

"Not enough. I can still feel the pain." Nick's hand fell off the side of the board as two men hoisted him up. "I need more beer."

"What an asshole he is," Marnie said under her breath. She shook her head and backed away to allow the men to carry Nick to the dock then get him on the boat.

Jack continued to help Marnie along as they walked behind the group. "What is it with you people up north and breaking limbs?" He laughed. "You two are done, right?"

"Most definitely. Nick came here asking me to go back with him but this is one of the reasons I wasn't too upset that he left. He drinks too much."

"He seems like a fun guy." Jack slowed his stride.

"Oh yeah, he's a fun guy. Always the life of the party, the last one to leave." She smirked.

"Marnie," Nick moaned. "Marnie, where are you? I love you."

Jack released his hold on her and she sighed. "Let me get them on board." He guided her to the dock handrail and made sure she could stand. The pain in her ankle was tolerable.

She ignored Nick's plea but couldn't turn her

back on him completely in his condition. The least she could do was get him to the hospital. And then she could leave his sorry, drunken ass there for his family to deal with. She sat on a bench at the rear of the boat as the men lowered Nick to the floor.

"Got him secured?" Jack hollered out to the men as he revved up the boat.

"Ready to go," one of the men yelled back and gave a thumbs-up. Jack waved and waited for them to disembark before pulling out of port.

Nick moaned and she placed her palm on his forehead. "I think you'll live. What the hell were you doing anyway? Showing off as usual?" What at first she'd found endearing about him had become annoying. The short time apart had given her a clearer sense of what their relationship was—she was surprised that it happened so fast. She knew she was making the right choice. She felt bad for him but she wasn't buying his apology, no matter how persuasive he tried to be. His drunken state definitely wasn't going to win her back. Since the beer fund was cut off when he left, she saw an immediate improvement in her financial status. Score for her bank account.

"I love you, Marnie." Nick reached up to her, barely able to lift his arm more than a few inches from where it lay.

"Stop. I don't want to hear it. My only purpose at this point is to get you to the hospital and then you're on your own."

"Aw, come on, Marnie. You know I love you. I made a mistake."

His garbled, liquor-induced speech made her shoulders tight with annoyance. She leaned over him and stared dead into his eyes. "No, I made the mistake. Two years ago. I mistook your charm and my caring for love. I've finally figured it out. We're done. Period." She tolerated a lot but once her mind was made up she could sever a tie like it was never there.

She glanced toward the cabin. Her goals had changed.

The roar of the engine quieted. Marnie looked to the cabin to see if he was still at the wheel. He was.

"I even had Jen change the locks so don't think you can just show up and surprise me there." She turned her back to him and laid her arm on the rail with her chin resting on her fist.

That reminded her—she'd have to call Jen and tell her he'd showed up. She peeked at him from beneath her fist. *Such a child.* She'd spent the greater part of her adult life working and living in the city. Love was never a priority and then she'd met Nick. She thought she needed a man to protect and take care of her. Someone to provide for her, and she had mistaken that for love. He'd failed on most fronts and she knew it wasn't his fault. They just weren't right for each other. She needed someone who took life seriously, at least some of the time, but also had the ability to laugh. Someone who could make her laugh, and not by crushing a beer can on his forehead.

She looked to the cabin and watched Jack commandeer the small craft through the dark night. The sky was overcast with the threat of a storm. She could tell he was focused and serious about his work but something happened on the beach that told her he offered more and she wanted to find out what that was. He was genuine when he asked her questions. He wanted to know about her and not just what she did for a living but what interested her. She'd never had that with Nick, who had passed out from too much to drink.

Nick groaned as he tried to move but the straps held him in place. *Finding the perfect love is like chasing fireflies in the city. Possible but not likely.*

Nick was not her perfect love.

She strolled into the cabin and sat down. She felt somewhat guilty about leaving Nick all alone but she was compelled to be near Jack. It was as if she was pulled to him by an unseen force. She sat in silence and watched him skillfully man the boat. Even his silence was fulfilling. He said so much without having to speak. His confidence was intoxicating. *Oh, what am I doing?* She caught him glance at her.

"How's he doing?"

"Drunk and broken but he'll live." She didn't want to distract him. The water scared her even more at night. The moon was covered by cloud and she didn't like that she couldn't see past the boat lights. It brought back her childhood fear of the dark and water, not a good combination right now. She gripped the seat and examined the cabin without being too obvious that Jack was part of her focus.

"What are all of those lights on the dashboard?" she asked.

"The helm is the control center for the craft." He laughed.

A patch of cloud cover cleared and the moon poked through. "It's pretty out here. Quiet. Well, except for the engine noise."

He sat in the captain's chair and held the wheel steady with one hand. "There's nothing to worry about out here." He patted her knee.

"What makes you think anything is wrong?"

"Oh, come on. Your nails practically punched holes in your seat when you sat down. You couldn't have held that seat any tighter."

Damn, he notices everything. She thought she'd played it cool and kept her fear under control. She relaxed and realized she was safe in his capable hands.

The boat slowed as they approached the dock. A red flashing light circled the sky from an awaiting ambulance. Tomorrow she would have her talk with Nick, when he was sober. It would be a waste of her time and useless for him to have any type of normal discussion in his inebriated condition. She was too tired for this.

Jack expertly pulled the boat into a boat slip designed for water ambulances. She admired his ability and could tell he enjoyed what he did. It was a lifestyle for him, not a job. *That must be nice.*

Two emergency room techs removed Nick from the boat and onto a stretcher. Jack hadn't turned off the boat. Marnie walked up to him and rested her hand at the small of his back.

"I have to go in with him. He doesn't know anyone here and he's liable to piss someone off and he needs to get that leg…"

Jack held his index finger to her lips lightly. "I don't need any explanations. You do what you have to do."

"But how will I get back?" She wanted him to kiss her again. As she watched Nick being carted away into the hospital, she knew she had to go but she wanted to stay with Jack.

"Someone at the desk will know how to get in touch with me." He winked with a smile and turned from her then walked into the cabin.

She stepped off the boat and onto the dock. Lights from his boat grew dimmer in the night as he motored away.

It must have been a slow night because Nick was in an examination room by the time she got into the building. She gave the intake nurse his information then went outside. No boat lights to let her know Jack was within reach.

Her cell phone rang and startled her. "Jen? What's wrong?"

"Now what makes you think something is wrong?"

"Um, it's late."

"Okay, real quick because this is going to cost us a fortune. Your nice rent-controlled apartment is going condo. You have sixty days to buy or vacate. Bye."

"Don't you dare hang up!" Marnie yelled.

"Gotcha." Jen laughed.

"It's not going condo?" A sigh of relief escaped her lips.

"Oh no, it's going condo. I wasn't going to hang up."

"You're a sick woman. Well, there was talk about it, so I guess the rumors were true. Damn."

She ran her fingers through her hair. There was nothing she could do about it now. She'd have to wait until she got home. She'd try her best to enjoy the time she had left on Star Island. "I have my own disaster here. Nick." Marnie sat down on a bench craving a cigarette—she hadn't had one in ten years.

"Nick? What's he got to do with anything? And remember this is costing us so say it fast."

"He's here. He showed up to ask me to go back with him and then he broke his leg in a drunken attempt to win a limbo contest." She dug through her pockets looking for anything to chew on.

"Yeah, that sounds like him. So what are you going to do?"

Marnie looked out to the sea and then to the hospital. There was so much change going on. "I honestly don't know." She hesitated. "I met someone."

"Seriously?" Jen shrieked with happiness.

"Yes, and I don't think it matters." The urge for a cigarette grew stronger, as did her uncertainty.

"Why not?"

"He lives here." Marnie didn't take her eyes off the water. She knew Jack was out there and she wanted to be with him.

"And so do you for almost two more weeks. Don't be stupid. Go for it." Jen hung up before Marnie could respond.

It had been a long night in the hospital. Nick was settled in and she said goodbye. She headed back to the bungalow in the late afternoon. She didn't call for Jack but used the ferry service that ran only during certain times of the day; she couldn't face him right now with her crusty clothes from the night before and uncontrollable mane of hair. The hours spent watching Nick lying in the bed after his cast was set gave her time to think about their relationship.

He *did* come back to her but she was over him and she wanted more. She was positive about that.

They didn't fit. She was sure of that. They were from two different worlds and they didn't mesh well. She needed someone who would complement her life—not complicate it. Someone who got her and didn't treat her like a wounded bird just to make himself feel better. She needed—Jack.

She knew she was hard to please and rarely let anyone close to her. Nick had been safe because he was happy with the simplest things in life. She felt a bit guilty about leaving him alone in a strange place but it was his fault he was there anyway and it was ruining her vacation.

She kept searching for Jack's boat as the ferry made its way to Celestial Harbor. He wasn't around. How did her trip turn into the most frustrating and aggravating time in her life?

The ferry docked and she limped slightly down the plank and noticed her bamboo cane stuck in the sand at the end of the rail. *Jack.* She smiled as she thought back to their conversation on the beach the night before. She felt there was something there.

He was too interested in her. Or maybe she

was so used to little attention, that any was welcome.

She grabbed the stick and dug it into the ground with each step even though she didn't need its assistance anymore.

"Hello, Marnie. Good afternoon." Cecelia greeted her on the porch. "Your bungalow has been cleaned so you can relax. I'm sure it's been a long night."

No piña colada pitcher on the table but it was a little early to drink. Her stomach growled and hurt—she needed to eat. "Thank you, Cecelia. Yes, it was a long night but Nick will be released tonight and then I have to look into getting him home. Thank you again."

The room was free of sand until a trade wind kicked up again. She needed a shower, her clothes were crusty against her body, and she was getting itchy. She didn't even think to change last night after getting doused with seawater. Her immediate reaction was to get Nick the help he needed and she accomplished that. *What now?*

She walked into the bedroom and smiled. Cecelia hadn't let her down—not only was there a pitcher of piña colada but a plate of cucumber, tomato, and cheese finger sandwiches with potato chips, and a selection of fresh fruit. She scoffed down a sandwich and jumped into the shower. The warm salt-free water cascaded over her and she scrubbed the sand out of her hair, watching the suds swirl down the drain. If only her worries could disappear that easily.

Hunger forced her to cut her shower short; she felt light-headed and weak. At least the grittiness from the sand was gone. She sat in the rattan chair next to the bedroom window and realized that she hadn't even slept in the bed yet. She ate a few more sandwiches and poured half a glass of what was becoming her favorite beverage.

With her stomach satisfied with finger sandwiches and the dizziness subsiding, she picked up a sheet of paper and pen from the side table. She had to sort out her finances and figure out what to do with her apartment. She'd had enough of the Caribbean fresh air for a day and was comfortable curled up in a corner chair. She could appreciate the beautiful sky through the window without having to be out in the open.

A gust of wind blew through the room and the paper landed on the floor. *Omen?* She picked it up and crumpled it into a ball and tossed it into the waste bin. She took another sheet of paper and wrote down *New York Condo*—and stopped. Her stomach fluttered and she smiled as she thought about Jack and the beach.

Hours passed as she dozed on and off while curled up in the chair. She woke up as the sun dipped down and darkness filled the room. She turned on the lamp next to her then walked over to her suitcase on the bed and pulled out a sarong and sheer cover-up. Enough time had been spent in thought. She needed to get out and kick her toes in the surf. Her ankle was almost back to normal but she took her cane anyway.

The night air was warm but not stifling, the sand cool but not cold. Her gauzy cover-up gave little protection against the slight wind. She walked to the water's edge and drew circles in the sand with her stick, watching the water wash them away with each passing wave. She hadn't even thought about her living situation; no need to worry about that until she got home.

She plunged the bamboo into the ground in front of her, wrapped her hands around it, and closed her eyes. Her body absorbed the rhythm of the ocean and she felt light as she swayed to the motion of the water.

She'd been here only a few days but learned so much about herself. She wasn't as afraid of the water as the thought she was. She wasn't in love with Nick and she wanted more time with Jack, but she had to work on her fear of flying. It wasn't like Jack could scoot up the coast to New York on a regular basis. She had access to cheap fares. *Oh, who am I kidding?* He must meet hundreds of women visiting the island. Why would she be special?

"So are you over him?" Jack's comforting voice filled her silence.

She squeezed her eyes tighter and was sure she was hearing things. The sea could be so many things.

A hand slid around her waist and she recognized the subtle but firm grasp. She waited.

"Again, are you over him?" This time the question was softer yet closer.

She released her grip on the bamboo cane and he removed it from her hand. He turned her to face him and pulled her in closer—the ocean lapping at their feet. She opened her eyes and smiled. "Yes."

He tossed the cane on the beach not far from where they sat the night before. She sank into his body, waiting, unsure what would come next but eager to find out. It might take a few more trips to Star Island to know for sure but she was willing to get on a plane.

Suddenly, he reached above her and grabbed at the air.

She pulled back but he caught her, held her close, and opened his hand.

"Hmm, that's odd."

She peeked into the darkness of his palm and it lit up. "Fireflies."

"It's unusual for them to be out this early in the season." He closed his hand just enough to hold the fireflies without hurting them.

"Maybe not." She smiled. *I think Grandma could be right.*

She pushed in closer to him as the sea lapped at their feet and softly peeled back his fingers to release two fireflies into the wind. She took a deep breath, confident she had found her perfect love.

About…

Lita Harris spends her time between New Jersey and the Endless Mountains region of Pennsylvania, where she writes most of her books. She also lived in Alaska for a short time just for fun. An avid crafter, unused supplies clutter her basement and attempts at making pottery, jewelry, and stained glass are proudly displayed in her house, usually behind a picture or holding a door open. She also makes candles and homemade soap. With enough books to stock a small library she may need to construct a building to store her literary obsessions.

She writes in multiple genres, including women's fiction, contemporary romance, paranormal, and cozy mysteries.

For more information about Lita, please visit her website at www.LitaHarris.com or at twitter.com/litaharris and facebook.com/litaharrisauthor.

For more stories by Lita Harris, try *Love At Christmas,*
Available from Sweet Cravings Publishing.

Love at Christmas

Kristen Anderson is resigned to live a child-free
life in New Jersey. That is, until she's given
custody of her seven-year-old nephew after the
death of his mother. Christmas brings them to
their grandmother's house in Pennsylvania where
the family focuses on healing and reopening the
family inn in time for the holidays. Enter Luke
Baldwin, a man with a past that leaves him
uncertain whether he'll ever find love—until he
meets Kristen.

Kristen's and Luke's desire to be together is
complicated by Kristen's yearning to return to
New Jersey, her grandmother's determination to
keep Kristen in Brookside Falls, and a family
secret that is revealed on Christmas Eve. Will the
deceit that threatens to break them apart change
their lives forever? What will Christmas bring
them?

In Her Dreams

Emma Kaye

❧

Author Winnie Boyle finds more in the U.S. Virgin Islands than the inspiration she sought for her latest novel. When she reads from an old journal she finds on the beach, she's transported to another time and place—literally. She assumes it's all just a dream when she finds herself in Regency England. Surely the gorgeous Viscount Bastian Caulfield and his sweetly innocent sister couldn't be real.

The dream quickly turns to a nightmare when she can't wake up and realizes something sinister is at work. Someone's trying to kill Bastian and Winnie's been brought back in time to save him. How? She has no idea. But time's running out.

Can she escape this crazy dream with her mind and body intact? Because it may be too late for her heart…

❧

Dedicated to ~

The man of my dreams and our wonderful children. I love you.

My family and friends, who have always supported my dreams.

The Scribes, who make the Timeless books such a pleasure to write.

Mallory Braus, whose edits were killer but right on target.

In Her Dreams
by Emma Kaye

Winnie Boyle threw her pen and notebook onto the towel next to her. She tugged the lever to lower her beach chair but it didn't give.

She yanked harder.

The lever gave with a snap and the back of her chair crashed down.

So did she.

She yelped, her legs lifted in an effort to keep herself upright that failed miserably. The strap of her bikini tugged at her neck. A quick glance reassured her that she was still decent, but it was a near thing. She ceased her struggles with the chair to set herself to rights.

The bright island sun beamed upon her like a spotlight. Her cheeks blazed with the heat of embarrassment. Maybe nobody saw?

Of course the lever now moved with ease as she maneuvered herself into a more comfortable position.

Cough. Cough.

So much for her discomfiture escaping notice. She twisted toward the sound, shielding her eyes from the brilliant Virgin Island sun.

A teenage girl hovered over the recliner next to her. She wore a long, flowing white cover-up over a pink swimsuit that peeked through at the shoulders. The wind blew her wavy dark brown hair across her face. She flipped back the errant strands and tilted her head to keep them out of the way. A leather-bound book pressed against her chest, clutched tightly in her hands. "Good morning," she said with a British accent.

"Hi," Winnie greeted her.

The girl gestured to the seat. "May I sit?" A beaming smile made her seem awfully excited for someone simply asking for a seat.

Winnie forced herself to not look at the dozens of empty chairs scattered across the beach. The day was young and most of the Celestial Harbor guests hadn't made it down to the beach yet. "Sure, no problem."

"Thank you. It's a lovely day, is it not?" The girl studied Winnie's face as if expecting something.

Winnie was at a loss to know what. "Yes. Gorgeous."

"My brother and I arrived a short time ago."

"Are you here for the wedding?" That could explain it. Maybe she thought Winnie was a distant relative and wasn't sure how to greet her.

"Wedding? No. We're here to meet someone, but it appears we're a bit early." Her smile slipped. Sadness swept across her face, making her appear even younger and more vulnerable.

"You might want to check with Captain Jack." Winnie nodded toward the small dock where she'd been greeted upon arrival a week ago. *Jack's Craft* bobbed in the water as the captain helped a guest disembark. "He'd know if your friend has arrived yet."

The girl shuddered. "That won't be necessary, thankfully. The captain was quite— intimidating." She wrinkled her nose. "And dirty."

Winnie chuckled. "He's a character, that's for sure." Easy on the eyes, too. He'd make a great secondary character in her novel and probably end up with his own book somewhere down the line.

The girl lowered herself to the chaise. She perched on the edge, her posture ramrod-straight. "Oh my. This chair is frightfully low."

"It's a recliner. You're supposed to lie back and relax." Winnie suited her actions to her words, resting her head on her sunbaked towel.

"Yes. Well. I'm afraid I'm not used to such furniture." Her smile returned. "I shall adjust." She rearranged her cover-up until her legs were completely covered. She laid her book down on the small table between them and lifted her face regally to the sun.

Winnie squashed a twinge of jealousy. Damn. Why did she feel like the awkward teenager all of a sudden?

She closed her eyes and tried to find the sense of peace she'd been looking for when she'd put on her bathing suit and headed to the beach. Why couldn't she relax?

The edge of her notebook dug into her thigh

and she sighed. That would be why. The darn thing wasn't as distressingly empty as it had been when she'd arrived a week ago, but it certainly wasn't as full as she'd hoped. And none of it was useable. A whole bunch of character notes, story ideas, and crappy dialogue. If she didn't get on the ball real quick, she was going to miss her deadline.

Her characters weren't working for her. Well, the heroine was okay. It was the hero. He was an ass. All he cared about was money. There was no way *her* heroine would ever fall in love with him. And if she did, Winnie would be tempted to smack some sense into her.

She needed inspiration.

A cool breeze wafted over her skin. The scent of the ocean tickled her nose. If she couldn't find inspiration here, she was doomed. She forced her eyes open and took in the view.

Palm trees and hibiscus lined the edge of the secluded beach. The buildings were kept back beyond the foliage, which gave the illusion of undisturbed beauty. Her room was a short walk back along the weathered wooden walkway, but from here, she couldn't hear a thing from the busy resort. Surprising given that they were in the midst of repairs.

Winnie scratched at a scrape on her arm. Her own bungalow was in decent shape, but the roof of the main building was getting an overhaul. None too soon. The weather channel said a freak tropical storm was heading their way.

She scanned the beach. Towels and beach bags lay scattered over many of the chairs now as guests greeted the day by enjoying the sparkling water and frothy waves. A man came out of the surf a dozen or so feet away. She started to move on, but his antics grabbed her attention. He was an adult, but he played in the surf like a child. Running in and out of the waves, diving under and popping back up.

Too playful for a hero? Maybe not. Her heroine could use some playfulness in her life. And he definitely had the body of her imagined hero. His baggy swimsuit hung low on his hips, clinging to his legs and showing off his tight abs and muscular calves. Very nice.

She grabbed her notebook and pen as she watched him cavorting at the waterline. She'd give him green eyes. A perfect complement to his dark hair. She couldn't tell if it was black or dark brown with it all slicked back from the water. Short, anyway. She scribbled away, a smile tugging at her lips.

Yes. Finally.

She alternated her attention between her notes and the man. Her fantasy probably had no link to reality, but it didn't matter a bit. All that mattered was that she was finally getting into this story now that she'd found a hero her readers could love.

The teenager's gasp broke the spell. Winnie glanced over when the girl jumped up from her chaise. Her eyes were huge in her pale face. Her gaze fixed on the water. Winnie turned to see what had her attention.

Walking toward them with long, purposeful strides was the gorgeous stranger. He glanced neither right nor left, his focus clearly on the two of them.

No, not them.

Holy crap, he's staring at me.

Impossible. She had no idea who he was. She'd certainly remember if she'd ever met someone that looked like him.

Longing swept through her. The expression on his face…pure joy. He definitely thought she was someone else.

The girl ran toward him. She grabbed hold of his arms, forcing him to a standstill. He resisted for a moment, his gaze still glued to Winnie. Then something the girl said snagged his attention. His smile transformed into a fierce frown. The girl pulled him away and within seconds they'd disappeared among the trees toward the resort.

Winnie's mouth gaped open. She clamped her jaws shut. *What the hell?* That was the girl's brother? She suddenly wished she'd been a bit friendlier.

Her notebook dropped to the sand with a soft thud, bringing her attention back to the present. She should try to capture that joyful look of his in her notebook. A look like that belonged at the end of the book when the couple got together forever.

The description flowed from her pen like water from a faucet. She'd been writing romances for years, but the words had never come so easily. Of course, she'd never had a look like that turned in *her* direction before.

She tossed her notebook on the little table and realized there was already something there. The teenager's book.

Winnie picked up the tattered, leather-bound volume and turned it over in her hands. The girl was long gone and Winnie had no idea who she was. Still, this was a private beach, so she must be staying at the resort. She'd ask at the front desk.

Hmm. They'd need a name, though. She scanned the inside covers and flipped through the handwritten pages. Maybe she could find a name in there somewhere.

The girl had the strangest writing. Pretty. Not like her own barely legible scrawl. She squinted at the small, flowery script.

The pages fell open somewhere in the middle. A small, dark green bag that smelled strongly of pine, cloves, rosemary, and sage fell out. She picked up the tiny pouch and studied the writing on the page. She read aloud in an attempt to make out the strange script.

> *" 'I say this spell of my free will,*
> *To keep his heart from harm or ill.*
> *Through time and space we'll fear no threat.*
> *Our strength will protect and guide us yet.*
> *For thirty days we'll have our chance,*
> *To right the wrongs or make our stance.*
> *On thirty-one the time has come,*
> *Friend or foe the spell is done.*
> *Spirits of the heavens, hear my plea.*
> *I seek your help, so mote it be.' "*

The scent of sulfur and beeswax drifted across the wind. She could swear the young girl's cultured British voice repeated the phrase she'd read, but no one was around. The light dimmed. Dark enough that she pushed up her sunglasses to the top of her head. It didn't help—the light faded even more.

The storm, already? She squinted at the book, but could no longer make out the words.

The lines of writing swirled and faded. It was too dark to see.

Her heart fluttered wildly in her chest. She fought for breath. She wanted to get up, go inside, but she couldn't make her body respond. She sat there, pinned to the lounger.

The world faded away…

∞CR

Winnie clutched her roiling stomach and squeezed her eyes shut against the whirling blackness. A cold draft wafted up her legs, raising goose bumps up and down her body. She shivered and clutched herself tighter.

"Oh my goodness! You poor dear. What happened to your clothing?" asked a softly accented British voice.

Winnie's eyes popped open. *What the hell?*

The beautiful, pristine white-sand beach of the Celestial Harbor resort was gone. In its place was a large bedroom filled with heavily carved dark wood furniture.

A young woman dressed in a full-length empire-waist gown sat at a writing desk a few feet away. The light of four large white candles flickered across her somehow-familiar face. Her dark brown hair was pulled back into a severe bun at the base of her neck. She bit her lip. Her hands twisted in her lap.

"Where…where am I?" Winnie asked. Had she fainted? Too much sun? Was she dreaming? She pushed up against the soft, plush fabric of a golden paisley chaise lounge. Where was the wooden beach chair and her bright orange towel?

"Oh! I'm dreadfully sorry. Please. Allow me to introduce myself." The girl stood, took a delicate hold of the sides of her dress, then curtsied.

Curtsied?

"I am Lady Jane Caulfield. You are at the country estate of the Earl of Wallingham. I do apologize for the suddenness of this call. I expect I summoned you out of your bath? You wear the strangest garment." She rattled on, but Winnie couldn't follow. Jane crossed the room to a large armoire, yapping away the entire time. She swung open the doors and took out a dressing robe. "You may borrow this for the moment. I will summon my maid to alter a few of my dresses for your use while you stay with us. We appear to be of a similar size."

Jane held out the peach-colored garment with an inquiring look on her face. Eyebrows raised, a slight smile on her lips.

Winnie stared. Moving didn't seem possible quite yet. Her mind was in a whirl.

"And you are?" Jane asked.

The door crashed open. Winnie jumped at the resounding bang. She swung around and her heart tripled its throbbing beat. The gorgeous man she'd seen on the beach stood only feet from her. She didn't think he'd caught sight of her, with his back partially toward her and his focus on Jane.

Winnie forced herself to stay still. Avoiding attention seemed like a good idea at the moment.

"What the bloody hell do you think you're doing?" He waved his arm in the direction of the writing desk, the candles still lit upon it.

Now that Jane had moved, Winnie could see

a book lay open in the middle of the desk. The barest hint of rosemary told her the small flecks scattered across the tabletop were likely a mix of herbs. The scent was familiar. Winnie sniffed the same odors on her hand mixed with her suntan lotion.

"I felt the power of your spell wash over me all the way out in the stable. There are consequences to your actions, Jane. Magick is not to be handled lightly. Nor by children."

Spell? Magick? What the hell is going on?

"I am not a child, Bastian." Jane stood straighter. Winnie wouldn't have thought it possible. It was like the girl had a metal rod stuck to her back. "You chose to ignore my warning. I had little choice but to see to your safety myself. I am your sister and I care too much for you to allow any harm to befall you."

Bastian sighed. He winced when he ran a hand through his thick, dark hair. He cupped his upper arm but stopped almost immediately and crossed the room to stand directly in front of Jane. "I know you worry for me. It is needless. Father has done nothing to warrant this fear you harbor."

She shuddered but stared him down. "What of the stray bullet as you hunted the other day?"

Bullet? And I thought this couldn't get any worse. Winnie clapped a hand over her mouth to muffle any involuntary noises.

This isn't happening.

If she said it often enough, it would be true.

"An accident, no more."

"I am not convinced." She poked his arm and raised a brow at his pained expression.

Now would be a really good time to wake

up. *Wake up!* Desperation fueled her panic. He was bound to notice her at any moment. What would happen then?

He strode over to the desk and flipped the journal closed. "And what did you hope to accomplish using our mother's magick book?" With his thumb and forefinger, he pinched the wicks of each candle, snuffing their meager light. When done, he looked up. Straight at Winnie.

She froze like a deer caught in the headlights. He was close enough now that she could see the crystal clear blue of his eyes. Not the green she'd imagined for her hero. They were a blue she would have described in her book, but had never seen in person. Movie-star eyes.

Only it wasn't love shining in those ocean-blue depths this time.

She forced her chin up and met his glare head-on. That's what her heroines would do. They wouldn't crumble. Or cry. Or scream. Like she wanted to. She couldn't stop the tremor in her hands.

His fierce frown was at complete odds with the man on the beach that morning. This man didn't mistake her for someone he loved. And he apparently wasn't the playful type.

Somehow, she missed seeing that look on his face. Ridiculous since it had never been for her anyway.

His gaze raked her from head to toe, pausing at her midsection where the dangling ruby-red gemstone on her belly ring matched the polka dots on her barely-there bikini.

She wasn't as brave or brazen as the heroines in her novels. They'd have stuck out their chest and propped a hand on their hip before asking the beast if he liked what he saw.

She crossed one arm across her stomach, the other over her breasts.

But damn it! She was on vacation.

Or dreaming.

Why should she be embarrassed? Her bathing suit wasn't exactly modest, but she'd seen worse.

Only, she wasn't on the beach. Standing next to two fully dressed people—actually, two overdressed people—was unnerving. Not to mention how the image of him in his own clinging bathing suit was seared on her brain.

Red crept up his neck and spread across his cheeks as he watched her squirm. He dropped his gaze. "Jane. Who is this person and why is she practically naked?"

Jane threw the dressing gown over Winnie's shoulders. Winnie shrugged into it, tightening the waist with a vicious yank on the belt. Pissed at herself for feeling so self-conscious. She clutched the neckline together with a trembling hand.

"The spell brought her here." Jane ran over to her brother and grabbed his hand. "She's here to protect you."

Winnie reared back in surprise. "I'm what?"

Bastian's laugh sounded like a bark. Short and surprised. "This is the result of that spell you cast? I can think of little she can do for me that is suitable to be discussed within your hearing."

Jane tilted her head and gave a small frown, Bastian's words apparently lost on her innocent ears.

Winnie wasn't quite so innocent. Fury boiled

up within her. "Excuse me? Holy crap, this is one messed-up dream."

"You will guard your tongue, miss." Bastian grasped Jane's hand, pulling her to his side and slightly behind as if to block her from Winnie.

"Oh, I'll *guard my tongue*, as soon as you do. I'm surprised I didn't dream you up some manners." She pinched the flesh of her bicep viciously and winced at the pain. "Okay. That was supposed to wake me up." *Why can't I wake up?* "How did I get here and why are you all dressed like it's the nineteenth century? Will someone please explain to me what's going on?" *Holy crap. Not a dream.* Breathe. She had to breathe. She sucked air through her nose and released it in a gush. Again.

"Oh, you poor dear." Jane twisted out of Bastian's grasp and flung herself at Winnie, screeching to a halt just shy of knocking into her. She took Winnie's hands and squeezed them lightly.

"What year do you believe it to be?" Bastian asked.

Winnie's head ached. She stared at them for a moment before his question became clear. "It's two thousand fourteen." She pulled her hands from Jane to rub her temples, ignoring their shocked expressions. "I must have hit my head. You're all a figment of my imagination. And you're dressed like that because my work in progress is a Regency."

"You must be terribly confused." Jane shook her head. "I believe you were about to share your name when we were so rudely interrupted." She cast a scowl in Bastian's direction.

"Confused!" She choked back nearly hysterical laughter. She had to hold it together. What had Jane asked? Name. "It's Winifred Boyle—Winnie. Don't call me Winifred, I hate it." *What the hell am I rambling on about?* "What I don't know is how I got here and why I can't wake up. Did I pass out or something?"

"My dear Miss Boyle—"

"Winnie." This situation was bad enough. She wasn't going to have some teeny-bopper make her feel like a high school science teacher. *Right, focus on the important things, Winnie.* She resisted the urge to roll her eyes at her own idiotic musings.

"As you wish. Winnie. This is not a dream." Jane pulled her over to a small settee at the foot of the bed. "Please, let us sit." She took a deep breath once settled. "The year is eighteen hundred seventeen. I have brought you back in time to aid us. I am sorry my spell caught you unawares. I must admit to not knowing quite what to expect when I followed the directions in Mother's journal."

"Exactly why you should not be fooling with such things in the first place." Bastian gripped the leather book then shook it in Jane's direction. "You mess with forces you know not. And what have you gained? A houseguest. Are you lonely? Was it company you sought?" Some of the steam left him as he studied his sister. "I'm sorry our father did not see fit to bring you with him to London this past season as he promised."

Winnie watched the emotions play out across his face. She'd bet he was awful at poker. She wanted to stay angry—it was easier. But he wasn't the annoying, blustery man who'd barged in here a few moments ago. He may have been upset, but he was guided by concern for his sister. Who could blame a guy for that?

"Oh, Bastian. Please don't fret. I have met the men our father considers suitable and I can assure you I have no desire to go to London to waste my time fending off their unpleasant advances." Her voice trembled as she continued. "You know my concern. I fear for your safety." She lowered her voice to say to Winnie, "Our father appears to prefer his new son over his eldest. I fear he plans to arrange an accident that Bastian is not intended to survive."

"What?" She'd dreamed herself into a plot for her next novel. Maybe she should let it flow. See where her imagination led her. "Why would he do something like that?"

"He would not." Bastian shot his sister a quelling stare. "This conversation is inappropriate in the extreme. We will not besmirch Father's name in such a manner."

Jane gave a decidedly unladylike snort. "I heard them, Bastian. Our stepmother wishes a title for their son and our *father* seemed inclined to agree." She twisted her hands in her lap, then seemed to realize what she was doing and smoothed the fabric of her dress before folding her hands neatly once more. "Lady Wallingham will not rest until her son is heir to an earl. And with all the activity planned for the house party in two weeks, there will be ample opportunity to see to it. Winnie has arrived not a moment too soon. We shall barely have enough time to acclimate her to our ways before Father returns from

London."

Winnie had spent years researching this time period for her novels. And now a Regency lord and lady wanted to teach her how to behave at a Regency country house party. Too bad she'd never enjoyed reenactments. They made her feel awkward and out of sorts. While she loved reading fish-out-of-water stories, she'd never wanted to be the fish.

She tried, but failed, to stifle a near-hysterical giggle.

Brother and sister stared at her like she had two heads, though Bastian's gaze dropped a bit lower. She glanced down. The robe had gaped open to reveal the swell of her breasts peeking out of her bikini top. She twitched the neckline closed and lifted her chin to stare him down.

He averted his flushed gaze, his focus suddenly glued on the leather book in his hands. He picked at the fraying edge of the cover. His teeth caught at his lower lip. She'd swear he fought back a grin.

Now Winnie stared. Without the angry scowl, he looked like the fun-loving man on the beach rather than the angry brother who'd burst in here. Yum.

He cleared his throat and she jumped. How was it possible for her mind to wander in the midst of a dream?

"We'll have to send her back right away," he said.

Jane gripped her arm and Winnie winced. The girl was stronger than she appeared. She was also remarkably pale. Winnie shifted in her seat to put an arm around the girl.

"That's not possible, Bastian." Jane's smile was shaky as she patted Winnie's hand and watched her brother. "We need her."

"For what?" he asked. He shook the book in Jane's direction. "It is apparent you missed some facet of Mother's magick. What possible use could we have for a half-naked woman?"

Winnie raised her eyebrows.

There came that adorable blush and semi-smile. He cleared his throat again. "What I meant was, how are you supposed to keep me from this terrible danger my sister believes our father poses? She would have been better served purchasing a new puppy."

"A puppy!" Screw that. Winnie sprang up, hands on hips, heart pumping. "Are you comparing me to a dog? You think a *dog* would be better company than me?"

Bastian held his hands out in front of him. He chewed on that lip again and then stammered, "N-no. That's not what I meant at all. You are beyond lovely. I couldn't possibly… I only meant a dog would be better capable of guarding me. Not that I'm in any danger, of course." He shot a helpless glance at Jane, who rose to the occasion.

"Bastian meant no offense, dear Winnie." Jane glared at him. "He is awkward at best when speaking with a lady. His compliments are dreadful and generally misunderstood as insults." She forced Winnie to turn around, so her back was to Bastian and whispered in her ear, "We must get you into something more appropriate. I believe your lack of attire has deprived my dear brother of his wits."

Winnie could hear Bastian sputtering behind

her, but a quick glance down at herself showed her nipples clearly outlined by the thin material of the robe. The neckline plunged dangerously low, so she resisted the urge to face him.

"Bastian," Jane said. "You will leave us immediately. Can't you see I must get our guest properly attired? You should not see her thus."

"There is no reason. You will reverse your spell at once and return her home where I'm sure she dresses in the height of fashion," he said, the sneer in his tone clear.

A short bark of laughter escaped Winnie's lips. "I was at the beach, so yeah, this bikini was appropriate. Thank goodness I hadn't decided to take my nap on one of the nude beaches so popular with the locals." Oh, how she wished she could see his face when she heard the choking noises he made. Still, she resisted.

Out of the corner of her eye, she saw Jane bite her lip, struggling to keep her own laughter at bay. She wasn't entirely successful. Her body shook with suppressed mirth. She coughed delicately into her hand. "I am sorry, Bastian, but that will not be possible. Mother's spell included a time frame for assistance. Winnie will be here for one month, no less."

₧₨

Winnie smoothed the skirt of the pastel-blue empire-waist gown she wore in an attempt to still the shaking in her hands. If this had been a dream, she would have woken up a while ago. At the very least, her dream self would have skipped the lengthy, and boring, dressing process. Making

Winnie look *proper* hadn't been easy.

During that time, she'd decided she was either hallucinating or she'd traveled back in time and everything that was happening was real.

She didn't know which was worse.

The hall seemed to go on forever. The urge to peek into any one of the dozens of doors leading off it was tremendous, but she didn't want to get caught spying. She'd be under enough scrutiny as it was. Despite Bastian's demand that Winnie confine herself to either Jane's or her own room for the duration of her stay, Winnie was determined to make the most of this trip into la-la land. Whether it was real or not. She had a new book to finish and her situation was bound to spark her creative juices.

Beginning with Bastian.

She should call him Lord Caulfield since he was the heir to an earldom and carried his father's secondary title of viscount, but she couldn't seem to help herself. Jane had called him by his first name and Bastian was now stuck in her head.

He was the embodiment of a romantic hero. Tall, dark, and handsome. She'd generally avoided that phrase as too clichéd for her novels, but damn if they didn't fit him perfectly.

Add to that, he was smart. According to Jane, he'd single-handedly brought their rather dismal fortune back from the brink.

Winnie was going to pick his brain, study his mannerisms, and basically follow him around like the freaking puppy he would have preferred.

The hallway veered to the left. Winnie paused at a window overlooking an expansive garden. She gasped in delight. Flowers of every color bloomed in neat and tidy planting beds.

Winnie breathed deep, imagining she could smell their perfume. Her own garden was tiny in comparison, but she tended it with loving care. She could picture herself caring for the roses climbing an archway that sheltered a picturesque bench set in a secluded corner. She figured the spot had a decent amount of privacy from the ground, though nothing was left to the imagination from her vantage point.

Like the maid and footman making out like teenagers. Winnie brought her hand to her lips to stifle her smile. Naughty, naughty.

She rushed on. She didn't want to draw attention to the lovebirds. They could get into a decent amount of trouble if caught by the wrong person.

The *swish, swish* of her skirts sounded loud to her ears. She shortened her stride to accommodate the restricted range the dress gave her.

Finally, she came upon a grand staircase, the likes of which she'd only ever seen in movies. She clutched the railing with one hand, her skirt with the other. The banister was smooth, dark wood. She wished she could hop up and slide down, but figured that wouldn't go over too well.

Jane's voice echoed down the hall when she reached the bottom. It didn't take long to find the right door. She took a deep breath, then sauntered into the breakfast room with her head held high. If Bastian were there, she didn't want to slink in as if she were wrong to have come.

Jane glanced up at her approach. "There you are, Winnie! I was about to send a footman to assist you." She waved a young man away. He slipped through a different door without a word. "I'm afraid this old house can be a terrible maze if you're not used to it. Did you take a wrong turn?"

"No, just getting used to walking in this dress." Winnie's stomach took that moment to growl, loudly.

Jane stifled a giggle and indicated the platters of food on a sideboard along the outside wall of the room. "I beg your pardon. Listen to me going on and on while you must be perfectly famished."

"Thanks." Winnie helped herself to a selection of breakfast pastries. A place setting was beautifully arranged about halfway down the table. Winnie positioned her plate at a spot near Jane and maneuvered the rest of what she needed to her new chair.

Jane gave her an odd look, so she said, "I doubt I'd be able to hear anything you said all the way down there. This is much cozier." *Cozy* wasn't a word she'd normally use to describe the space. The table was monstrous and the chair so delicate she was half-afraid it would splinter when she sat.

She breathed a sigh of relief when it held. Not a very deep breath, however. The corset restricted her breathing. She inched her seat forward, giving a yelp of surprise when a footman seemed to appear out of nowhere to help. She smiled her thanks before turning her attention to the food.

"How do you manage in all this clothing?" she asked Jane after slaking her initial hunger pains with a few bites of a buttered roll.

"Whatever do you mean?" Jane asked. She

smoothed the shawl wrapped around her shoulders, then took a delicate bite of sausage. Her eyes widened and she all but dropped her fork back onto her plate. "Do you mean to say the attire in which you appeared was not donned for bathing? I thought you referred to it as a bathing suit."

She laughed. "True. Just not in the strictest sense." The laughter died on her lips as a rustling at the door caught her attention. Bastian glared at them, a paper dangling from one hand, the leather-bound *Book of Shadows* in the other, his mouth slightly agape. She cleared her throat before continuing, "I'll tell you all about the fashion at home a bit later. I don't think your brother could handle it."

"I thought I told you to keep her in your room." The words came out in a mild tone, but the frown on his face was anything but gentle.

"Yeah," Winnie responded before Jane had a chance. "And I thought we told you to forget it."

₲ℛ

Well, that had gone well. Winnie chuckled to herself as she strolled through the garden she'd spotted from the upstairs window.

Bastian hadn't exactly been thrilled at finding her and Jane—*gasp*—eating breakfast together. He was cute, but damn, the man had to lighten up. Winnie had read, and written, enough Regency novels to keep herself out of trouble here. He hadn't wanted to hear it, though.

She turned a corner and came upon the lover's bench. She'd been right. Tucked away as it was, it afforded a great deal of privacy. Then again—she looked up at the manor and spied the window on the second floor. Nope, no privacy at all.

So no bringing Bastian here for privacy.

Whoa. Where had that thought come from? She sunk onto the slatted-wood seat. Sure, Bastian was gorgeous, but was she really interested? They hadn't exactly gotten along so far.

She closed her eyes. His face immediately filled her mind's eye. The picture was much too clear, meaning she'd paid way more attention than she had any right to. What was the point? She'd be going home in a month.

And home wasn't precisely around the corner. There'd be no long-distance romance in this case. When she went home, he'd be long gone.

A picture of a man frolicking on the beach in his baggy swimsuit came to mind. What was that all about? That guy had seemed to know her, but when she'd arrived here, he'd had no clue.

She groaned, burying her head in her hands. Thinking about what it all meant had her head pounding. Ibuprofen would come in handy right about now, but she wasn't going to get it.

The yapping of dogs reached her ears moments before a knotted-up ball of frayed rope landed with a splat at her feet. The dogs she'd heard came careening around the corner, followed closely by a laughing Bastian, walking with a noticeable limp.

Her heart sped up, her eyes widened. One of the dogs, a puppy actually, snatched the ball and, tail wagging, bounded off to join the group prancing around their owner.

Another attempted to wrest a length of rope from Bastian's hand. The puppy's rear wagged frenetically as tiny growls emitted from his miniature throat.

Bastian straightened and let go. The dog gave a startled yelp as his momentum dropped him onto his butt, his prize hanging loosely from his jaws.

Bastian ignored the dogs at his heels and gave a formal, stiff bow in her direction. "I apologize for disturbing your solitude. I was unaware anyone was back here."

He turned to go, his ankle obviously giving him trouble as he turned on it.

Winnie held out a hand to stop him. "You're hurt! What happened?"

"I'm fine."

"Then why are you limping?" She slid over to one side of the bench and indicated the spot next to her. "Have a seat." When he hesitated, she continued. "Would you like me to fetch Jane?"

His lips pursed together, but he dropped onto the seat next to her.

She leaned over to get a look at his leg, but other than a bit of mud on his boots, everything looked fine. Puppies clambered over each other, staging a mock battle over the rope toys.

He grabbed the ball, then threw it down the path. The puppies scrambled over each other to chase after it. The sounds of battle continued, but thankfully somewhat muffled by the surrounding bushes.

"Are you going to tell me what happened?"

His shoulders slumped in defeat, but he

quickly pulled them back and settled more comfortably on the bench. "Will you promise to keep this to yourself? I have no wish to add to Jane's concern."

Uh-oh. That didn't sound good. "I promise."

"My horse threw a shoe and I was thrown." He stretched out his leg in front of them, twisting the ankle back and forth with a wince. "I landed poorly."

She frowned. "You're worried Jane will think it was an attempt on your life?" At his nod, she continued. "Was it?"

He shrugged. "Accidents happen. However, they are happening a bit more frequently than usual. Magick has consequences, Miss Boyle. In my sister's attempts to help, she may have caused more problems than she solved." He looked off into the distance for a moment, then turned toward her. "Such as your presence here. I apologize for the trouble we've caused you."

A smile tugged at her lips. Any reference to her situation made her want to laugh. Either that or she'd cry. "Well, now that I've realized I'm not nuts, I suppose I can deal with it. It's only for a month, after all."

"You speak in the oddest manner, yet I believe your words are meant kindly. Thank you."

Their gazes met and she had trouble looking away. Her breath caught. She wanted to lean forward to be closer to him.

The swarm of puppies charged around the corner, yelping and fighting over the rope. They skid to a stop in a heap at her feet. Bastian plucked the toy from their midst, gave her a quick bow, then threw the ball and limped away with the pack.

She blinked. Maybe it was better if he kept up the stiff, formal facade around her. She found his other side far too appealing. And that could lead exactly nowhere.

೩೦

Winnie took a deep breath as she walked beside Jane. They'd been working hard getting Winnie up to date on all the important social issues of the day while altering a portion of Jane's wardrobe to fit Winnie.

The past few days had taught her that she'd barely touched the surface of Regency life in her books. She'd thought she was fairly well versed in the era, but that turned out to be a joke.

Since she was stuck here for a month, she was eager to get all she could out of it, though she'd been thinking more along the lines of researching dialogue and social customs.

Not this.

"Is this really necessary?"

"Yes, most definitely," Jane answered. "You can't possibly stay in the country for very long without going for a ride. Why, I generally take my horse out at least once per day. And when Father returns in a few days for the house party, there will be plenty of outings scheduled. It would be beyond rude to excuse yourself from all such outings. Your absence would be noted."

"And you want me to stick around your brother in case your dad tries something."

Jane blushed. "I admit to having that motive as well. Bastian is an accomplished rider and spends a great deal of time in that pursuit. Ample opportunity for an arranged accident to make my new younger brother heir to an earldom."

"I don't understand. I mean, Bastian's his son, too."

Jane pulled her to a stop, her cheeks crimson as she stammered, "I'm afraid that's not entirely true." She paused as if collecting her thoughts, or gathering her courage, before continuing. "Our mother was rather headstrong as a young woman. She wished to marry someone of whom my grandfather did not approve. She thought to gain her way by giving herself to that man. Bastian was the result."

Oh. "So Bastian's illegitimate."

"No! Of course not," Jane said in a shocked voice. "He's simply not the true son of Lord Wallingham."

"I'm confused."

"Our father had little money, but he had a title our grandfather coveted for his descendants. So my mother, and her dowry, were given in marriage to Lord Wallingham. Bastian was born but a few months later."

"And since your mom and Lord Wallingham were married at the time of his birth, he's the heir."

"Yes, that's it exactly. And now that Lady Wallingham has delivered a son…" Jane shrugged and they continued on their way. "Well, now you see the reason behind the danger to Bastian."

"What exactly do you think I can do about any of this?" Winnie pulled at the short-sleeved, bolero-style jacket she'd borrowed. It was a bit tight around the bust and neck. The second she was out of Jane's sight she'd slip the top button open. She swallowed and grimaced at the tightening around her throat. She and Jane were of like height, but Jane still had a teenager's willowiness. Winnie hadn't considered herself willowy for, well, ever.

"I am sure I do not know," Jane replied. "However, you were brought to me in answer to my spell so I must assume your presence will be of benefit in some manner."

Soft neighs and the stamping of hoofs permeated the otherwise quiet stables. The earthy smell of hay and—Winnie wrinkled her nose—manure greeted them when they entered.

"Bastian?" Jane called.

"Here."

They strolled down the long aisle to the final stall on their left. Bastian stood within, brushing the neck of a beautiful, glossy black horse.

Winnie leaned next to the half door. A head popped out of the next stall and butted against her back. She laughed and turned to pet the persistent animal. Big, soulful brown eyes begged her to stroke the soft skin of its nose under the halter strap. "Aren't you a sweetie?"

"She's searching for a sugar treat." Bastian's strong arm grazed her shoulder as he reached around her to display a handful of light brown lumps. "Here. Give her these and she'll become your devoted slave."

He kept a respectful distance, but she could still feel the warmth of his body so close to hers. Her heart raced. Her mouth turned dry, as if she hadn't had a drink of water in weeks. "Thanks," she managed. He dropped the sweets into her open palm. She shivered.

The horse lapped up the treats in less than a second. Bastian's approving smile kept her from jerking her hand back as the horse's whiskered nose tickled her palm. The horse lipped at her hand, then nudged the buttons on her coat when she didn't find any more sweets. Winnie stepped back with a laugh and gently pushed the horse's head off her chest.

"This is Blossom. I'll have one of the grooms throw a sidesaddle on her and we'll begin our ride."

What? "Did you say sidesaddle?" She responded to his nod with a negative shake. "No way. Are you nuts? There's no way. I've been on my fair share of trail rides, but there's no way I'm getting onto a horse perched like a squirrel on a fence."

The frown was back on his face. For half a second, while he'd watched her feed Blossom some treats, he'd actually seemed to like her. Nope. Not anymore.

"I thought we agreed you would learn to blend in to our way of life? Riding a horse is an essential element of our plan." He propped his hands on his hips and glared.

She straightened her back to face him head-on. "That was before you said I'd have to do it sidesaddle."

Jane, who must have slipped out while Winnie was getting acquainted with Blossom, rushed out of a nearby stall. "Bastian. Winnie. Please lower your voices!" She darted a glance up and down the area.

Bastian took a deep breath. He bowed toward

them each in turn. "I beg your pardon, Miss Boyle. Please excuse my rudeness. I do forget that you are unaccustomed to our world. This must be a great inconvenience to you and I would do well to remember such."

Now Winnie didn't know what to do. He was hard to deal with when he went all prim and proper and *nice*. "Thank you. The idea of perching up on that huge horse with my legs dangling uselessly over the side scares the cr—" She cut herself off. They were back on decent terms. Best to keep the cursing to a minimum. "Well, the thought frightens me."

Jane gave Winnie's shoulder a squeeze. "Of course it does. But Bastian is a wonderful teacher! In fact, he taught me to ride. And Blossom is as gentle as a lamb. You won't have any problem with her." She gently moved Winnie aside to open the stall door. Blossom stood still as Jane entered, not moving until Jane had a firm grip on the halter.

It took only a few minutes for the efficient groom to ready the horse. She did have a gentle way about her. She plodded along next to the groom as he led her to a mounting block outside the barn entrance. Winnie followed. She rubbed her shaking hands against her thighs. Sudden warmth on her lower back made her glance up. Bastian stood at her side, his hand at the small of her back, barely touching. His presence somehow gave her comfort. She took a deep breath and nodded.

Bastian stepped to the side of the mounting block, near the horse's shoulder. He held out his hand to her. Winnie squeezed it hard enough to make him blink. He was quick to hide his reaction and helped her take the two steps up. She stared at the strange saddle. At a loss on how to get on the thing.

"Like this," Jane said from her other side. She mimed the act of getting on the horse and settling her skirts.

Now Winnie knew what to do, but she wasn't going to manage it anywhere near as gracefully as Jane indicated. She took another deep breath and gave it a shot.

ℂℂ

The sidesaddle wasn't quite as bad as she'd assumed. There was a hook for her leg, so she felt some amount of security perched up high on Blossom's back. She didn't love it, but she could manage. Now if Bastian would stop being so damn polite, she could actually enjoy herself.

Hard to believe she wished someone would be less polite, but he took it to the point of seeming like an automaton rather than a real, live person. This cold, detached *gentleman* was annoying the crap out of her.

Jane had discovered a rip in her riding habit about five minutes into their ride. She'd insisted they continue on without her. She was supposed to have sent a groom along to keep things *proper*. Winnie thought it ridiculous but she'd done enough research to know they took it seriously.

"If you look to your right, you will see the northernmost border of our property. Our holdings extended far further once upon a time. Much of the un-entailed property was duly sold off in my great-grandfather's day. However, through my father's *management*," there was a bitter note to his voice that rang out in contrast to his words, "we have regained much of what was lost. The land to the north remains a bone of contention for my father. We have been unable to regain it from its current owner."

Winnie's ears perked up. The horse's twitched as if it too was suddenly interested in the lecture they'd been subjected to for the past hour. "I take it your father's better at managing the land than your ancestors?"

Bastian snorted. "Hardly. My father has no more business sense than that horse you ride. No. My father is simply more ruthless than his forebears. He married my mother for her fortune. Once he had it, he bought back what land he could and treated her as little more than a slave while burning through her money."

Winnie clapped a hand to her mouth, but quickly returned to grasping the reins in a white-knuckled grip. "I'm so sorry. That must have been horrible."

Bastian didn't seem to hear. They'd come to the edge of a pond surrounded on three sides by a grove of trees. A table and chairs had been set up under the shade, close to the bank. It was a picturesque little spot. Perfect for a picnic. The thought of getting off the horse made her sigh in pleasant anticipation.

Then she gaped at the ground, so extremely far away, and gripped her saddle tighter. "Um, how do I get down?"

The groom took hold of Blossom's head and smiled. He was cute, probably not much older than Jane, with light blond hair and laughing eyes. He stepped closer and held out a hand. "Let me help you, miss."

"Take Charger, John. I shall help the lady." Bastian tossed his reins to John before turning to Winnie. Rather than simply offering a hand, he grasped her under her arms and lifted. She twitched her skirt off the saddle. He may have already seen her half-naked, but having her skirt twisted on the saddle above her head would have been beyond embarrassing.

He lowered her to the ground slowly, and if she knew anything about the proprieties of the time, indecently close to his body. This was definitely something worth writing about. She tried to capture the moment by focusing on all the small details that delighted her. The warm, hard length of him as she slid against him. The clear, ocean blue of eyes that didn't waver from her own. She'd heard of people being unable to break away from a gaze, but hadn't believed it until now. She certainly didn't want to break the eye contact—he had her more breathless in those few seconds than from the hour of keeping her seat on the sidesaddle.

He smelled of leather and hay with a hint of sandalwood. She could have stood pressed against him all day. She nearly stumbled when he stepped back abruptly.

"It looks as though my sister has seen fit to arrange a brief repast during our tour." He gestured toward the intimate table for two.

"Looks like." Her voice came out huskier than normal. She steadied herself with one hand against the horse until Bastian made a gesture and

John walked the two horses a decent distance away to graze.

The way her body felt she didn't know if she'd ever again have her characters have a tryst in the woods after galloping across a field. Every bone in her body ached from the exercise.

Bastian cocked his elbow in her general direction, so she placed her hand lightly on top to be led to lunch.

A young woman curtsied when they neared. "May I be of any further service?"

"No, thank you, Betsy. That will be all."

Betsy left to join John with the horses after one more quick curtsy and a smile.

"Please be seated." Bastian held out a chair for her.

The setup was ridiculously intricate for a picnic. The place settings were fine china, with a flowery rose pattern along the golden-lined edge. She had no doubt the silverware was actual silver. An array of food cluttered the table, all beautifully arranged. Bastian took the seat opposite her and proceeded to pile her plate high with a sampling from each dish. Slices of chicken, some kind of meat pie, several vegetables drowning in various sauces. She didn't eat so much on Thanksgiving, let alone on an impromptu picnic after an hour-long trail ride.

She picked at her meal as Bastian continued his lecture about the estate, occasionally interrupting himself to correct her use of the wrong fork or shake his head with a frown if her elbow touched the table. She finally couldn't take it anymore.

"Enough!"

Bastian raised an eyebrow, but his ceaseless discourse thankfully stopped.

"I'm sure the running of an estate this size is extremely important and interesting. But I'm done." She tossed her napkin on the table. The chair resisted her attempts to push it back. Bastian struggled out of his. He was quicker, but then he wasn't hampered by a ridiculously long skirt and tight top. She was dying from the heat in her getup. The weather was nothing like the hot sun and cool breezes of the tropical beach she'd so recently lounged on, but it wasn't cold enough for a jacket. She flicked open another button, scandalizing Bastian in the process if she accurately judged his frown. She'd already received a warning that her loose collar bordered on the indecent, but breathing took precedence over an overblown sense of dignity, in her opinion.

"This behavior is completely uncalled for," Bastian blustered. "I do not know what passes for manners in your home, but here, this is the height of rudeness."

"So it's considered polite to bore your guests to tears and pick on every movement they make for hours? I always thought the definition of a gentleman was someone who went out of his way to make those around him feel comfortable."

"I—" He clamped his mouth shut. His face glowed beet red, most likely a combination of anger and being trussed up in as much clothing as she was. He plucked a small white handkerchief from his pocket to mop at the sweat beading his brow.

Remorse washed through her. When had she

turned into such a harpy?

"I'm sorry," they both said at once.

He chuckled. "It appears neither of us is completely comfortable with this position in which we find ourselves. I will endeavor to improve myself. Please, resume your seat so you may finish your meal. I promise I will not utter another word about the estate or make any further attempts to turn you into a nineteenth-century maiden."

She considered his offer, but couldn't stomach the thought of sitting. She rubbed at the small of her back. Her butt was in dire need of a massage, but she wasn't about to go there with him watching. "I'm not all that hungry. And, honestly, I don't know that I can sit anytime soon."

He held out his arm. "Then perhaps you will honor me with a stroll?" He nodded toward a rise in the property along one edge of the woods. "There is a lovely view of the manor from above that hill. I would be delighted to show you."

She took the proffered arm. "That would be very nice. Thank you."

They strolled in silence for a few minutes. She loved walking along at his side with her arm tucked up against him. Holding hands had always seemed childish and awkward, but this was different. When he offered his arm, she felt cherished. He could out-distance her in three strides, yet they strolled along at a comfortable pace.

This wasn't a dream, but it certainly felt like one. Being with him made her heart race and her thoughts swirl. He was exciting and comfortable, yet confusing and surreal. Much like this whole time-travel craziness.

What did it mean that she'd been summoned here at a teenager's whim? Stolen through time. What must they be thinking at the resort? Had they even noticed she was missing? When would they?

It was a depressing thought. She was pretty sure her absence wouldn't be noted until she failed to turn in her manuscript to her editor. She had friends, and family, but she was a loner. When she was deep into one of her books, she might not emerge for weeks. People had learned not to worry if she failed to return a call or missed an appointment when she was on deadline. She'd always thought it was great that they knew her so well.

Now she wondered what that said about her. She couldn't imagine Jane treating anyone so shabbily. When Winnie had landed in their laps, Jane had done everything in her power to ease Winnie's fears and make life here as pleasant as possible. Would Winnie have done the same? She liked to think so, but had doubts.

Bastian was trying as well. True, he had a tendency to wax on and on about mundane things, but what should she expect? They barely knew each other and he was an intensely private person. That much about him was obvious.

Yet he'd spent the day doing his best to entertain her. He'd also spent hours poring through his mother's magick books trying to find a way to send Winnie home more quickly. He may not be worried about his own safety, but his actions showed he worried about hers.

The wind picked up when they reached the slope's top. Bastian cursed under his breath. The soft neighing of horses and call of voices drifted up to them. Mayhem ruled at the manor's front door. Servants rushed about unloading a series of four carriages.

"You have visitors?" she asked.

"Father." He frowned as he studied the scene below them. "I'm afraid we have less time than anticipated to acclimate you to our way of life." He must have seen the worry on her face because he patted her hand, which still lay upon his arm. "You shall do fine. My father will likely take little notice of you." He returned his attention to the commotion below.

"Should we head down?"

He gave a start. "What? Yes. That's an excellent idea. We will go around by way of the music room. We should freshen up before greeting Father."

They skirted around back of the huge house to a wide-open set of French doors. Potted plants lined the edges of the cobblestone patio. She stopped to smell a beautiful pot full of yellow primrose. The fresh spring scent calmed her nerves.

Bastian didn't believe what Jane said about their father. Winnie had to remember Jane was a teenager, though she seemed so much older. Weren't teenagers notorious for their drama? A stepmother and a new baby brother were definitely events that would set any teenager to rebelling.

But the uneasiness in her stomach didn't entirely go away. Winnie didn't know a whole lot of teenagers, but Jane didn't seem like a drama queen.

Bastian paused at the doors. He held out his hand. So chivalrous. She wasn't used to it. She smiled in response and hurried her steps.

They'd barely stepped foot through the doorway when Jane rushed up to them. She skidded to a stop not a second too soon. Her delicate face was pale, a section of her long brown hair escaped from her neat little cap and she fought for breath. A large white shawl draped around her neck, trailing all the way to the floor behind her.

"I saw you from the window." She panted. "Father has returned," she declared as if the world would stop with her statement.

Bastian smiled and took her hands. "I know. We saw him from the hill. Take Miss Boyle to change her gown into something more appropriate. I will wash up and meet you downstairs at—" he pulled a watch on a golden chain from his pocket and consulted the time, "—half past the hour."

Meals were apparently a much bigger deal when the lord and lady were in residence. Winnie jogged to keep up as Jane rushed to her room muttering, "Half past the hour! How does he expect us to be ready in so short a time?"

"I take it we have to change?" Winnie asked, panting slightly at the exertion.

"Yes, Lady Wallingham insists we dress for dinner." Jane burst through the door to her room. "And of course all the servants are assisting *her*.

We shall have to make do."

They muddled through together and in short order Winnie felt glamorous in a low-cut pastel-pink gown with a delicate creamy lace overlay.

"Lady Wallingham will be terribly jealous," Jane said as she put the finishing touches to Winnie's hair. "So be careful, she's likely to spill something on you out of spite."

"She sounds awful," Winnie said. She wasn't looking forward to meeting the woman. "How long has she been your stepmom?"

"Several years. She was Father's mistress while Mother was alive. He married her within days of Mother's passing." She shuddered. "It was indecent. He did not even allow Bastian and I to observe a proper mourning period."

Winnie squeezed Jane's shoulder comfortingly. "I'm sorry."

"Thank you. As I said, it was several years ago. She was pregnant at the time and he wished to be sure he could claim the child."

Confusion wrinkled Winnie's brow. "But I thought she just had the baby?"

Jane nodded. "She lost the first child, if she even carried one to begin with."

"You think she faked a pregnancy to get your father to marry her?"

"Bastian believes so. Father was furious. Over time she became increasingly desperate to have a child. Her relief was tremendous when she discovered she was pregnant. When she delivered a boy, she became even worse. I do not believe she is of right mind."

"Postpartum depression?" At Jane's confused look, Winnie explained, "It's when a woman suffers a period of melancholy after giving birth. It can be very serious."

Jane shook her head. "She was terrible before she became pregnant. If she were not so awful to myself and Bastian, I could find it in myself to feel sorry for her. Father is not the easiest of people to love."

೮೦೧೮

Jane wasn't kidding, Winnie realized as she listened to Lord Wallingham at dinner that evening. If the man made one more derogatory comment about his children, she was going to smack him. If the table hadn't been so damn long, she might have done it already. As it was, she was thankful for the distance.

"How long do you plan to stay, Miss Boyle?" Lady Wallingham asked from her position at one end of the table. Her voice was low-pitched and breathy. She sounded like she'd had a carton-a-day cigarette habit her whole life. She leaned forward so her ample breasts spilled out the top of her emerald-green gown.

Winnie wondered if the woman hadn't taken account of her increased bust size now that she had a newborn, or whether she actually thought it was a good look.

It wasn't.

"I'm not certain." Winnie peeked at Bastian. He didn't seem entirely pleased, but he made no motion that she should discontinue her answer. "Bastian—Lord Caulfield—has been kind enough to invite me to stay for the duration of the house party."

"He has, has he?" Lord Wallingham mumbled. He tipped his head back to take a long draft of his wine. He'd emptied at least two bottles entirely on his own since they'd sat down. They were barely through the second course, with several more to go. The man's face was an alarming shade of red. "You and Caulfield seem remarkably close. I don't recall ever hearing your name before today. Where did you say you're from?"

Bastian came to her rescue. "She's from America, Father. Near Boston. You'll recall the rather lucrative investment I made there? She is the cousin of one of my business associates from that venture. He requested our assistance in entertaining Miss Boyle during her stay. I assured him that you and Lady Wallingham would be happy to extend your hospitality."

Well. He'd obviously given her backstory some thought. She'd meant to discuss it with him ahead of time, but they'd been caught off guard by the father's sudden arrival. Good thing Bastian was a quick thinker.

"Ah, her family's in trade. I see." Lady Wallingham sneered. "Yes, I'm sure we will all enjoy the addition to our frivolity." Obviously not at all pleased. "That dress looks lovely on you, Miss Boyle. Is it not one of Jane's? Might I ask what happened to your own wardrobe?"

"I'm afraid my own luggage met with a mishap at sea." She placed a hand over her chest and played it up. "It was dreadful. All my lovely things dropped into the water as I came ashore. Of course, nothing was salvageable. Dear Jane was so kind as to let me borrow a few of her gowns."

"I'm surprised it fits you. Jane has all the curves of a stick," Lord Wallingham said.

Poor Jane's face burst into flames, but other than that she remained as calm as if she hadn't heard the awful comment.

Lady Wallingham's smile made Winnie sick to her stomach. *Bitch*. She took way too much pleasure in her husband's nastiness.

Bastian cleared his throat. "Perhaps we should go over some of the details of the upcoming party? I understand…"

Winnie let her mind wander as they discussed the events to come in the following days. She was already exhausted and she'd yet to play croquet on the south lawn or charades in the drawing room. She'd have to make a point of having one of her Regency heroines too tired to participate in every single event of a country house party. Usually she wrote them as eager to attend everything in order to spend time with the hero. Ugh.

When dinner finally ended, she breathed a sigh of relief. Until Lady Wallingham stood and said, "We shall await you in the drawing room, my lord. Enjoy your port and cigars."

The men stood when she did. Each bowed to her as she swept out of the room. Jane and Winnie trailed in her wake.

Winnie would have rather followed a gator into a swamp.

ഇരു

After more than a week of these dreadful dinners, Winnie had reached her limit. When they retired to the drawing room after dinner one night, she saw her chance for an early escape.

"I'm terribly sorry to cut the evening short, Lady Wallingham. I have a terrible headache and fear I must retire." She grabbed hold of Jane's arm, pulling her along, but pretending to lean on her for support. "I'm sure you won't begrudge me Jane's assistance? I'm not sure I could make it on my own." She dipped her head in farewell and dragged Jane from the room before Lady Wallingham could recover.

Jane put a hand to her lips. A smile tugged at the edges and she emitted small choking noises. The minute they'd reached the safety of the upper corridor, she burst out laughing.

Winnie followed suit and they stumbled their way to Jane's bedroom. Jane immediately collapsed on her bed. Winnie sank onto the paisley lounge that had become her perch whenever she joined Jane in her room.

A hiccup sounded from the bed. Jane managed to get her breath back first. "Oh my goodness. That was a great deal of fun. I don't think I've ever seen Lady Wallingham quite so astonished. I never would have had the nerve had you not been with me, dear Winnie."

"I wasn't taking the chance of still being there when the men came in. Poor Bastian. He's all alone with both of them."

The door opened and Bastian came through. "I thought Miss Boyle might manage to find you a way out of entertaining Lady Wallingham this evening."

Winnie grasped the hand he held out to her. The laughter died on her lips and she pulled back her shaking hand quickly. "Yes. Well. I knew we had to get away quickly. Your stepmother wouldn't have liked what I would have said to her if she'd said one more thing to me tonight. I'd have likely gotten myself kicked out."

He rubbed his hand against his leg absently. Winnie wondered if he'd felt the same jolt she had when they'd touched.

Jane sighed and pressed a shaky hand to her cheek.

"Are you okay?" Winnie asked.

"I am rather tired. I believe I shall retire early this evening." Jane regarded Bastian. "You won't mind keeping Winnie company, would you?" She strolled over to her dressing room, waving her hand airily at them on her way. "Have a lovely time. I shall look forward to our morning ride."

Winnie and Bastian were left alone standing next to the enormous bed. Winnie's stomach fluttered and her gaze darted over the room, anywhere but at him. "Um, what about a walk in the garden? It's a nice night and I'm not all that tired."

"I would be delighted." He bowed in that formal way he had and held out his arm. She was getting used to it. She placed her hand on his forearm and they left the room together. They strolled quietly down the hall, content to simply be with each other. He'd certainly grown on her the past two weeks. She wasn't sure how she was going to feel when this all ended and she got back to her own time.

Speaking of time... "I wonder what the people back in my time are thinking? They'll know right away that I didn't get up and go home.

I would have had to have Captain Jack give me a ride." She looked up to study Bastian's profile but caught him watching her, a sad smile on his face. She kept eye contact. She couldn't have turned away if she'd wanted.

He brought them to a halt by the window that overlooked the garden bench. "They won't have missed you at all."

"No? Well, that's a bit depressing. I'll have been gone a whole month."

He shook his head. "No, you misunderstand me. I've studied Jane's spell. You will return to the exact moment you left. It will be like this never happened."

"Oh." That was depressing in a whole other way. She dropped her gaze. His cravat was tied as expertly as ever. She ran a finger along the intricate fold near his neck.

He pinched her chin with his thumb and forefinger, gently guiding her head up. Once she gazed into his eyes, he cradled her jaw with a tenderness that brought tears to her eyes. "This has happened. I shall never forget."

Ever so slowly, he lowered his mouth to hers.

Their lips joined in the lightest of caresses. The kiss couldn't have been more perfect if it had been coordinated in a movie studio. No awkward nose bump, no fumbling, no embarrassment. Only a wealth of feeling that nearly overwhelmed her.

She brought her arms up to circle his neck. Her eyes drifted shut when he pulled her to him and deepened the kiss. Her heart thundered in her chest. Liquid heat poured through her limbs. He gripped her hair, not quite to the point of pain.

The passion in his grip excited her. He'd never lost control, but seemed on the verge now. His long, muscular thigh pressed between her legs, forcing them open. She groaned at the pressure the movement created against her core. He pushed her up against the window frame. The edge bit into her back, but she didn't care. A warm breeze through the open glass washed over her, but did nothing to ease the fire within.

He stepped back. She whimpered at the loss of contact and tightened her arms around his neck.

Success! Yes. He crushed her to him, taking her mouth in an onslaught that left her breathless and dizzy.

Her hair came swirling down. He used both hands to caress her face, the hair caught between his fingers silky against her cheeks. She released her death hold on his neck to trail one hand over his shoulder, down his chest, and push the fabric of his evening jacket to the side. She slipped her hand against the warmth of his stomach, frustrated by his waistcoat. She wanted skin but wasn't likely to get it. They stood in the middle of the hall, in full view of the garden below them.

When he eased back once more, she let him go. He didn't release her immediately. He took his time. Nibbled softly on her bottom lip. Kissed his way along her jaw, to that spot below her ear that made her shiver and tilt her head back to give him greater access.

They both breathed heavily when he finally pulled away. He propped his forehead against hers, his eyes closed, as they both struggled to regain their breath.

"I've wanted to do that since I first saw you

in Jane's room that day."

She chuckled lightly. "The fact I was barely dressed probably had nothing to do with it."

He laughed. "Certainly not. I made a valiant attempt to keep my eyes off your body so that I could focus on the matter at hand."

"Right." She rested her head on his chest. The new angle gave her a perfect view out the window. The countryside was beautiful. The hills rolled out beyond the hedgerow that marked the boundary of the intricate flower garden. She squinted in the direction of the little pond where they'd had their picnic, but could make out only the faint line of trees peeking out over the hills.

Movement out of the corner of her eye caught her attention. She glanced down toward the little bench to see if the maid was meeting her lover there once more.

Not the maid. She gasped as she looked directly into the face of Lady Wallingham, who stared at her with such blatant loathing that Winnie's skin crawled.

ഇ൦ര

Winnie didn't mention the look that had passed between herself and his stepmother, but it took a long time for the uneasiness to pass. She'd reassured him that she was fine, but she wasn't sure whether he bought it. He'd continued to give her cautious glances as they strolled around the garden. When he made a motion toward the little bench, she shook her head and steered him in another direction.

"Winnie?" He halted in the middle of a path,

forcing her to stop since he held her arm captive against his side where she held on to his forearm.

She refused to look at him. She didn't want to admit how much his stepmother had scared her. It was silly, really. What could the woman do?

But that wasn't the only issue.

The kiss. She needed some time to process that kiss. She'd been kissed before, of course, yet no man had ever made her feel the way Bastian had.

She'd written about the subject a million times. That first kiss. She'd described it in so many ways. Always trying to keep the descriptions fresh. She'd thought she knew what she was talking about. The rush in the veins during the seconds leading up to that initial meeting of lips. The fluttering in the stomach. The heat that washed over the skin.

Bullshit. All of it. She'd had no clue.

Because none of those outward descriptions were enough. It was the feeling in her heart that was so indescribable. She, a woman who wrote love stories for a living, had no words.

He stood quietly in front of her until she couldn't stand the silence anymore. Patience was much more his suit than hers. She peeked at him through lowered lashes. She focused on his chin, maybe strayed a bit to his lips—she couldn't resist—but she avoided his gaze. He'd see too much. She wasn't sure how much she wanted to reveal. She was leaving soon. What was the use?

"Perhaps we should discuss what has happened between us?" His lips tilted down at the corners. It wasn't a fierce frown, as he often wore when upset. He seemed infinitely more sad.

Her heart tore. She wasn't going to return home whole. A part of her would stay here. With him.

She nodded. He was right. Whatever happened, she needed him to know. "Yes. I suppose we should."

"I didn't mean to distress you with my advances." His chin dipped. He twisted his hands together, an uncharacteristically nervous motion.

Her head shot up at his words. What?

"I realize I should have restrained myself. I'm afraid I felt so strongly that I let my desires overcome my manners. I had no wish to make you uncomfortable or to force my attentions where they were unwanted. I value you too much for that."

"You're kidding, right?" She couldn't believe what she was hearing. Unwanted? "I've wanted to kiss you forever, it seems."

He pulled her into his arms. The extra-tight set of his shoulders relaxed and his mouth spread into a huge grin. "I am relieved to hear it." He brushed her hair behind her ear, letting his fingers linger to caress her cheek.

She leaned in, her eyes closed. "We're still shit out of luck, though, aren't we? The spell's going to send me home in two weeks."

He hugged her tight, resting his chin on top of her head. His chest rose and fell in a great sigh. "Perhaps. I am working on a solution, but I am uncertain of its success."

"Do you think there might be a way for me to stay?" She leaned back to scrutinize his face. He was an awful liar. She'd know right away.

He struggled to get his features under control

and she grinned. He knew how much his face betrayed his thoughts. He grinned back. "I am looking into the possibility. I found a way to send you home early a few days ago." He winked. "I found I didn't care to cut our time short. The wording of my sister's spell leaves room for different interpretations. Yet it is not something that can leave any room for doubt. Magick extols a terrible price. If done improperly, the consequences can be severe, and unpredictable. I am not willing to risk your safety."

"What if I'm willing?" She warmed at the thought that he could have sent her home but hadn't.

He brushed his thumb across her lips. She took his thumb gently between her teeth and flicked her tongue against the pad. He hissed, his eyes widening, his body stiffening against hers. His arousal pushed against her stomach. She smiled at his wide-eyed gaze. She stood on tiptoe and kissed him lightly. "I'd be willing to take the chance. For you." She dropped back and lowered her head. "If you wanted me to."

Slight pressure under her chin brought her head up. She stared into those deep, gorgeous, movie-star blue eyes and could have died happy. That look was back. The one she'd seen on the beach. And it was directed at her. Swoon-worthy.

"I'm torn," he whispered. "I want you. I can't imagine allowing you to leave." He ran a hand through his hair, his expression pained. "But how can I risk your well-being?"

She traced the frown lines next to his mouth. "I've always been a romantic at heart. I'd have said it is worth risking everything for love." She shook her head. "But a part of me didn't believe it could be real. I didn't believe I'd ever find someone I'd be willing to risk everything for." She kissed him again. "Then I met you. And now I know love is worth the risk. *You're* worth it."

&⨀⨀

The next week passed in a blur of activity as the house filled with guests. Every moment was scheduled with some game or another. Bastian kept to Winnie's side as often as possible. The one dark spot on what would have otherwise been a magical time were the outraged stares and nasty comments made by Lord and Lady Wallingham whenever they spotted Winnie and Bastian together.

But Winnie did her best to ignore them and enjoy herself. She treasured every moment spent with Bastian. They discussed everything, from favorite foods to childhood traumas. He couldn't get enough of her descriptions of the wonders of the twenty-first century and she learned everything she'd ever wanted to know about Regency society.

On most days, Jane joined them. At night she pleaded a persistent headache and retired early. Winnie suspected Jane was playing matchmaker, but didn't mind in the least.

Once Jane was settled, Bastian and Winnie avoided the evening social whirl to stroll about the gardens or spend pleasant evenings in his study while he researched ways to keep her with him. Other guests strolled in and out—Bastian insisted it wasn't proper to be alone in a closed room with her. Winnie laughed, but didn't argue. If she did end up staying she'd have to get used to those ridiculous restrictions.

That didn't stop them from sharing some steamy, hot kisses. She felt like a teenager sneaking around for make-out sessions with the boyfriend—not yet ready to go all the way, but testing the limits. Only, she wasn't so sure she wasn't ready.

She didn't have the opportunity for more. Bastian was a Regency gentleman. He treated her like a lady. She wasn't used to it. But she sure liked it.

Time was running out. Only one more week before the spell would send her back home unless Bastian and Jane found a way to break the return portion of the spell. So far, they hadn't had any luck. Tonight, Bastian thought he'd made a breakthrough. She'd left him reluctantly to finalize the spell he believed could allow her to stay with him forever.

Unbeknownst to him, she'd asked one of the servants loyal to the Caulfield siblings to stand watch over his study. Bastian wouldn't see the need, but she felt better taking that small precaution.

She smiled as she ambled down the upstairs hall on the way to her room. He hadn't been able to concentrate with her nearby. They'd been cuddled up next to a roaring fire in his study while he read through his notes. He'd nearly jumped when she ran her hand along the inside of his thigh. She couldn't help herself. She covered her mouth to stifle her laughter.

He really was awful at controlling his

expressions. She loved it. She'd never felt so desirable in her life. He made her blood sing and her heart pound.

Voices from up ahead jerked her out of her thoughts. She hurried her steps to avoid running into anyone this late at night. Seriously, the amount of traffic between rooms was worthy of one of her novels.

She wasn't paying attention as she rushed through the open door to her peaches-and-cream-decorated guest room. The door slammed shut behind her and she jumped, emitting a shriek of fright.

She started to turn around but something struck her from behind. Pain exploded in her head. She crashed to the ground.

"Winnie? Winnie? Are you all right?" The words echoed oddly in her ears. Like they came down a long tunnel. "Oh, thank goodness. She appears to be coming to."

Someone rubbed her hands briskly. She lay on her back, the thick carpet soft under her. She forced her eyes open, squinting at the overly bright light of a candle held too close to her face. She snatched her hand away from the person to shield her eyes.

"What happened?" Her voice came out weak, barely audible.

"Oh, Winnie. Thank goodness!" Jane's voice spoke in her ear.

Winnie blinked and turned her head toward Jane. She winced as the movement rubbed a tender spot on the back of her skull. "Jane? What happened?" She struggled to sit. She felt vulnerable lying on her back. She needed to get into a better position.

"Do lie back. Bastian has summoned Mr. Marsley, the physician. He should be here momentarily."

"Help. I want to sit." She fought the nausea that threatened with the movement. Her head throbbed.

Jane helped her into a more comfortable position propped against a corner of the four-poster bed. Her face wavered in and out of Winnie's spotty vision.

A draft of warm air swept through the room as the door opened. Bastian rushed in, dropping to his knees at her side. He put a hand to her face. "Are you well, my dear?" he asked in a whisper.

Nodding hurt, so she answered, "Been better."

"Mr. Marsley will make sure you recover." Bastian gathered her up and carried her to the bed as if she weighed no more than a ream of paper.

"The doctor? No, I don't want to see a nineteenth-century doctor." She snuggled against his chest, his warm, solid form comforting and safe. He placed her down gently, her head on the fluffy pillow. He spread the warm quilt over her legs. She grabbed his hand when he made a move to leave. "Stay."

An older gentleman stepped up next to Bastian. "I must examine you, miss. It would not be proper for Lord Caulfield to be in the room."

"I have a bump on my head. How's it going to get improper?"

"Miss Boyle and I have recently become

engaged. My sister can remain as well to ensure nothing untoward occurs."

Winnie's eyes widened. *Did anyone else notice the wink Bastian sent her way?*

The doctor beamed and clapped Bastian on the back. "That's marvelous. Now. Please step over to the side with Lady Jane and I shall endeavor to ensure your bride-to-be recovers to enjoy her nuptials."

Bastian backed off while Mr. Marsley gave Winnie a cursory examination. Soon enough, he declared her in relatively decent health, instructing her to rest easy. She was not to leave her bed for a week. Given that she'd had images of him sticking a fleam to her arm and spilling out half her blood, she figured she'd gotten off lightly.

"We should all be thankful the damage is not as bad as it first appeared. A little harder and you may not have recovered." The doctor patted her on the hand, then gestured for Bastian to follow him from the room.

Winnie tried to give Bastian a reassuring smile as he walked away. She didn't like the worried look that came over his face at the doctor's words.

Jane took hold of Winnie's hand and sat on the edge of the bed. "I'm so sorry, Winnie. This is all my fault." She suddenly hunched forward, bursting into tears.

Winnie's head ached, so she made do with patting Jane lightly on the back. "Don't be silly. Of course it's not your fault!"

"Had I not brought you here, you never would have suffered such an accident." She shook her head. "I don't understand how you injured yourself so badly."

Winnie flashed back to the expression on Lady Wallingham's face after she'd seen Winnie and Bastian kissing. She hadn't seen who bashed her on the head, but she knew why they had. Were she writing the story, she'd say the Wallinghams were worried Bastian would get married and have a kid of his own. Then they'd have more people to kill in order for their son to inherit. But she wasn't about to say anything to worry Jane. "I tripped on the edge of the carpet and managed to hit my head on the bedpost."

The door opened and Bastian strode in. He stood at the foot of the bed, staring down at Winnie and his sister.

"What did Mr. Marsley say?" Jane asked.

"Miss Boyle will be perfectly well in short order." He rubbed the back of his neck and shifted from foot to foot. He held something in his left hand, but she couldn't make out what it was. "And when she returns to her own time, it will be as if this were all but a dream."

Winnie's heart stopped. A ball of ice dropped to the pit of her stomach. The nausea worsened. "My own time? But, Bastian, I—I thought we agreed—"

He made a slashing motion with his hand. "The risk is too great. The doctor told me you could not have injured yourself in a fall. Someone tried to kill you. I will not expose you to the dangers of this house a moment longer." The candlelight glinted off unshed tears in his eyes.

"I'm willing to accept that risk." She wasn't as successful at keeping her own tears at bay.

They ran across her cheeks to wet the pillow propped up behind her. "I thought you wanted me to stay," she whispered.

"I do." The tears ran down his face now as he held out his mother's *Book of Shadows*. It fell open and he pulled out a small pouch.

When the scent of cloves and rosemary reached her, she knew what he planned to do. She held out a hand to stop him, but he was too far away. "No!"

He murmured words too low for her to hear. The light faded. Her hand dropped down to her side. The last thing she heard was Bastian's voice. "I love you."

℠℞

Winnie started awake. A warm breeze stirred the air, bringing with it the scent and sound of the ocean waves. She put a hand over her eyes to block the glare from the bright sun. "Bastian?"

Her head felt muddled, like she'd had too much wine and blacked out only to awake with little memory of the evening. The light wasn't right. Too bright. Where was the rolling English countryside? Or the four-poster bed piled high with soft sheets and fluffy pillows?

She squinted as she scanned the beach. A couple walked by, arm in arm. The man gave Winnie the once-over, but quickly dragged his attention back to his wife when she elbowed him in the ribs.

Winnie glanced down at the bright red polka dots of her bikini and her matching red belly ring. But hadn't she taken that out? It had caught uncomfortably against her corset.

"Bastian?" she whispered. Her heart twisted. Had it been a dream? She felt her cheeks and her hand came away wet. She used her bright orange beach towel to wipe up her face, unashamedly wiping her runny nose on the edge.

She swung her legs off to the side of her lounger. She hissed as her feet hit the sun-soaked sand. Almost too hot to take. A worn, leather-bound book lay beside her. She picked it up and wiped sand off the cover, then clutched it to her chest. She could go back. The book held the key.

She jumped up, jammed her feet into her sandals, and rushed back to her bungalow. It seemed the whole staff was hard at work. She had to jump to the side of the faded wooden walkway to avoid a group of them hauling chairs and tables to the beach.

The clambake was tonight. She stopped dead. That meant absolutely no time had passed while she met and fell in love with Bastian Caulfield. But how was that possible? She'd been gone almost a month.

But hadn't Bastian said something about the spell returning her to the exact moment she'd left? That would explain it.

He'd used the book to return her a week early. Surely she could use it to return to him.

The leather warmed in her hands. She stepped off the wooden walkway onto the crushed-shell path that led to the bungalows. She fumbled with her key. Her hand shook as she tried to force it into the lock. She managed at last and shoved open the door, sucking in the cold blast of air-conditioning.

She'd forgotten to turn off the light when she'd headed to the beach a month—no, that morning. She left her sandals on to protect her feet from the frigid tile. There was a small desk next to the TV. She pulled out the rolling chair, almost sending it flying across the room and catching it at the last minute. She lay the *Book of Shadows* down and let it fall open to the page with Jane's spell.

She read the spell aloud, clutching the bag of herbs. She waited for the world to fade away.

Nothing.

Her head dropped to the table. *Thump.* She'd have a bruise in the morning. She bolted up. Bruise. She felt the back of her head, expecting a huge lump but found nothing. Like she'd never been hit.

It had been a dream. She'd fallen asleep on the beach and somehow managed to dream up the whole damn thing. Her hero from the beach had somehow woven his way into her subconscious and she'd made up the whole sick fantasy.

Sobs tore at her throat.

Her heart didn't know it was a dream. Her heart told her it had been real. That he'd been real.

And she'd lost him.

It took Winnie quite a while to pull herself together. A shower and a change of clothes should have done a world of good to clear the cobwebs from her head, but after crying for nearly an hour, she was as fuzzy as ever.

She flipped through the pages of the journal, the writing somehow comforting, despite the fact she now knew it was the work of a stranger rather than her dear friend Jane.

The handwriting changed several times in the journal. Jane's writing she could identify because of the spell. But before it there were two different sets. Mother and grandmother?

But was it Jane's writing? Did Jane, as she knew her, exist? Or was she a figment of Winnie's imagination based on a brief encounter on the beach?

Winnie turned to the spell toward the middle of the book. Whether it was Jane's writing or not, Winnie wanted to follow her entries. She didn't bother reading at first, just traced the letters with her finger without taking in any meaning.

Then she spied her name. Winnie. What were the chances? She slowed down and took the time to read, word for word.

Her eyes widened and her pulse sped up. The book recounted the details of her time with Jane and Bastian. From the moment she'd arrived in Jane's room to the day Bastian sent her home.

And beyond.

ഇരു

They'd searched for a way to join Winnie. Jane wrote down all the details. How furious she'd been with Bastian when he'd sent Winnie home without consulting her first. And how quickly she'd forgiven him when she saw how devastated he was at Winnie's loss.

Bastian had barely survived another attempt on his life. Winnie gasped. He'd been poisoned, but they'd been unable to prove it was deliberate.

As soon as he'd recovered, they'd left. Hopped a ship to the Caribbean without a word to anyone.

According to Jane, the title would go into abeyance without the heir. Because Bastian had left, not died, the earl would never get his wish for his real son to inherit. Bastian felt bad about this, but he had no wish to die in order to give his baby brother a title.

The journaling part of the diary ended and it was clear Jane was working on creating a new spell. Words were blotted out all over each page, her thoughts on what might work written up and down the sides. Lists of ingredients took up a handful of pages.

Then, on a page all by itself, were four words.

Winnie is the key.

It was underlined three times.

After that, nothing. A section was torn out, the remnants still caught up in the binding.

Winnie flipped through the few remaining pages. All blank. Until the very last page. A completely different handwriting. Written in large letters.

I'm at the beach. Come to me.

Winnie's hand spasmed on the page, almost tearing it out of the binding. She knew that writing. She'd sat with Bastian while he worked on the spell and handled estate duties.

He was here.

She slammed the book shut and bolted out of the chair. It crashed to the floor, but she let it lie there unheeded. She had to get to Bastian.

The door swung open with ease and she didn't wait for it to swing shut before launching herself down the path to the beach.

The clambake was in full swing. She brushed past a crazy lady swinging a bamboo stick at some drunk. The drink was definitely flowing tonight.

She scanned the beach frantically. People stared as she pushed past—her muttered "excuse mes" bordering on downright rude. She couldn't care less.

"Bastian?" she called. But the music was too loud. He'd never hear her.

She climbed onto a chair to get a better view. It wobbled dangerously below her.

"Winnie!"

His voice. She spun around to find him, but the chair was unstable. It slipped and she cursed her clumsiness. The ground rushed up to greet her, then suddenly—he was there.

His strong, amazing arms wrapped around her. He swept her off her feet while the chair tumbled on its side. She got a glimpse of Jane standing off to the side, a huge grin on her face.

"Did you miss me?" he asked. She'd thought she'd never see that look again. The pure joy and unalloyed love. For her.

"Bastian!" That was all Winnie managed to get out before his mouth covered hers and swallowed anything else she might have said. So she answered him the only way she could.

With her whole heart.

About…

Emma Kaye is married to her high school sweetheart and has two beautiful kids that she spends an insane amount of time driving around central New Jersey. Before ballet classes and tennis entered her life, she decided to try writing one of those romances she loved to read and discovered a new passion. She has been writing ever since. Add in a playful puppy and an extremely patient cat and she's living her own happily ever after while making her characters work hard to reach theirs.

For more information on Emma, please visit her online at www.emma-kaye.com, on Facebook at www.facebook.com/emmakayewrites, on Twitter at www.twitter.com/emmakayewrites or on GoodReads at www.goodreads.com/emma-kaye.

Love time travel? Try another Emma Kaye time travel story—***Time for Love*** is available now from The Wild Rose Press!

Time for Love

Alexandra Turner will do anything to save her twin sister. Even when she's transported back in time to Regency England. Rescuing her sister and finding her way back to her own time will take all her concentration. Falling in love is not an option.

With the death of his brother, Nicholas Somerville became the ninth Marquess of Oakleigh and must return to England to take his place in society. Part of his responsibility will be to find a wife. It never occurs to him he might actually discover a woman he could love—until he meets Alex on his voyage home.

Can Alex and Nicholas find a way to bridge the gap of time and circumstance? Can they overcome their fears to realize that true love transcends time? Or will a dark secret from Alex's past rear up to separate them forever?

Poseidon's Strength

Nicole S. Patrick

❧

Former Marine Ryan Masterson is building a successful business, trying to be a supportive big brother to his now-widowed sister, Jenna, and finding the strength to overcome the grief of losing his best friend, Sam, who was killed in combat. But something is missing from his busy life. When he heads to the U.S. Virgin Islands to help his very-pregnant sister fix up her resort, he finds more than he bargained for—Faith Reagan. Sam's sister may be beautiful, but they've never quite gelled. However, Ryan may find what he's looking for at a place—and with a woman—he least expects.

Faith Reagan is trying to dust herself off and pull herself together. First her brother's death, then a tragedy strikes in her professional life. When she escapes to the U.S. Virgin Islands to help her sister-in-law, she thinks she's finally found peace. But when her longtime crush—bad boy Ryan Masterson—comes to town, will Faith be able to maintain the delicate balance she's worked so hard to achieve?

When Jenna's baby arrives early, Ryan and Faith must work together and discover that strength is found in many different ways, and love blooms in unexpected places.

❧

Dedicated to ~

My incredible partners for another fun ride on the second stop on our venture. It's an honor to call you friends.

My support system—my friends and family. Thank you for your inspiration and ideas. And of course, Joe, Patrick, and Sean—you are my world.

Our terrific editor, Mallory Braus, who helps me hone my skills to become a better writer with each story. Thank you!

Poseidon's Strength
by Nicole S. Patrick

"Mr. Masterson, call on line two," the newest college intern's voice sounded through the intercom.

Ryan pressed the button on the phone. "I'll take it in a minute."

He bit the pencil permanently attached to his mouth and grimaced. Good ole number-two yellows instead of nicotine-killer-sticks. Seven whole days and counting since his last cigarette and the cravings were subsiding, slowly.

Yeah right, keep telling yourself that.

Just last night he'd foraged like a freaking squirrel looking for the stale pack he *knew* was in his old computer bag. No such luck.

He swung his feet off the desk and tilted his head to the side with a crack. Damn cursor on the screen blinked—mocking him. Why was the new prototype of *Combat Bust Up II* kicking his ass?

The design wouldn't flow no matter what he tried. Had the concept run its course? Considering the hefty design fee the client paid up front, the idea of changing the game probably wasn't going to fly. They expected more bells, whistles, grenades, and Uzis than the last version. The code, the graphics—it all had to be perfect. And this version was far into the stratosphere of happening anytime soon.

Video games, websites, custom systems, whatever it took to keep RMT-Designs on top, and he designed them all. For the second year in a row his company had won the coveted award for systems design.

So why was this version not flowing? His mind wasn't focused. At all.

Could it be the crazy nightmares about his days in combat making an unexpected appearance had something to do with it? Those firefight scenarios in *Bust Up* hit way too close for comfort.

Ryan regarded the shadow box on his desk housing the flag from Sam's casket and a tingle of grief crept into his scalp.

Sam had been his best buddy in high school. They enlisted in the Marine Corps together eons ago, and then Sam became his brother-in-law—more like a brother, really. Sam had died in a firefight in that overseas hellhole. And now Ryan's dreams were taking a trip down memory lane? *Wonderful.*

He cracked his knuckles, resisting the urge to flip his computer the bird. Maybe a few days' vacation to blow off steam was in order. That pretty waitress at the coffee shop came to mind.

Her number might still be in his phone. Tedious nights and tons of work—*Combat Bust Up* sure was busting up his social life.

Spitting out the pencil, he looked away from the latest code worth of crap and clicked on the wireless headset.

"Ryan Masterson."

Static crackled in his ear. Damn. This was a brand-new earpiece. He fiddled with the device and upped the volume.

"Hello."

"Ry, are you there?"

His radar went up at the stress level in his sister's voice. "Jenna?"

"Did you listen to your voice mail?" The message light on the phone blinked steadily.

"What's wrong?" A quick glance at the calendar and he let out a breath. *Phew.* Her baby wasn't due for another few weeks.

"Haven't taken your head out of the hard drive lately, huh?"

That she was able to tease him was a good sign that maybe it wasn't too serious. "I've been knee-deep in this latest design. Why?"

Jenna sighed heavily through the receiver. "I've got issues."

"Issues?"

"The reservation system has the hiccups and some fluke storm is heading here."

Great. The last storm had done enough damage to her place. "Is it a hurricane?" He hoped not.

"No, thankfully," she said, then hesitated. "But some of the roof fell off again."

"What! Are you hurt?"

"No, no, I'm fine," she said, but her breath hitched.

"Jen?"

"And add to the mix," she said with a pained laugh, "these damn contractions...doctor calls them Braxton Hicks."

"Braxton who?"

"They're like what I'll feel when I'm in labor."

"Oh." He knew less than nothing about babies and contractions. He typed the term she'd used into the search bar and his stomach clenched. *Ouch!* "Um, maybe you should go to a hospital? Like, now?"

"Relax." She chuckled. "They're perfectly normal, although tell that to my bladder. This little guy's gonna be a punter for the Steelers."

While Jenna went on about her future baby boy's football career, his fingers flew across the keyboard looking for flights to St. Thomas. When Jenna needed him—something she had a problem actually admitting—he'd move heaven and earth to help.

"I'm looking for a flight now," he told her. "So far none have been canceled."

"Thanks, Ry. The rain isn't supposed to start until tomorrow night."

The U.S. Virgin Islands—tropical paradise—was a great getaway most of the year, but when storms hit, he sure as shit wouldn't want to be there.

Jenna Masterson Reagan, his crazy little sister, had always done things most would consider "interesting." But her decision to relocate there permanently was simply irrational. Granted, he loved a good vacation as much as the next guy—sunshine, girls, margaritas—but living it every day? No way. His high-rise apartment and access to civilization was the way to go.

Jenna, on the other hand, loved nature. Scuba diving, surfing, rock climbing—she did it all, in exotic places. It was why she and Sam had been a great match. He traveled a lot with the Marines, which was perfect for them.

"So how did the roof get damaged?" Celestial Harbor, the resort she'd purchased—on a whim, in his opinion—was in fairly good condition.

"Lousy repair job," she admitted in a tone bordering on embarrassed.

"And as usual you didn't ask for my help." Why was she so stubborn?

Jenna certainly had the skills and knowledge to run a resort, with her degree in hotel management from PSU. That she'd taken the time out of traveling and bungee jumping to finish college was the most rational thing she'd ever done. But owning a resort on an island in the middle of nowhere? Alone? Mind-boggling.

However, like a good and supportive brother, he kept his opinions to himself when she'd set up shop—and designed the reservation system and instituted payroll, even though he missed her something fierce.

He prepared for an earful. Jenna made no bones about touting her independence whenever he offered support she didn't *think* she needed. But he knew deep in his gut she was lonely.

"Ry, I need you." Her voice was grave.

He stopped typing. Wow, that was a first.

"But it won't be for long. I swear," she added quickly.

Something inside his chest hitched. In that instant he knew—the games, the stress, the clients, would have to wait for now. "I'll stay as long as you need."

"Thanks." She sounded relieved. "Love you."

"Back atcha." He clicked off the headset and grinned. Score! One first-class ticket booked for the 9:00 p.m. out of Pittsburgh International, with one stop in Charlotte, then on to St. Thomas.

He swiveled his chair around to catch the boarding pass printing behind his desk.

Something thumped from across the room.

A picture frame was facedown on the carpet, next to the file cabinet where all his other pictures were displayed. Maybe the vibration from rolling his chair on the plastic floor mat had rattled it?

He crossed the room, bent, and turned it over. A cold blast ran through his body.

Sam.

Ryan placed the picture on his desk, sat, and leaned back in his chair. A hot sting hit the backs of his eyes.

Damn. Would the sharp knife of grief ever subside? Jenna hadn't gotten the chance to tell Sam she was pregnant before he was killed on his last deployment, and merely thinking about it was too much to handle sometimes.

Going through each day, working like a dog, trying to be normal again, wasn't cutting it lately. The small things—like a Steelers or a Penguins win and not being able to text Sam the score—hit him between the eyes like a ton of bricks.

He exhaled on a huff. The photo was one of Sam's last: all geared up and ready to ship out, and so proud to be a Marine his face beamed.

Unlike himself, Sam was a career Marine. He'd loved the Corps—lived it, and knew there was no other place for him.

Wouldn't it be nice to feel that sure about something?

Aw hell, what was he complaining about? He'd done his time and earned his uniform. And now as a civilian, he was just as driven to build his own business. It was all about the next deal and the next system to design, not the long-term stuff.

So why was his subconscious nagging at him? Perhaps being so driven came with a price—like missing out on what Jenna and Sam had shared?

He chuckled to himself. *Get over it, Masterson. Real love is not for you.* He sure as hell wouldn't find a love like Sam and Jenna experienced in a bar, or at Pittsburgh's newest vodka lounge.

Besides, finding someone who could put up with his creative-genius moments, which usually struck in the middle of the night, was a long shot. Casual dating and women with no attitude, no judgmental overtones, and no commitment expectations was his mode lately.

But Jenna? She deserved more. Would she ever be able to move forward with her life without Sam? Not in the Virgin Islands in some falling-apart resort—that was for damn sure.

Maybe she'd consider selling the money-sucker? He breathed in deep and his jaw locked.

Brilliant idea.

His little sister had stopped being his responsibility when she married Sam, or so he'd thought. But now, no matter if Jenna wanted it or not, it was time to step up to the big-brother plate. Family shouldn't be far away from each other, especially now that most everyone in his was gone.

He stared back at the photo. "You trying to tell me to get her the hell outta there, buddy?"

Silence followed. What did he expect, Sam to float into the room and slap him on the back with an "atta boy"?

He rubbed his eyes. "Way to go, talking to an empty room."

But the more he digested the idea of moving Jenna back home, the more he liked it. Ever since Mom and Dad died and now Sam, worrying about Jenna was eating him up inside. She needed to be closer—she and the baby.

Uncle Ryan. A warm feeling invaded his chest. That sounded kinda nice. He couldn't wait to meet the little guy.

He'd teach baby Reagan about his incredible father. How honorable and courageous Sam had been—the rock of the family. And, of course, that Sam was a stellar Marine.

On the flip side, the little guy would also need to learn to value a sleek sports car and a large bank account from good ole Uncle Ryan.

The ache inside eased a bit and motivation came over him in waves. In fact, he felt more motivated about something other a computer program than he'd felt in a long time.

"Don't worry, Sam, I'll take care of them.

No matter how bat-shit crazy I am talking to your picture." He chuckled to himself.

Better get moving.

"Yes, Ryan," Deb answered when he beeped the intercom. She must've gotten back from lunch.

"I'm heading out tonight to see my sister."

"How long will you be gone?" she asked.

"Not sure." No need to ask for time off when you owned the company.

"I'll clear your calendar."

"Thanks. I'm bringing my computers, so tell Mitch and the others they'll get their code to test as soon as it's done."

She tsked. "Workaholic. I assume you'll need a ride, or do you plan on leaving your car at the airport?"

He wasn't about to store his new Porsche at Pittsburgh International. As always, Deb thought of everything. "No. I'll need a ride, thanks."

"What time is your flight?"

"Nine."

"I'll have Gerald pick you up at seven. Ryan, stop working and go home and pack."

He chuckled. "What do I need, a few shorts and a bathing suit?"

Clicking on a keyboard sounded through the intercom. "Better bring some rain gear," she told him. "According to the weather online, there's a tropical depression occurring off the coast of St. Thomas. If it's upgraded, they predict Tropical Storm Samuel."

He looked back at the picture and the little hairs on the back of his neck stood on end.

"Did you say Samuel?"

There was a long pause. "I did."

ℰᎧᏣᏫ

St. Thomas airport was chaos. Ryan's shoulder tightened under the weight of his two computer bags as he rolled his suitcase behind him and dodged people along the way.

A bunch of college-aged girls sprawled on the white tile of the airport floor with earbuds sticking out of their heads. Guess their Memorial Day weekend vacations were done.

God, he needed more caffeine. He glanced down at his watch—6:00 a.m. already? Nine hours en route and counting, but he'd arrived.

Rows of shops lined the sides of the walkway. Was that newsstand open? Too bad the iron security gate was down. The cigarette cravings had turned into a gum emergency since the TSA agent had confiscated his pencil.

Ryan padded along the walkway, looking for a sign with his name on it. Deb said she'd arranged for pickup. She was an amazing assistant. Yes, taking her with him from Celion Technologies in New York City to start RMT-Designs back home was the best thing he'd ever done for his company. She never complained about the nonstop working, especially lately, as more and more clients wanted his time.

All the schmoozing had paid off, though—his client base was bigger than ever. But in truth, he was a bit tired of the days and nights of partying. Coming into the office with a killer hangover more times than he'd admit under oath, was taking a toll.

Boy, he was getting old.

He squinted and reached into his shirt pocket for his sunglasses. Large picture windows lined the airport and the sun reflected off the blue-green water at the edge of the runway. As soon as he'd stepped foot off the plane, the tropical feel in the air helped to ease the wicked stress headache forming in his frontal lobe.

His pocket vibrated, but he ignored it. The twenty-seven voice mails since he'd left home could wait. At least his "strategy" to convince Jenna to move back home was in the works. James, the manager at the Omni William Penn, Pittsburgh's newest luxury hotel, was more than happy to hire Jenna at any time. The Omni's reservation system was stellar and *he'd* made it happen.

With renewed energy and purpose, he picked up the pace toward baggage claim and ground transportation and ticked off a list in his mind: fix up Jenna's resort, convince her to put it on the market, and take a mini vacation.

Everything would fall into place. Maybe there would be a hot girl or two to pass the time with in the process. When was the last time he'd had any female companionship? Sadly, he couldn't recall.

A man wearing a flowered shirt, shorts, and sandals held a sign with his name on it. Ryan approached with a smile.

"Mr. Masterson?"

Ryan propped up his suitcase and held out his hand "Hi, I'm Ryan."

The man shook his hand and handed him a business card. "I'm Max."

"Sorry it's so early, Max. I was delayed."

"No problem at all." They walked out of the airport to a black stretch limousine. Max popped the trunk hatch, put in the bags, and held open the back door.

"Mind if I sit up front?" Riding in the back of any car made him want to puke. It was a lovely souvenir from military jeeps.

The man looked surprised. "Not at all, sir."

"Please, call me Ryan. I haven't heard someone say *sir* since my days in the Corps."

He beamed. "My oldest boy's a Marine. In Afghanistan now."

"You must be proud." And more than a bit worried, too, he suspected. War was never easy to deal with, no matter what side of the pond you were on.

Max maneuvered onto the main roadway and nodded. "I sure am."

Ryan gazed out the window as Max touted the good things the Corps was doing for his son.

He'd never felt that way about the Marines. Sure, he'd done his time in combat, but in truth, the Marine Corps had merely been a way to get college money, and sometimes he felt guilty for admitting it. Sam always assured him military life wasn't for everyone. Leave it to Sam to help him feel better about himself.

"And my son's commanding officer looks out for the whole unit…" Ryan caught the tail end of Max's words.

"Having a good CO makes the time over there a bit better," he agreed.

Max smiled. "Did you lead a unit?"

"I didn't have that kind of responsibility."

No, Sam took that honor. He had a gift for taking care of people and protecting them—a natural born leader.

"But you served, and that's responsibility enough. So I thank you, sir."

Sam is the one he should be thanking, not me—he made the ultimate sacrifice.

As they headed off the exit ramp, a small branch ricocheted off the windshield. "Whoa." Ryan flinched. "Is the storm kicking up?" Palm trees along the sides of the road swayed like crazy, but the sky was cloudless.

"Not yet. It's not supposed to be a big one," Max commented.

"Have you lived here long?"

"All my life," Max said with pride.

"My sister relocated about six months ago. She owns Celestial Harbor." Those first three months after Sam died had been the worst. Jenna had cried nonstop, then out of the blue, hopped a flight and never came home.

Max smiled. "Ah yes, Miss Jenna…she's a lovely lady. My wife cleans the bungalows on her property and my daughter Cecelia works there, too. She's doing good things with the place."

"So I've heard." And, if he had his way, Jenna's improvements would help sell the resort.

Ryan spotted a sign for the Charlotte Amalie ferry dock, the only way on and off Star Island, where Celestial Harbor was located.

Max parked near the dock where a boat called *Jack's Craft* was moored. He handed Ryan his bags. "Have a good stay."

"Thanks." Christ, could it be any more humid? Jeans seemed like a good idea last night, but now—not so much.

Welcome to the tropics.

"Morning." The captain nodded when Ryan stepped on board. It took a minute to get his sea legs. He spotted a vacant seat at the back of the boat and rolled his suitcase past the other few passengers.

The captain jumped down, unhitched the line, and started up the engine. Less than fifteen minutes later, the dock at the edge of the pebbled walkway of Celestial Harbor came into view.

After the captain helped the last guest disembark, Ryan stepped onto the dock. "Thanks. Jack, I presume?"

The man nodded. "Yep. If you need a ride back or anything, just tell the front desk to call me, anytime."

Ryan heaved his bags off the wooden dock, passing the resort guests being met by their personal concierge service. His sister knew how to pamper her guests.

As he followed the path lined by palm trees and other foliage, the surroundings started to look familiar. He recalled from his one and only time on the island the beach area located at his left. He sidestepped it, but not before he noticed a few die-hard sunbathers stretched out on lounge chairs in the sand. One in particular, with a great body in a small polka-dot bikini and sexy belly ring, was in the midst of a wrestling match with her lounge chair. *Note to self: See if she's around later.*

He continued around the main lobby building to Jenna's residence—the largest of the bungalows she called home. He rapped on the door once then entered, rolling his suitcase behind him. "Hello? Anyone home?"

"Ry, is that you finally?" Jenna called out from the hallway.

She appeared and reality hit him in the face like a grenade. His little sister was going to be a mom—unbelievable.

"You're huge!"

"Never say those words to a pregnant woman." Her smile was wide and she glowed.

He and Jenna were a mere twelve months apart—Irish twins, Mom used to say. She had the carbon copy of his jet-black hair, although hers fell in waves down her back, and silver-blue eyes, which turned gunmetal gray whenever she was emotional or angry.

"That rule doesn't apply to sisters." He dropped his computer bags on a chair with a thud as she waddled toward him. She wrapped her arms around his waist and put her ear against his chest. Her enormous belly poked him in the stomach.

He closed his eyes. Sam's absence was a profound void, stabbing at the middle of his chest. *Keep it together.*

"I'm so glad you're here," she squeaked out.

"Me, too," he said against her hair.

She pulled away and swiped at her eyes. "Phew."

Oh no. Tears were his downfall. "Hey. What's with those?"

She sniffed and waved a hand at him. "Just raging hormones. You want coffee or something cold?" she asked and turned to the kitchen area adjacent to the living room.

"Caffeine, please." He groaned. Her

bungalow was quite spacious. She'd added a new sectional couch and a big-screen TV. "The place looks great."

"Thanks." She smiled. "I changed a few things and updated the appliances."

Sam had wisely taken out a substantial insurance policy, which pretty much set up Jenna for life. He glanced around the living room and stopped short. A large blue blow-up pool sat in the corner. "Are you having a keg party?"

She stopped pouring the coffee as a look of confusion crossed her face.

He pointed to the pool.

"That's my birthing pool."

His mouth slid open. "Your what?"

"Where I'm going to give birth." She handed him the cup and sat on the couch.

Her words sunk in and the preposterous idea took a moment to settle into his brain. "You're not a fish," he blurted out.

Her eyes narrowed.

Oops. Guess pregnant woman are supersensitive. He cleared his throat and approached the couch. "What I mean is, why not go to a hospital on the main island with, you know, doctors, and monitors, and pain medications? Right?" *Get the shovel to dig yourself out of this one.*

She patted his arm. "Spoken like a typical man. I want this birth to be an easy and spiritual experience, not one filled with medicine and bad vibes."

Bad vibes? *What a load of...* No way in hell his nephew was going to be born like a guppy. "Tell me you're joking. You've never been this 'hokey' before."

"Hello, Ryan."

He swung around. "Well, that explains things," he mumbled under his breath.

Five feet eight inches of long legs, blond hair, and the smallest bikini he'd ever laid eyes on walked into the room and the oxygen was sucked out.

Faith Reagan.

Sam's sister was as beautiful as ever. She gave him a cool stare and walked into the kitchen. And apparently just as warm and fuzzy, too. *So much for a little R & R.*

He shot a glance at Jenna, who pretended to study the condensation on her iced tea glass like it was a pirate's treasure map.

"Earthy-crunchy girl" was the name he'd made up to tease Faith with when he was young and stupid. He felt bad about that. A little.

However, Faith had no problem expressing what she thought of him—a shallow, animal-eating, fast-car-loving, mucking-up-the-environment jerk.

Ah, the memories came tumbling back. *Thanks, Sam. Torture me some more, will you? Where's your picture-throwing skill now?*

"Why hello, Faith. I didn't know you'd be here. Are you still a vegetarian, or have you come over to the dark side?"

She smirked. "Very funny. It's a healthy way of life. You should try it sometime." She opened a cabinet, grabbed a glass then headed to the ice machine.

He shot a what-the-hell look at Jenna, who merely laughed into her glass.

What in God's name was she doing here?

Last he'd heard she'd joined the Peace Corps or some crap.

As if reading his mind, Jenna spoke up. "Faith's my masseuse and yoga instructor. Plus, she's a certified doula."

He arched an eyebrow.

"Like a midwife. You know, someone who helps with birthing?" Faith explained to him like she was speaking to a child.

"I know what a midwife is," he grumbled.

Jenna darted a nervous look between them. It was no secret that he and Faith didn't quite gel. He never fully understood why, but he wasn't about to be her whipping boy, either.

"Plus, she's helping me put together a plan to use one of my storage buildings for a new school here on the island."

He didn't like the sound of *that*. "Why would you need a school? This is a vacation spot."

"The one on St. Thomas was destroyed in the last storm," Jenna relayed.

With Jenna hosting a school on her property, she'd never agree to relocate.

"Jenna, I'll fix breakfast after I clean up?" Faith asked as she rubbed her face with the towel draped around her neck. Her skin held the healthy glow of a deep tan, like the rest of her body. He, on the other hand, had the Pittsburgh vampire look down to a science.

"Oh yes! I'm craving one of your smoothies." Jenna laughed.

"Hey, what about me? I'm hungry, too."

Faith pinned him with a stare and the hairs on the back of his neck rose. "Sure. I'll fix you something, too," she said a bit too sweetly.

"Forget to mention she'd be here?" He nudged his sister's foot as Faith and her perfect ass exited the room.

"Long story."

"I've got time."

Jenna bit her lip. "Not my tale to tell."

Wonder what that was about. "Are you busy enough to hire her?"

"There's a big wedding booked this weekend, which is why I need your help." Jenna rubbed her stomach and stifled a yawn. "Get my laptop." She pointed to the counter. "I'll show you what's happening with your reservation system. Oh, and the supplies for the roof repair are waiting for you too."

"Jeez, you're bossy," he muttered, then logged on to her computer and did a quick inventory of the website for Celestial Harbor. He scanned the online form before moving into the back coding. "You've got a virus."

"No! Your special software was supposed to avoid that."

He dug some more, located the problem, and swore. "Looks like a tracking device. Damn. I thought I had this stuff covered. Hmm…it originated from a server belonging to a real estate broker on St. Thomas."

Jenna's mouth flew open. "No way. There's a shady guy coming around asking about buying properties."

His ears perked up but he kept typing. Someone was looking to buy her out? *Interesting.* "I'll disable the system and set up a temporary database."

Jenna sunk into the cushion. "You're the

genius."

He heard the shower start up. "Does Faith stay here with you?"

"I thought it would be best if she were close, since I'm due soon," she said without opening her eyes.

"Hmm..." Great. She'd be right down the hallway. "Go take a nap or whatever it is pregnant ladies do while I fix this."

Jenna laughed. "Ha! Like clean the bungalows and restock the towels?"

Jenna playing maid didn't sit well with him. At all.

"Maybe this place is too much for you. There might be some credence to selling it." At her shocked look he decided to tread lightly. "I'm not saying to that sleazy guy, but just think about it."

She waved a hand at him. "Stop being such a big brother."

He leaned over to kiss her forehead. "Not gonna happen." With Sam gone, it was his job to protect her again.

She wrinkled her nose. "You smell. Go put your clothes in one of the guest rooms and take a shower. I need my roof fixed today and there's a clambake tonight at five. Oh, and *please* try and be nice to Faith. She's a big help."

He shrugged and raised his hands. "I'm being nice. Maybe you should worry about your brother."

Jenna winked. "You're a big boy. You can handle it."

The question was, did he *want* to handle Faith?

Showered and ready to get to work, he headed back to the kitchen a half hour later.

The blender roared and something smelled—well, not quite good. Faith had on a muumuu thing that hid her legs, but at least exposed one tanned shoulder. *Why does she look good even in a sack?*

He placed his duffel bag on a stool and pulled out another to sit, as she poured a thick liquid resembling snot into a glass. She plopped in a straw and slid it across the countertop.

"Bacon and eggs in a glass?"

She rolled her eyes. "Hardly. That's a heart attack waiting to happen. This—" she sipped from her own glass, then flicked out her tongue to lick her upper lip, "—is healthy."

A twinge of heat simmered in his lower body. What the… *Think of algorithms. Think of code. Do not think of Faith's tongue.* "As it turns out, I'm trying to be healthier. And I quit smoking."

Her eyebrows rose to her hairline. Was that a snort?

"When? Yesterday?"

"Over a week ago, as a matter of fact." *What is she, the health police?*

She studied him for a moment as if she was gearing up to give a lecture. He recognized the expression. She shrugged instead. "It's not a good idea to smoke near an infant."

Did she honestly think he was that much of an asshole? *Play nice, for Jenna's sake.* "This is…interesting." He eyeballed the glass, trying not to grimace. "Any strawberries in there?" He cautiously sniffed the contents.

"No. Why? Are you allergic?"

"Quite deathly," he admitted.

She put her elbows on the table and held her chin in her hands. "Oh? Do tell."

He leaned away from the glass, suspicious. "Why? So you can do me in?"

She sighed heavily. "Don't be ridiculous, Ryan."

When she said his name with that whispery thing in her voice, something funny happened inside—like indigestion, only without the need to burp. Her hair fell in loose waves against her bare shoulder and smelled like some kind of coconut stuff.

She *seemed* innocent enough, but he was hardly the best judge of women, admittedly. Whenever he'd tried to be friendly to Faith in the past, she'd blown him off with an icy comment. "Sam never told you the story?"

She straightened and tapped her fingers on the granite. "If it had anything to do with your many bimbo escapades, then I'm sure he hadn't."

Bimbo escapades? Granted, he and Sam had had their share of fun, before Sam fell head over heels for Jenna. "I wish." He chuckled, but ceased when she harrumphed.

He cleared his throat. "No. It was at boot camp, actually. We were scared shitless, or at least *I* was. Sam was always so cool under pressure, you know?"

One of her hands rose to grab her necklace—a thick, gold choker with a seahorse pendant. A somber expression crossed her face. "He was."

Did talking about Sam make her upset? Come to think of it, he'd never seen her cry—not once at the funeral—or mention Sam again. Ever. "You really want to hear this story?"

She crossed her arms. "Go on. You've piqued my interest."

His stomach growled, but he ignored it. Anything to avoid drinking the green stuff was fine with him. "Well, we only had, like, five-point-two seconds to eat, stow our trays, and get out of the mess hall each meal. I'm chowing down—didn't even see or taste the food. I could've eaten my boots at one point."

The corner of her mouth lifted.

Whoa. Where was this coming from? He *never* talked about his time in the Marines. "So, we go back out to drill," he continued. "Which is nonstop marching," he clarified at the question in her eyes, "and I start to feel funny, and not in the 'ha-ha' way. Sam glances over and his eyes bug out like one of those puffer fish."

She laughed out loud suddenly and her whole face changed, like a light had turned on. Her green eyes were bright against the flush of her cheeks.

All coherent thought left his brain.

"Well?" She poked him in the middle of his chest. "Don't leave me hanging."

Was she flirting? Nah. *Snap out of Faithdom, you idiot.* "The next thing I know the drill sergeant is picking my sorry ass off the pavement, and none too gently. He takes one look at my lips and curses to high heaven. Took a good week for the swelling to go down. My throat closed up and everything."

Her eyes widened. "That's dangerous. You really *could've* died."

He shrugged. "Death might have been easier

because for the next eleven weeks Sam called me Bubble Lips. I got my ass kicked by the sergeants more for that than anything else I screwed up." He smiled at the memory. "Sam was a real smart-ass at times."

Her smile disappeared as the elephant in the room dumped in his lap. "Hey, I'm sorry. If you don't want me to talk about him, I won't."

She seemed vulnerable, which he'd never witnessed before. "No, it isn't that. It's just…I miss him."

"Me, too," he said softly. They stared at each other in silence for a few seconds, like some kind of connection was growing.

He didn't know if he liked it or not.

She gestured to his glass. "I thought you were hungry."

"You *swear* there are no strawberries in here?"

She shook her head. "Nope. Just kale, celery, cucumber, and apple."

"Sounds delicious," he muttered. The texture was think and sludgy and bits of vegetable that hadn't gotten pulverized crunched in his teeth. *Holy…* This shit would stick to his insides like tar. Maybe it'd work for Jenna's roof repair.

He took a long chug, bit back a choke, and swallowed. The last clump of ick went down and he forced himself to keep it that way.

"Like it?" There was a hint of challenge in her voice as she sipped from her glass.

"Absolutely." He wiped his mouth with a napkin. "So, um…how have you been?" It might not be the worst thing to play nice in the sandbox with Faith. *Only for Jenna, of course.*

She eyed him suspiciously. "Do you really care?" There went the ice-queen tone again. Jeez, what had he ever done to her? He exhaled heavily. Enough was enough.

"Listen, Faith, I just have to ask you—this is kind of frustrating for me, and I'm not one to admit it often…"

"What is?"

He looked at her square. "Why don't you like me?"

She reacted so quickly that if he weren't already on high alert because of her awesome smell and that two-second burst of a smile earlier, he'd be wearing her smoothie.

She'd knocked over the glass, and the lavalike substance made its way across the counter toward him and onto the floor.

"Crap," she muttered and grabbed the roll of paper towels from the holder. He jumped off the stool and commandeered a dish towel, which Jenna probably kept for show since it was brand new—*who could understand the female mind?*—and wiped up the mess. Faith's head was bent next to his and they almost bumped.

Cold ick oozed through his fingers. Her arms were so near to his that he itched to reach out, after he washed his hands of course, and caress the skin of her delicate wrist. He'd never noticed the cute seahorse tattoo there before.

Snap. Out. Of. It. He just needed a good day of hard work, a beer later, and then some cute girl to shoot the shit with.

Not Faith.

Yet if she gave an indication that she'd want that, he wouldn't say no.

Not a thought he was willing to explore right now.

However, she hadn't answered him, either. Why *did* his question rattle her?

"So?" He tossed the filthy dish towel in the sink and turned to face her.

"I never said I didn't like you," she said tightly and sopped up the rest of the mess.

"Could've fooled me."

Her lips flattened. "News flash. Not every female falls over you. Although it's probably not what you're used to."

"You'd be surprised." Lately, his dating life was in the toilet.

"Yeah right," she muttered under her breath.

He tilted his head toward her. "I'm sorry, what was that?"

"I just know your type, that's all." She crossed her arms.

"And what type is that? Supportive brother? Successful business owner? Disgusting smoothie drinker?"

At least she grinned at the last comment.

"Faith, honestly, what did I ever do to you? Run over your cat by mistake? Or maybe fed you a hamburger when you weren't looking, which wouldn't be a bad thing, if you ask me."

Her lips pursed. "Oh come on, Ryan. You think I haven't overheard through the years about your many escapades. Even Jenna's told me some tales."

He'd deal with his sister later. Besides, it wasn't as if he had a harem. "You keep saying escapades. What's the problem with dating? You *don't* date?"

"Who says I don't date?" she sputtered, all defensive now.

It was his turn to cross his arms. "Let me guess. You like guys who eat like birds and meditate?"

Her eyes darted to the counter. "You don't know anything about what I like."

Her regarded her in silence. Wait a minute— her crossed arms, her foot tapping on the floor, her super-defensive stance—she'd been *dumped*.

For some reason, the thought of some jerk hurting Faith made him want to punch the asshole.

"Give me his name, I'll beat him up for you. Since Sam's not here, I'll take the place of your big brother." *With not-so-brotherly urges. Sorry, Sam.*

"That's…not…" she stammered.

Her leaned in closer and smiled. "Don't judge a book. We're not all bad, you know."

He grabbed his bag off the table and ignored her stunned look as well as the rumble of his stomach.

္‣

Faith draped the basket over one arm and rewrapped her sarong tighter around her waist. At the end of the pebbled path was the banquet hall—well, not quite a banquet hall, more of a building Jenna had decorated in warm Caribbean colors of sea-foam-green and peach, and perfect for parties.

Since Ryan was busy working most of the day on the roof to fix it in time for the wedding, it was only fair to do her part, too, for Jenna's sake.

Are you done pining over him yet? And yeah, just great. He thinks of himself as your big brother now.

Ryan loved fast cars and faster women, judging by the stories she'd overheard throughout the years. One of her girlfriends even went out on a date with him...once. He probably didn't remember it.

What was she, chopped liver? Sam knew she'd had a crush on Ryan forever ago. What he hadn't known, or what she'd never told her brother, was that it'd never ceased. She still carried the torch, but apparently Ryan wasn't interested in making it ignite.

For all the organic lifestyle she'd carefully lived every day, her one weakness was bad boys. And unfortunately, Ryan-the-bad-boy-Masterson was just the kind of man she liked. *No, scratch that. Used to like.* Leo, the asshole ex, crept into mind along with the urge to hit something.

Now all she needed was a safe, boring guy—a vegetarian for sure.

Ryan Masterson?

Nope.

No way.

So why, then, was she bringing him lunch? *It's for Jenna.* Plus, he'd been somewhat nice earlier. It was easier to act like a bitch than to admit he wasn't really *that* bad. Maybe he'd grown up and left his jerk tendencies in Pittsburgh?

Steady banging and loud music blasted from the roof as she approached the building. She wanted to plug her ears as he crucified a Rolling Stones song. The man was seriously tone deaf.

Should she yell up to him?

Out of nowhere, a piece of shingle flew over the side of the building and landed close to her foot. She jumped back with a yelp.

"Oh shit, Faith! Did you get hit?"

She shielded her eyes from the sun, looked up, and forgot to breathe. Ryan's sweaty white T-shirt clung to his cut muscles. With his bandanna and ripped jean shorts with holes in places she had no business thinking about, he looked like a pirate.

A long and lean, six-foot pirate, with a crooked smile that did stuff to her equilibrium. A split second later he was next to her. Had he *jumped* down?

He tore off his sunglasses and searched her face. "Are you okay?"

No words formed inside her brain. "Fine," she choked out.

"Oh good. What's in the basket?" He gestured to her arm. "Another breakfast enema?"

Busted.

"The smoothie didn't agree with your digestive system?" Might as well play it off.

The corner of Ryan's mouth lifted. "I'll get even."

His eyes skimmed down her body and her stomach fluttered, but she lifted her chin. She was hot and grungy from teaching yoga on the beach, but it had nothing to do with the bead of sweat trailing down her collarbone into her bikini top. Either he was planning her slow death, or something else entirely, which couldn't be possible. *Remember, you're his little sister now.*

"Seriously, if there's anything green in there,

please go away."

A laugh slipped out. *Okay, so he's a little funny.* "Jenna made you lunch. She's tired, so she asked me to bring it."

He pointed to a bench under a large hibiscus tree. "Want to keep me company?"

She blinked. "Um…sure." No big deal. *It's only lunch. He's a player, and lives the fast life, even if he was a great brother to Jenna.*

"Phew! It must be ninety degrees today." He wiped his face with the bottom of his shirt and she caught a glimpse of skin. She studied her pedicure. *Let's face it—you are so attracted to him it's ridiculous. And he's never given you a second glance.*

So far this job at Celestial Harbor was a godsend, away from the drama she'd left behind, and noneventful—great for her zen.

Until now.

Ryan's presence upset the balance she'd carefully established in her life and her psyche the past few months.

He unloaded the basket and dove into the sandwich with gusto. He cracked open a bottle of water and offered her one. "I was thinking about booking a massage later."

Visions of him lying naked under a sheet flashed into her mind. The water went down the wrong pipe and she choked. "I'm pretty filled up today." She swallowed hard.

"Can I ask you something?" he asked in between chews.

His tone made her suspicious. If he thought she was about to explain Leo, he'd be disappointed. How had he guessed anyway? Jenna would never spill, and it wasn't as if she had *I've been dumped* stamped on her forehead. "I guess," she said instead.

"Whose idea was it to have my nephew born like Shamu?"

She bit the inside of her cheek. "It was actually Jenna's," she answered truthfully.

He shook his head. "Yeah, about that. I just don't know—"

"Water birth," she interrupted him, "is quite soothing to the mother, and a natural way to bring forth the child." She stated her mantra, but a familiar knot of stress invaded her core and she gripped the bottle.

She'd performed only one water birth, and had learned tragically that it wasn't always the best option depending on how the baby was positioned. But Jenna trusted her wholeheartedly, despite when she'd voiced her fears. Nothing would go wrong with this birth. She reached up absently to touch her necklace. *Oh, Sam, how am I going to do this?*

"If you say so." He didn't sound convinced. Neither was she.

"Your shorts are vibrating."

His eyebrows shot up. "What? Oh." He reached into one of the least-ripped pockets and pulled out his phone. "Damn," he muttered and clicked it off.

Who had called? One of his bimbos? *Jeez, what did she care?*

Ryan got up and stretched with a groan. "Thanks for lunch, but I'm burning daylight. Are you going to that clambake thing?"

Crap. She'd forgotten all about it. She rose

from the bench and gathered the basket and his garbage. "Probably," she mumbled. Jenna insisted she mingle and move on with her love life. But the idea wasn't as appealing now that Ryan had arrived.

"Hey, listen, Faith—" he seemed uncertain, "—since I plan to be here awhile, how about we try to, you know, get along, or at least pretend to, for Jenna's sake?"

Wait a minute. What? Pretend to? A few hundred snippy answers came to mind, but before she spoke up, a group of female guests rounded the corner.

"Hi, Ryan," a redhead, who clearly needed a bigger bikini top, sang out and jogged up to them. Faith took a step back. The woman didn't even acknowledge her. She leaned into Ryan and the others closed in behind her.

"Will we see you at the clambake later?"

He laughed and her stomach sank, and then anger simmered.

Big brother, my ass. She didn't want another big brother. She also didn't bother sticking around to hear his answer.

∞○∞

Ryan rubbed his stiff shoulder through the ugly Hawaiian shirt Jenna insisted he wear. He really needed that massage, but Faith had been MIA since lunch.

"Hey, Mr. Masterson." Theo passed by with a tray of empty glasses. Jenna's small staff was efficient and always smiling. He was beginning to understand why she loved it here.

But dealing with annoying guests was harder than he'd expected. How she kept her cool was anyone's guess. He'd almost ripped the ridiculous mounted swordfish off the wall in the lobby and bashed the shit out of the groom-to-be. Some guests were downright rude.

If—no, *when*—Jenna came home to work at the Omni, she wouldn't have to worry about this crap. She'd stay at his condo, and he'd hire a nanny if she wanted. It was time to bring up selling again, and soon.

Crickets chirped and a gazillion bugs buzzed as he made his way back to the beach. The calypso band by the pool was on their last song, and torches surrounded what was left of the pig roasting on a spit. Theo and crew had set up tables laden with platters of shellfish and other fixings. It was his kind of party.

A welcomed cool breeze wafted off the surf as he stepped onto the beach. Jenna's idea to host the clambake as a fundraiser for the Storm Relief Fund was a success. He'd manned the donations desk, and now it was time to think about Caribbean rum and *not* Faith Reagan and her laugh.

He looked up and down the beach. Jenna wasn't around. Guess she'd probably hit the hay.

The local couple he'd met at the donations table earlier, Alan and Eloise, were walking away, probably heading home. Funny how the guy mentioned knowing of RMT-Designs. Guess his company's reputation was growing. He couldn't be happier about the success.

Speaking of happy, he'd thought Faith would be *thrilled* about his peace offering, but she'd disappeared before he could get rid of those annoying girls.

Why was she so tense around him? He'd hoped to take the pressure off her to *really* be nice to him—which sucked now that he thought about it. The small glimpses of pleasant Faith were few and far between.

Face it—she barely tolerates you. Why else would she have tried to poison him?

He grabbed a piece of pineapple from the display and popped it into his mouth.

Coolers filled with beer, water, and soda sat on the sand next to the tables. He lifted the lid on a large punch bowl and dipped in the ladle. Pieces of mango, cantaloupe, and pineapple floated around in the mix. He sniffed. No strawberry, Jenna had made sure. Good to go.

The kick of alcohol hit the back of his throat. Too bad there was no cigarette to go with his drink. Willpower. *Once you're over the hump, it'll be clear sailing.*

"I guess you finished the roof? Jenna seems much happier now that you're here." Faith appeared next to him and filled a cup with punch. She took a long drink.

He scanned her from head to toe. Her dress was red and sheer and flickering torches behind her highlighted the silhouette of her curves underneath. The strapless top defied the laws of gravity and, yeah…her cleavage showed zero tan lines. All sorts of images flashed into his mind of her sunbathing…nude. *So much for that cool breeze.*

"Glad I can help," he answered shortly.

The band finished the song and people

clapped. Her gaze shifted to the pool area and he tried not to stare at her perfect profile. Where Sam had been built like a blond, brick shithouse, Faith was the opposite—graceful and ultra feminine.

Her long mane was in some kind of bun thing, which left the column of her neck exposed and so sexy his palms started to sweat.

It was practically old-man creepy to think of Sam's sister in such a way. Christ, he was at least five years older than her, not that younger women were necessarily off-limits…but still.

Never, ever, had he breathed a word of his growing attraction to Faith to anyone—especially Sam and definitely not "nosy Jenna"—that would have been a disaster.

So he gave Faith a hard time in front of everyone instead. Better to play the jerk card than face any kind of feelings.

Sam dating Jenna wasn't a big deal. He'd trusted the guy with his life. Plus, Jenna had her own mind about things.

But he and Faith? That was crazy. He had to admit, though, that she was super caring to Jenna, and Sam had worshipped her. Maybe she was the kind of woman he could see in his life, minus the no-meat part. *What?* He must've gotten too much sunburn today, because his rational thoughts and good sense had left the building.

"Don't you have a company to run back home?" She fiddled with her necklace and his eyes glued to it, but no lower.

"I took some time off."

And there went the lecture-to-be expression of hers. "Hmm…how noble of you. Jenna's been worried lately, a whole lot worried, if you hadn't noticed."

What's with the attitude? "She's fine each time I call," he said warily.

She gulped her drink again, wiped the dribble from her chin, and grumbled.

"What was that?" he asked.

She looked at him all wide-eyed. "Oh, nothing."

His eyes narrowed. "No, no...I believe you said something. Don't hold back now."

She refilled her cup and lifted her chin. "Well, I've been here three weeks and I don't believe you've called once."

His mouth opened and closed like a striped bass on a line. "I send email." Why in the hell was he defending himself? Hadn't he just busted his ass all day on the roof?

She shrugged. "Oh well, you know how that can be," she said coolly, and surveyed him over the rim of her cup.

"How what can be, an email?" Judgmental-female alert. Why did the beautiful ones have to be so messed up? He sighed and took his own gulp. He should have followed Jenna back to the bungalow.

"Impersonal technology." She waved her hand in the air as if to make a point, but it only caused her to tip over slightly before she righted herself.

Was she drunk? Could be. She'd downed, what...at least two cups of punch since this conversation began.

"What I mean is, Jenna's chi is totally off."

Ryan scratched his head. "Her chi?" Now *he* needed another drink and quick. And she needed a chair before she fell over.

She looked him square in the face—or she *tried* to. "The energy she emits and then gives to the baby."

No way did he understand any of that hocus-pocus, holistic garbage.

She blew out a breath. "We all give off a chi to the world and an aura. Like yours, for instance, is…well, never mind."

Thank God. He didn't need the 411 on feng shui, or kung fu, or whatever. "So you're saying Jenna's been unhappy and I didn't pick up on it?"

She nodded and bit at her lip. "She's nervous about the birth."

He knew it! That stupid water thing. This deserved more in-depth conversation.

Ryan held up a finger. "Hold that thought." Spotting two vacant lounge chairs, he sprinted down the beach and dragged them back. Most of the clambake guests were either gone or milling around the pool. They'd have privacy for this heart-to-heart.

He motioned to the chair and tilted his head. She started to protest then sat anyway—more like plopped down and her legs shot out. Her skirt inched up her thighs.

Focus.

His chair creaked under his weight. "About this birth thing…in the water…in the living room. Are you planning to do this without any medical help?"

She took a long sip of her drink and stuck the empty cup on the sand. She studied the waves before asking, "Why? Do you think something could go wrong?"

An unsettling thought took root in his gut, but he hoped to hell he was wrong. "Do *you* think something could go wrong?"

Her panicked eyes met his. She swallowed hard—hard enough for him to see the muscles in her neck move. Then she reached up to touch her necklace before vaulting out of the chair.

What the...

He shot up and trailed her as she raced down the beach. She didn't stop at the water's edge, but continued straight into the waves. He reached out and grabbed her arm before she took a swan dive into the surf.

"Whoa, hold up." Water lapped his calves, warm and foamy. The bottom half of her dress plastered to her body like a second skin. His pulse hammered.

"What's the matter? What did I say?" Hell, he had no idea how to deal with any of this stuff. Computers were so much easier than women.

First, a pregnant, emotional sister, and now Faith, who was acting strangely—icy one minute, flirty the next—it was confusing as shit. Either Faith was seriously drunk, which led to this midnight dip, or she was upset about something.

Face it, Masterson, you have no clue how to act around her. You never have.

She poked a finger in the middle of his chest. *Ouch!* "It's what you didn't say. What, am I not good enough?"

He tensed. "Not good...wait, what?"

"Oh, I'm sorry, perhaps I'll shave off a few hundred points from my IQ. *Then* you'll want me," she slurred.

Where was this coming from? Too much

alcohol, that's where. "Did you have anything to eat today besides that sludge drink?"

"Too upset to eat," she mumbled and waved a hand at him.

He frowned. "Let me walk you back to the beach. You need something to soak up the rum." *Sam, buddy, I am now taking care of your drunk-ass sister, just for the record.*

He steered them out of the water and held her against his side when she stumbled. Holy crap, she was polluted. If she ate a steak once in a while, she'd be able to hold her liquor better.

She dug her heels into the sand, forcing him to stop short. Then in an instant, she was all over him, plastered against his chest like a wet suit. She wound her arms around his neck and her breath against his lips sent a bullet of heat between his legs.

"Oh I do need *something*."

He pulled away. *Oh boy, this is not good.* Concentrate on anything but her sexy, begging-to-be-kissed lips.

She tilted her head to one side and puckered those sexy lips. "What's the matter, Ry, not interested in earthy-crunchy girl?" A hint of uncertainty invaded her eyes for a split second, before her tongue flicked his lips. "You taste good."

His body tensed and he leaned his lower half away from her, but she reached around and grasped him tightly. Jeez, she was strong. Must be all that yoga. "Ah, Faith, this isn't a good idea."

She smiled. "You're a liar," she whispered.

He gritted his teeth and prayed for restraint. "You need some sleep."

"Sleep?" she purred. "You're right. I've wanted to do *that* with you forever."

The top of his head detonated at her words—and with her rubbing against him like a cat, she was the most incredible feeling he'd had in a long time.

Aw hell, sorry, Sam.

His head swooped down. He couldn't fight the need. She tasted like rum and pineapples and pure heaven. She sighed into his kiss, and something in his chest rippled. He pulled her flush against him and braced his feet apart in the sand. How could a kiss feel this right, this intense?

What the hell *are you doing?* Despite how incredible the feelings were, Faith was clearly drunk, and their lip-lock was wrong on so many levels.

He broke away, by some flash of willpower, and cupped her face. "Look, Faith, you're not entirely sober and I know you'll regret this in the morning." Plus, he doubted this is what Jenna had meant by "being nice" to Faith.

Saint Ryan? Who knew?

"Please, come and sit down while I clean up." Cups and plates were strewn onto the beach. Good idea to keep his hands busy, and not on Faith's body. "Okay?"

She seemed dazed and rubbed her swollen lips.

Stop looking at her lips. "Here." At the lounge chair, he helped her sit. She sighed and closed her eyes. He turned around to pick up a few discarded beer bottles to keep busy and give his body a chance to settle down. Wow, she was going to have some hangover. When he turned around again, he froze.

Holy! Faith was at the water's edge—buck naked. Her dress lay on the sand next to the chair. Naked drunk girl, rough surf—a recipe for disaster. "Faith, wait! Stop!"

She looked at him over one shoulder and let down her hair. He swallowed hard. In the moonlight she was sex personified.

And going to drown, unless you get your lecherous ass in gear.

He shrugged out of his shirt and sprinted to catch up to her, but she dove into the dark surf.

"Faith! *Crazy*-crunchy girl," he muttered under his breath. His heart pounded and he shot into the water after her. Man, he should've quit smoking sooner.

Her head broke the surface.

"Stay right there," he ordered.

She swam toward him and rose out of the water like a siren. He blinked and forced himself out of the trance. "What in the hell..." he started to give her what for, but was cut off by her lips sealing to his like a lifeline.

He groaned into her mouth and caressed her bare back. She broke the kiss and ran her fingers through his hair.

"Ryan, I—"

"Mr. Masterson," someone called out farther down the beach.

He shoved her behind him.

"Oh no." She groaned and put her forehead against his back.

"Don't worry. I'll intercept whoever it is, and you go put your clothes on."

When she didn't respond, he turned and

searched her eyes. "Faith, honey, you with me?"

She seemed to have sobered up in two seconds flat, and nodded.

"Good girl." He couldn't resist and bent down to give her a quick kiss. "Go. Now." She scooted out of the water and he dragged his eyes away.

Theo appeared at the spot where he'd thrown his shirt.

"Mr. Masterson, Captain Jack needs to transport someone to the hospital and wanted me to let Miss Jenna know, but she's not answering her phone."

"She's probably asleep." Ryan stepped in front of Theo's view of Faith. "Lead the way."

Finally, the stupid drunk guy who broke his leg doing the limbo was en route to the hospital. Maybe now he could get some sleep.

He padded along the hallway and put his ear to Jenna's door and heard...nothing. *Good.*

At Faith's door he hesitated, then knocked softly. No answer.

"Faith," he whispered. He cracked it open and his eyes adjusted to the dim light from her nightstand. After entering, he closed the door behind him with a soft click.

Faith was dead asleep and snoring away. He smiled at the sight. She hadn't bothered to undress. He pulled the sheet over her legs and bent to kiss her gently on the forehead. "Sleep tight, earthy-crunchy girl."

This evening was sure up there on the crazy meter. Hell, he'd had plenty of girlfriends—*well, not lately*—so why was Faith the one woman who made his chest ache? The run-a-marathon, been-through-boot-camp kind of ache? This trip was turning into more than he bargained for. He exited her room and closed the door.

"Sam, buddy, what am I gonna do now?" Way to go again—talking to an empty room.

༺ོ༻

Ryan cracked open an eyelid at the sound of rain pelting the windows. At least the roof was fixed, or that wedding party might be a little soggy today. And *someone* was going to have a killer headache.

The memory of Faith coming out of the ocean, with drops clinging to her perfect…

A crash sounded from the living room. Vaulting out of bed, he pulled on shorts and a shirt and ran into the hallway.

Jenna was near the couch, a broken bowl lay on the tiled floor, and her cereal and milk pooled under her feet.

"You dropped your breakfast." He grabbed a paper towel to sop up the milk.

"Ry." She gave him a worried smile. "I think my water just broke."

He backed away from the puddle. "Whoa."

"Please go get Faith," she said, more calmly than he felt.

He stared at Jenna's stomach. *Get with the program, idiot.* "Right." He ran down the hallway and knocked on Faith's door. No answer. *Screw this.* He threw it open as she was coming out of the bathroom in a pair of shorts and a T-shirt.

"Ryan, what are you doing…" Her eyes were guarded, but she must have seen the frantic look on his face. "What's happened?"

He took a deep breath. "It looks like baby Reagan may be coming a bit early."

Stark fear crossed her face. He'd seen that look in combat, years ago. Hell, he'd lived the fear. She reached for her neck and turned white.

"*Faith*, what's wrong?"

"My necklace. It's gone." Tears formed in her eyes.

She's worried about some necklace? Now? "It's probably somewhere in here," he suggested impatiently.

She shook her head and sat on the bed. "No, you don't understand. I *never* take it off. Sam left it for me…" Her voice trailed off.

"I'm sure it's sentimental but…well…maybe it fell off when we were, you know, in the water…last night." What a way to bring up an awkward moment.

Her eyes shot to his face. "Oh no." She groaned and covered her face with her hands.

Oh God, please let her keep it together. *I don't have a clue here.* "Jenna's in the living room. She's asking for you."

"It's too early, Ryan," she moaned. "I promised Sam I'd take care of things, and I don't know if I can." Fat tears rolled down her face.

Promised Sam?

He knelt at her feet. "Hey, hey," he said as her shoulders shook. He held both her hands. "Look at me. Whatever it is you have going on, you need to push past it, for Jenna."

The internal struggle mirrored on her face

was killing him. She hugged her stomach and rocked back and forth.

"And for Sam." *Sorry. I had to play the Sam card, buddy.*

At those words, she snapped out of the hell inside her mind. She blew out a breath and nodded. "Okay. I'm good. What's up with Jenna?"

"Um…her water broke?"

"It's time." She got up, grabbed a bag from the bottom of her closet, and quickly headed out the door.

On Faith's nightstand was a picture of her and Sam when they were kids. "Wish you were here, buddy."

"I'm going to need you, Ryan," Faith called out from the hallway.

Jeez, everyone needed him lately. Time to get moving.

In the living room Faith lifted Jenna's feet onto the couch and plumped a pillow behind her back. "Take a load off," she told her.

Jenna sat back, panting slowly. She gave him a serene smile. "Guess this is happening. With the storm and the wedding this afternoon—talk about timing, huh? Ryan, you need to tell the staff to secure the buildings."

"Concentrate on you right now." Faith smoothed a lock of hair away from Jenna's sweaty face.

Then Faith went into autopilot mode, pulling things from her bag and setting them on the counter. "Ryan, I need your assistance. Can you handle it?"

Whatever demons Faith had faced back in

her bedroom were gone. She was calm and collected, and in charge. Quite amazing. "Uh, sure I can."

"Get clean towels and a few big pots of water ready to boil. Oh, and wash your hands really well." She barked out the orders and returned to the couch.

Oh, *that* kind of assistance. Faith raised Jenna's nightshirt up around her waist and he shot around like a bullet. "Whoa…what the hell?"

"How long have you been laboring?" Faith asked Jenna.

"My back started to hurt at the clambake," Jenna answered. "But I thought it was more of those false contractions."

Ryan heard the snap of gloves and a long *hmmm*. "Is it safe to turn around now?" he asked through gritted teeth. His heart pounded in time with the tick in his jaw.

"Yes," Faith answered. She pulled a blanket up high on Jenna's belly and turned to him. "There's a water valve on that tub. Please turn it on now."

"You're not actually doing this in *that*?" He pointed and glared at the stupid tub. "I mean, is there time to get her to the hospital?"

At those words the lights went out and every appliance sputtered to a halt.

"Oh shit. Now what?" What a freaking nightmare. This was why people lived in cities, with backup generators. What if something went wrong? His stomach roiled. If anything happened to his sister or nephew…he couldn't think straight.

"Plan B," Faith said, steadily.

"And that would be?" Plan B would be...*funny, a rhyme.* He was about to lose it. *Combat Bust Up* didn't seem so bad right about now.

"Omigod," Jenna blurted out. "Faith, I think I need to push."

She licked her lips and nodded. "Okay, you're fully dilated, so let's do this." She glanced up at him. "To answer your question, no. There's no time for the hospital. And since you're so squeamish," she said with a smirk, "you can catch the baby."

He felt the color disappear from his face. "Please, I'll drink one of your smoothies every day for a week straight if you're kidding."

She and Jenna laughed. "Faith, stop torturing him."

Faith removed some foreign-looking objects and a vial of oil from her bag of goodies and explained to Jenna what to do.

The windows rattled. "Ry, close the shutters tight. The last thing we need is glass breaking and flying in. And grab the battery lantern from under the sink."

Ryan crossed the room to do Faith's bidding. Anything to get out of the labor and delivery fray was fine with him, even Tropical Storm Samuel. *Shit, Sam, you are here after all.*

Dark, ominous clouds sat low in the sky and the wind whipped as he pulled the squeaky shutters closed. Hopefully the guests were smart enough to stay the hell inside their bungalows.

"Ry, get back here and position yourself by Jenna's head. She knows what to do, but try to keep her mind off the pain."

For a moment he thought she was going to come off with something teasing or smug again, or lecture him about what he was doing wrong, but all she did was give him a sweet smile. "We can do this. Together." An emotion that he couldn't quite identify shone in Faith's gaze. Her confidence in him made a dam in the middle of his chest burst.

She put a sheet over Jenna's knees to block his view.

"Mind. Pain. Got it." He smiled back and handed the lantern to Faith, then reached over and took Jenna's hand. *If only Sam were really here.* That knife of grief reared its ugly head and he blew out an unsteady breath.

"I know." Jenna squeezed his hand. "Seems unreal that he's not here to see this," she said sadly.

A short laugh escaped him. "Yeah, he loved this stuff. Would be on that roof like Ben Franklin in a hurricane, for crying out loud."

She laughed through the sheen of tears, which had suddenly appeared, and his heart lurched. Memories of Sam flashed in his mind. "They used to call him Patch in the Corps because he could fix anything."

"He told me," Jenna replied. "Remember that time my car broke down at PSU?" She smiled.

At least she was smiling now. Smiling he could handle—tears, not so much. "That POS was held together by spit and tape. I could never understand why you drove it."

"But Sam got it up and running before Dad even knew what happened. He was amazing." Her lips turned down.

"Hey, only good thoughts. Plus, I'm dying to meet my nephew, so whatcha waiting for?" He brought her hand to his lips.

She winced and the fun started.

Jenna was a trouper, breathing through each painful moment. *Thank God he wasn't female.* One last drive to the goal line and she held on to deliver her future Steeler.

He and Faith shared a smile as their new nephew took his first breath. He tasted salt and realized it was coming from his own face. Samuel Ryan squawked like a chicken.

"He's got your temperament," he told Faith. She glared at him, but only halfhearted as she cleaned up Jenna.

"And *your* appetite," Jenna piped in. The little man's fuzzy head was under a blanket against her. She was radiant holding her son.

The lights buzzed to life, along with the refrigerator and air conditioner. His grin broadened. "Well, all right!"

"Ryan, see if the phone works. Call the hospital, Jenna's doctor, and Captain Jack. All the numbers are on the fridge," Faith ordered.

"Gotcha."

ഇൻ

Jenna and baby Sam were safely aboard *Jack's Craft*, the island wasn't in terrible shape, and the sun was trying to peek out.

All in all, it was a good morning.

Ryan walked back to Jenna's bungalow and felt like crashing for a week. But he knew he couldn't. There was cleanup and the numerous things he'd been left to take care of in Jenna's absence. He'd gotten the verbal list as she'd left the dock.

Where was Faith?

She'd said she wanted to shower before starting the wedding preparations, but there was no sign of her.

The beach.

For some reason, he was nervous to face her. Between the excitement of Jenna and Sam, Jr., he'd barely deciphered the crazy thoughts and events from last night in his mind. Did she regret kissing him? Did she even remember it? He'd never felt this kind of pull toward any woman before.

Her strength, her fortitude—hell, she had it all. When had Sam's little sister become such a phenomenal woman? And how had he failed to notice it before?

For all his teasing about her hocus-pocus, it was her abilities and natural grace which pulled them through and made Samuel, Jr.'s birth go so smoothly. Grace under pressure.

She sat on the sand close to the surf. Her hair blew like silk strands in the leftover wind. He sat next to her, but didn't speak. She drew circles in the sand with her index finger and glanced up at him over her shoulder with a weak smile.

Uncertainty hit the pit of his gut. "What did you mean you promised Sam?"

Her back straightened and he thought she might bolt for the water again. A short burst of laughter came out. "You're going to think I'm nuts."

He raised an eyebrow. "More nuts and twigs

than usual?"

Her eyes narrowed.

"Just kidding. I'll listen."

Her face became serious. "A few months ago my patient lost her baby in childbirth…a girl."

Oh man.

"After that happened, I couldn't function. Just slept a lot. Didn't eat much. But then…I'm not sure if I dreamed it…or if it really happened."

"What?" Her hand shook and he reached over and entwined his fingers through hers.

She licked her lips and looked at him squarely. "Sam was there. And he asked me to take care of the baby, and made me promise to help Jenna when her time came."

He shivered. "But he never knew about the baby."

"I know," she said softly.

He digested her words in silence.

She pulled away and brushed sand off her legs. "It sounds hokey. Which I'm sure you're *so* surprised about." She rolled her eyes.

He smiled. "Your hokey stuff isn't that bad anymore, at least not as bad as your smoothies."

"Which will be waiting for you later, if I recall your promise," she said with a devilish grin.

The breeze blew a lock of hair into her mouth and he reached out to tuck it behind her ear. She took his hand again, brought it to her lips, and something shifted inside his chest.

"The next morning, it felt like a weight had lifted. That's when I looked over on my nightstand and there was the necklace and I had no idea how it came to be—the same one I lost," she said sadly.

"Oh, Faith, I'm so sorry." And he probably had something to do with that loss. Gently grabbing her legs, he tucked her feet between his legs and rested his hands on her thighs. It was so natural to touch her now, as if it were somehow second nature.

"When I was a little girl," she began, "I loved seahorses—was obsessed with them. They're amazing creatures, did you know that?"

He loved when her face lit up. *Wait, loved? Wow.*

He trailed a finger down her leg, and she sighed. "Tell me."

"The ancient Greeks believed the seahorse was characteristic of the god Poseidon, and stood for strength. Sam knew I loved them. He'd given me quite a few seahorse trinkets when he was…still alive." She turned her head to the surf. "But *that* necklace gave me strength…from Sam, just when I needed it most."

He took her chin and brought her eyes back to his. "You're wrong."

Her brows furrowed.

"Your strength was always there. He just gave a little nudge to bring it back out. I think Sam's been nudging people a lot lately." Great, now he was starting to sound hokey.

Her eyes widened. "What?"

He gave her a sheepish look. "Never mind."

"Listen, Ryan, about last night, and all that…" Her cheeks reddened. It was such a contrast from her confidence a short while ago.

He stopped her words with his lips. "Truth is, I've wanted to *do that* with you forever, too."

A smile bloomed across her face. "Why

didn't you ever say anything?"

"Are you kidding? Sam would've…well, let's just say because I liked my teeth where they were supposed to be," he admitted.

She bit her lip. "I'm sorry if I was judgmental. It's just that…well, I've wanted you to notice me…really notice me, for a very long time."

He reached up and caressed her cheek with one hand. "Oh I've noticed, you can bet on it."

She threw her arms around his neck. "You do know," she flicked at his lips again and he let out a growl, "we've got a few hours before the wedding and an empty bungalow."

Sorry, Sam.

Ryan stretched out, grabbed his pillow, and Faith's scent hit him full force.

Today they were doing nothing but R & R. He was chucking his cell phone, enjoying the tropics, and some more rum punch.

Maybe a midnight skinny dip was on the horizon, too.

The ping on his tablet sounded. He turned on the screen and the latest picture of Samuel Ryan popped up. How was it possible to love one little person so much?

Jenna had sent tons of photos from her phone—this one was of the little guy sleeping in his hat and striped blanket. Captain Jack would bring them home tomorrow. Home to Celestial Harbor.

He turned off the tablet and flopped onto his stomach with a groan. Thankfully, all the obnoxious wedding guests were finally gone.

How could he possibly convince Jenna to sell *now*? And would he even want to? The wedding turned out, by some miracle of fate—or Faith—quite extraordinary, from the buzz among the guests. One couple had already booked their affair for next year.

Perhaps this *was* the place for Jenna to be after all? But how in the hell could he be away from her and Samuel? And Faith? She was another story entirely.

He loved her.

It was like a battering ram had wacked him in the heart and there was no turning back. Sam, Jr.'s birth had brought him to the place he needed to be, and with the woman he'd always adored. Now he needed to figure out how RMT-Designs could set up an office in the Virgin Islands at least part of the year.

His body jumped as sturdy hands massaged his back. "Ahh, you have the magic touch." Her hair tickled his back when she leaned over and bit his ear. Hard. "Ouch!"

"Are you ever going to get up? I've taught two yoga classes already, you dirty, stay-up-all-night computer geek."

No sleep had been well worth it. "You had something to do with that, no?" He sunk deeper into the bed as she worked his muscles.

"True." She chuckled.

More importantly, the lack of sleep had also been productive. The newest RMT-Designs game was sold. Celion had bought it on proposal—*Poseidon's Strength*. Only, the hero was now a heroine instead of a soldier, and she rode a giant seahorse. *Combat Bust Up II* was officially a bust, and he'd never felt as sure of anything in his life.

Wasn't that what he'd wanted? To be sure of something, like Sam had been?

He turned over and smiled at the reason.

About…

Nicole S. Patrick has always loved to read, and in her teenage years, she "borrowed" her mom's books to sneak away and become lost in the world of romance. After more than ten years in the corporate world of tech recruiting and HR management, she decided to stay home and raise children. But with so many romantic stories and characters floating around in her head, when the kids napped, she was compelled to put those words on a page and pursue this crazy dream of becoming published. Nicole writes romantic suspense and her heroes are those alpha males in uniform. She lives in New Jersey with her real-life hero, her husband, and her two sons.

❧

For more information about Nicole, please visit her website at www.nicolespatrick.com.

❧

Coming soon from Nicole S. Patrick…

A Matter of Honor

A romantic-suspense novel about a Marine Corps captain and a traumatized investigative journalist—the daughter of the man he blames for his father's death. One of the core values of being a US Marine—honor—is tested as he is forced to help her solve a murder and do the honorable thing by keeping her safe.

A Pirate's Vacation

Julie Rowe

❧

A year ago, Emergency Room doctor Josie Zizzo lost her husband to the violence in war-torn Syria. Watching him die while bullets rained down on their makeshift hospital, left her suffering from Post-Traumatic Stress disorder. Returning to work in the ER proved impossible, the PTSD throwing her back in time to the awful day her husband died. In an effort to heal, Josie buys a B&B in the U.S. Virgin Islands, but the property needs more repairs than she anticipated. Her best friend promises to come help, but it's her best friend's brother who steps off the plane, firefighter Mark Durant. Mark is the last man she dated before meeting her husband, a man she loved, a man who walked away from her when she asked for more than a causal relationship.

Mark has come to help Josie because he's suffering his own PTSD nightmare and hopes the sun, sand and time spent with the most giving woman he's ever met will help him heal. It isn't until he steps off the plane and sees Josie's shocked face that he realizes his sister has set them both up. Now he's sharing a house with a woman he wants more than his next breath, who's also fighting her own terrifying memories. It isn't until a storm hits the island that they're forced to face their pasts and all the ghosts that haunt them. Can love survive nature's wrath and their personal demons?

❧

Dedicated to ~

Heroes everywhere—those people who give of themselves to help others until it hurts. You know who you are. I thank you.

A Pirate's Vacation
by Julie Rowe

It was a good day to be a pirate.

Not a cloud in the sky, the winds were fair and from the east. The late-morning heat was enough to put even the most athletically inclined person into a doze. The perfect time to land on the sand and hunt down some treasure—or in this case, fix it up, make it all shiny, and hope the tourists showed up.

At least, that's what Josie Zizzo hoped.

Then again, nothing had gone the way she'd hoped for the past year.

Oh, who was she kidding? Her life had virtually ended when her husband died in front of her eyes.

Both of them were emergency-room physicians, though at different Boston hospitals. They'd signed on to a medical mercy mission in Syria. One week into the mission, their makeshift hospital had come under fire by two different groups. Her husband, Adler, had been hit in the chest. Unable to move because of constant gunfire, she'd watched, every second a stab to her gut, a slash to her heart, as he bled out.

It had taken her a week to get home to Boston with her husband's body. Another week before his service and burial, then twelve weeks to realize she'd never be able to go back to life as she knew it again.

Her first shift back in the ER had made her new reality clear. The noise, the people, the blood—suddenly she was back in Syria watching Adler die. Again.

She'd screamed herself hoarse.

Again.

Post-traumatic stress disorder, they'd said. She needed therapy, time, and probably a different job, for a while at least.

So she'd left the hospital and began searching for something completely different from her Boston home. It took her six months to figure out what she wanted, but she finally decided on an entirely new way of life.

A bed-and-breakfast. The Caribbean. Pirates.

Of all the dreams she and Adler had together, running a B&B on an island that had once been home to convicts, rum runners, and the infamous pirates wasn't one of them.

She bought the first property that had appeared feasible. Something that needed fixing to make it nice. So when she arrived on the island of St. Thomas six weeks ago to take possession of her new home it had been with the hopes of getting the place ready for her first guests within a month.

That time frame had been unceremoniously dashed against the rocks. The Pirate's Cay, as her B&B was known to the locals, had needed a lot more repairs than she realized from the report and pictures the real-estate agent had sent her, but because the home had sold for a lot less than fair market value, she really couldn't complain too much.

The price had been too good to be true.

Fool's gold.

No treasure here.

Thankfully, she'd called on her best friend, Benita Durant, to come to the island to help her out for a few weeks. Benita had been her rock after she'd gotten back to Boston from Syria. Helped with the service and burial arrangements. Encouraged her to move to the Caribbean, saying the sunshine, heat, and slower lifestyle were just what the doctor ordered.

Between the two of them, they could get it all done.

Hopefully.

Possibly.

Maybe.

All Benita had to do was get off the plane and pick up her luggage, then they could get to work on making The Pirate's Cay the island's hidden gem.

Yeah, keep telling yourself that, Josie. You're just putting off the inevitable mental meltdown.

So here she was, at the airport stretched up onto her tiptoes, looking for Benita's brown ponytail among the passengers exiting the luggage carousel area.

So far, no Benita.

A group of laughing vacationers from somewhere cold—given their lack of tans—blocked her view for a couple of minutes. When they cleared out of the way, Benita wasn't in sight, but her brother was.

The sight of him kicked her in the diaphragm like a bad-tempered mule.

Mark Durant stood six foot two and had shoulders to match his height. Built like a football linebacker, he didn't need to tackle Josie to push her over. A puff of wind would have done the job. Mark was the last man she expected to see.

The last man she'd dated before meeting Adler.

A man she had wanted with every breath in her body, but walked away from because she wanted what he couldn't give her. A marriage. A home. A family.

A man who'd told her in no uncertain terms he wasn't ready to settle down.

"Hey," he said, staring at her with a gaze that never wavered and a smile that bordered on sinful. His voice flowed over her like dark chocolate, heady and rich.

She swallowed around a lump the size of Manhattan to say, "Hi." It came out like a croak.

He stared at her while she tried to process the fact that her best friend, whom she'd talked to only yesterday, had set her up.

Mark's expression slowly morphed into a frown. Then it dove into surprise. "Holy shit, you were expecting Benita."

"Yup," Josie said. She tried for a weak smile, but highly doubted it looked happy at all.

Mark, who had his duffel bag slung over his shoulder, dropped the bag on the floor. He shoved his hands in his jean pockets. "She told me you needed… She showed me pictures and an email you'd written asking for…" His voice trailed off and his gaze dropped to his bag.

"Help?" Josie finished for him.

He glanced at her with sad eyes and a grin curving his lips, and she caught her breath at the impact of his expression. "Yeah."

He had the best puppy-dog eyes of any man she'd ever met. Hands down, bar none.

Years disappeared and it felt like yesterday when he'd last kissed her, put his hands on her body, and made love to her. It weakened her knees and turned her breathing into something totally optional.

Well, wasn't this just ducky. Hell of a time for her libido to come out of hibernation.

Josie sighed, put some starch in her legs, and refused to succumb to the seduction of her memories. She would be polite and friendly, that was all. "Come on, you're here. You might as well get the nickel tour."

He didn't move. "Not necessary. I can grab the first plane going back to mainland USA."

That duffel bag was full. He hadn't planned a short trip.

She raised one eyebrow. "Did you take time off to come here?"

He froze like she'd just caught him with his hand in the cookie jar. "Um, yeah."

Shit. "How long?"

"Four weeks."

That rocked her back on her feet.

"From the pictures, I can tell your new place needs a lot of work."

Heh, she should have asked his opinion before she bought it. And he'd come all this way to help her, despite knowing the status of the B&B.

"What made you decide to help me?" She tried that smile thing again; maybe this time it'd work. "I mean, we haven't seen each other in a few years."

"Five."

"I beg your pardon?"

"We haven't seen each other in *five* years."

He kept track?

"Like I said," he continued. "I saw the photos of the place you bought and knew you'd need help. When Benita said you asked her to come down and give you a hand, well, I said I was handier." He shrugged. "I'm pretty good with electrical stuff and not bad with plumbing. But you weren't expecting me and you sure as hell…heck…didn't seem happy to see me just now, so—"

She tilted her head to one side. "You're already here and my main backup generator isn't working. After that, I have all the problems you mentioned. Electrical, plumbing, a leaky roof, some carpentry, and a lot of landscaping that needs to be done. Think you could handle a working man's holiday?"

"Can you?"

That was the question.

Could she do it without him? Yes, but it would take a lot longer, cost more.

He was an old friend who wanted to help,

that's all.

Yeah, keep telling yourself that, Josie.

"Yup. Let's go." She turned to lead the way to her tiny, ancient Japanese car, catching just the beginning of a smile crossing his face as he picked up his bag to follow her.

What the hell had Benita told him?

The drive from the airport took only fifteen minutes. The B&B was located up the hill, with a fantastic view of the harbor. The building itself wasn't new, which was part of the problem. It needed a new roof and some of the siding needed to be replaced. Probably damage done during the last hurricane to hit the island. Aside from the view, the property did have other high points. Built into the slope, the house had three main living levels with six bedrooms, each with an en suite bathroom, scattered throughout. There was a beautiful terrace, overlooking a pool located one level down, and a kitchen a chef would kill for.

She parked her car behind the house in front of the small garage, which was full of tiles for the roof, planks, a table saw, tools, and a whole lot of junk.

"I'm sorry things aren't as..." Her voice trailed off as she tried to imagine how it all appeared to Mark. The plants and landscaping had taken over the yard like they'd won the roundup and the cowboys had been evicted. She winced. "I haven't got much of a green thumb."

He shrugged. "Cleaning up the landscaping won't take long, a day or two. It's the roof we want to tackle first."

"The backup generator is at the top of my priority list, too." She took in a deep breath. "Okay, let's get your stuff in a bedroom so you can see the rest of the place."

He wasn't content to take a quick inspection—he knocked on the walls, inspected the ceilings, and stamped on the floors. They went through every room, all around the outside and circled the perimeter of the property.

"This is fantastic," he said, as they stood on the terrace, the ocean stretching out from the edges of the island to the horizon.

She blinked. The list of things to do was a long one. She should know, she'd written it. "Fantastic?"

He turned to her with an excited grin. "You're right, that was the wrong word. This is *awesome*. You can really do something with this place. Whatever you want."

She stared at him and said, "What have you been smoking?"

He laughed and punched her on the shoulder, which nearly knocked her to the ground. "Oops," he said, grabbing her around the waist and hauling her up against him.

Her hands landed on his chest, the muscles there hard and hot enough to scald. His scent teased her nose, drawing her in, making her want to taste. Strong arms held her close and her gaze rose to lock with eyes the color of the Caribbean Sea.

Adler's eyes had been brown.

Ice, cold and sharp, stabbed deep into her chest and she reared back.

Mark kept hold of her shoulders, but set her

carefully away a couple of steps, his voice a soothing balm on her wounds. "Sorry, didn't mean to knock you over."

Pulse pounding in her ears, breathing rapid and rough, she struggled to pull her frayed nerves together with little more than ghostly cobwebs of a woman who hadn't existed in a year. "I'm o-okay." It came out in a stutter.

He winced. "Really?"

She stared at him, the concern on his face turning his eyes and mouth sad. The invisible gash in her chest grew, the ice spidering out, making her arms and hands shake. "No." The word slipped through her lips. She really hadn't meant to say it, especially to this man, who'd come thousands of miles to help her.

"Hey," he said softly, drawing her toward him. "Hey, it's all right." His arms came around her. "It's okay for you to lean on a friend." One large hand cradled her head against his chest.

Through her tears she asked, "Are you my friend?"

His voice rumbled beneath her ear. "Yes."

She'd been so alone since Adler died—alone, adrift, and rudderless. No safe harbor. Could she trust a man who'd already broken her heart once?

She wrapped her arms around him and held on.

Minutes, or hours, later her tears finally dried up and she backed out of Mark's embrace. "Thanks for letting me get you all wet."

He glanced at his shirt and chuckled. "No problem. I'm not scared of a little saltwater."

"A useful quality, especially here."

He moved away to examine the roof. "Have

you had any storms since you arrived?"

Giving her a chance to pull herself together?

"A few rain showers, but no high winds." She wiped her face with the hem of her T-shirt.

He stared at it for another moment. "Roof or generator, which first?" When he transferred his gaze to her face, she realized he was waiting for her to answer.

"Roof. I've got all the supplies and I'm ready to go on it."

"Good."

"But first," Josie said, trying to follow Mark's lead and keep things casual. "Burgers and beer."

"Jo," he said with a huge grin. "You're talking my language."

It had taken them four days to finish the roof. Mark had spent the most time up there, but only after Josie had insisted on slathering him with sunblock.

Pure torture.

His muscles were taut and hard, yet supple. Her hands shook the first time she put the lotion on his naked back, but he never said a word. Her hands didn't shake the next day, but the rest of her did.

She'd forgotten how seductive stroking a man's body could be. How addicting. Warm skin over firm muscles drew her in, teasing her intimacy-starved body until it was all she could do to let him begin work every morning. Her body wasn't the only part of her starving for the comfort of a man. Her bruised and battered heart needed care and concern, and he provided it with effortless generosity.

He was familiar, a friend.

He'd also run from her five years ago when she'd wanted more than a physical relationship, and torn her heart out in the process.

Had he changed?

Had *she* changed?

The questions circling her brain were driving her crazy.

Luckily for her the roof was done, so her major temptation was more out of sight. Mark had moved on to repair the generator located in the lowest floor of the building. Not exactly a storm cellar, but also not a living space, either. The only thing she was certain of was that it was the oldest part of the house with heavy beams composing the walls and ceiling. The beams were dark, as if stained with pitch or oil. Between the beams was a primitive sort of cement made of local sand and crushed shells, or so the real-estate agent claimed.

The generator, which was large and heavy, had to be connected to the home's wiring manually and was used only if the solar power panels on one section of the roof were damaged or covered.

It hadn't been used in a year or two.

Mark had examined it, taking it apart before deciding he needed a few parts. He'd taken off to check a couple of shops that sold parts, electronics, and certified junk.

She'd decided to tackle some of the siding and even managed to replace a couple of planks before Mark returned, excited with his finds in town.

"I think I got this licked," he said to her. He held out some spark plugs, a wire brush, and some kind of cleaning oil. His smile was reminiscent of a little boy who'd discovered tadpoles in a pond and had scooped up a pail of them.

"You mean, the problem is…it's dirty?"

"I don't think that thing has been cleaned and the plugs changed since it was new."

"Wow, I hope it's that simple."

"I checked out some of the plumbing problems you're having in the upstairs bathrooms," he said, as if they'd done this a million times. He took the wire brush coated with a little cleaning oil to the spark plug connections on the generator. "Again, I think they're fairly simple fixes. A couple of upgrades on some of the pipes, especially the elbows, to copper. Right now some of it's copper and some is brass, and that is where the problems start."

"Will it be expensive to buy the new pipes?"

"It'll be a few bucks—copper isn't cheap—but you don't need too much of it, either, so…"

"Okay, okay." She walked the length of the tiny room and back again.

Mark watched her for a moment then went back to cleaning the generator. "What's going on in that head of yours?"

"What do you mean?"

"You're pacing." He glanced at her as he worked. "You've been a big ball of nerves ever since I got here."

That halted her in her tracks. "I have? I didn't mean to be. I'm worried about getting everything done and I have to watch costs."

"That's not what I'm talking about."

"Oh." She waited for him to continue, but he didn't. "What are you talking about?"

"Why buy this place? It's a long way from Boston."

She blew out a gust of air. "That's exactly why I bought it."

He stopped working to stare at her. "Have you gotten counseling?"

His question knocked all the air out of her lungs.

She had, but she'd only gone to see the counselor twice. Both times she'd ended up having a flashback followed by a panic attack.

"It didn't help," she finally said. "It only made things worse." Her face was wet. She wiped her hand across her cheeks. When had she started crying?

"Yeah," he said softly. "It can do that the first few times."

How did he know that? The expression on his face was one she'd never seen on him before. His eyes were dark and sunken, as if old with knowledge he didn't want. Knowledge that kept wounds festering long after they should have healed.

"What happened to you?"

He put down the brush and gestured toward the doorway. "Let's take a break. Go sit in the sun."

That was the best idea she'd heard in a long time.

They settled on the terrace above the pool. Josie got them both a beer, cold from the fridge.

Neither said anything for a long couple of minutes.

Mark sighed and stared out at the distant harbor. "So my ten-year anniversary at the firehouse was about four months ago."

"Congratulations."

He shrugged with a resignation he hadn't had five years ago. Back then, he was so excited and proud to be a firefighter. "Do you remember Drake? He and I joined at the same time."

"Yeah, you and he were thick as thieves when we…dated."

"Yeah," he said with a grin that came and went. "We got into some trouble, him and I." He turned to glance at Josie. "Did you know he got married? A couple of years ago, I stood with him. Her name is Sandra and she's a teacher. Anyway, we had a three-alarm about four months ago and Drake and I were on search and rescue. It was a run-down apartment building and we weren't sure if there were any people left inside."

He took a swig of beer and she noticed his hand shaking, though his voice was strong and even. "I found an elderly woman on the floor in the first-floor hallway. I was able to get her out and get her on oxygen. She revived quick. The paramedics took over and I turned around to see how Drake had made out. He wasn't there."

Mark's voice broke, but he kept talking. "I talked to the chief, who said Drake was late by seven minutes. I asked if I could go in and get him. He told me a team of two had already been sent in."

Josie watched as Mark clenched his beer can, denting the aluminum. She leaned forward and almost put her hand on his shoulder, but caught herself before she could do it. He was in the middle of something awful and any touch, any noise from her might very well trigger a startle reaction or panic attack.

Bitter experience had taught her that the strength of the reaction had nothing to do with the person trying to help and everything to do with something no one could predict.

How a person processed horror.

Everyone experienced trauma differently, dealt with it differently, and relived it differently. There was no scale or measurement that could be applied, or pill that could dull the pain for long. For anyone who suffered from post-traumatic stress disorder, the memories were often worse in some ways than the original trauma.

Stress responses in the moment of the event are automatic, usually fast and easy to regret. Much too easy. A person might have only seconds to react during the incident, but years to lament their actions, nonactions, words said, and decisions made.

Mark was reliving the nightmare inside his head, and the bad part hadn't happened yet.

"So I waited," he said, his voice rough. "And waited. The team came out, but…" His voice trailed off.

"No Drake," she finished for him.

"No, they had him. He was…" Mark's shoulders shook. "His oxygen tank was dented. The team had found him under some debris and had dragged him out. But he lost his gloves at some point and his hands were—"

"Burned," she whispered.

Mark's voice sounded shredded. "Destroyed. No hope for recovery." He stood and threw his beer can as hard as he could.

It splashed in the pool below, but she didn't give it a second thought. She was too busy staring at Mark as he lurched back, his shoulders and legs shaking. He spun and stumbled, and ended up on his knees in front of her.

She was ready for him, her arms open.

He didn't hesitate—put his head in her lap and wrapped himself around her.

He cried for longer than she expected, but eventually, he settled down, though he kept his head where it was and his arms around her.

"I hate it when people tell me it'll get easier as time goes by," she said to him in a soft voice that allowed no argument. "Or that I did everything I could and I shouldn't feel guilty. Or that I should feel lucky, grateful because it wasn't me." She stroked his hair. "Those people, I want to punch them in the mouth."

That startled a snorting laugh out of him.

"The ones I want to choke are the ones who think that a few months is plenty of time to make everything okay," she went on, "and that I'm being dramatic or high maintenance because I have a panic attack. They don't realize that the passing of time can make it worse instead of better."

"What triggers you the most?" He sounded like he'd been eating gravel.

"Sound, most definitely. You?"

"Smell. I'm a firefighter who can't stand to smell something burning."

"Inconvenient," she said as if it were a minor inconvenience, easily dealt with.

His body started shaking again and she

winced, thinking she'd triggered him again. Then he raised his head and she realized he was laughing.

Like a lunatic.

"You're the queen of understatement," he said, sitting back on the floor with his arms and legs out in front of him.

"Ha, you haven't heard nothin'. The first time I tried to go back to work a little kid slammed a bathroom door and scared the shit out of me so bad I, uh, shit my pants."

That made him roll around on the floor laughing. "The first time I tried to barbecue steaks after the fire, I threw up on the grill."

That made perfect sense to her. Still… "The poor grill."

He was laughing so hard now that tears were streaming down his face. "Not as bad as that time in college when Herbie Stubacker—the stinkiest guy I have ever met in my life—ate some kind of bean salad, and his farts after were chemical-weapon grade. It was so bad, when he let a really long one go, my buddy and I puked out the window." Mark was holding his stomach like it hurt, but that wasn't slowing down the laughter. "We were on the third floor."

"You didn't."

He nodded, laughing so hard he had to be having trouble breathing. "We did."

"Was anyone standing below you?"

He shrugged and she rolled her eyes at him. "That is the most ridiculous story you've ever told. And I'm never, *ever* serving you bean salad."

His laughter calmed a bit and he gazed at her like she was his favorite flavor of ice cream.

"Thanks. You have no idea how much I needed that."

"For what? Letting you tell me stories or laughing until your sides hurt?"

He grinned. "Yes."

"I think I needed to hear what you said, too. I've been alone since Adler died. Totally alone." She sucked in a deep breath and pointed an index finger at him. "But your sister is in trouble."

"Oh yeah?"

"Yeah. She set us up."

Mark's smile turned wicked in a heartbeat. "You think?"

She pressed her lips together. "You went along with it. Why?"

"I had to get out of Boston before I self-destructed. She came to see me last week and I must have looked terrible, because she got on my ass about not taking care of myself. I told her I didn't want to hear it. Then she mentioned you, this place, and the trouble you were having with it. She thinks you can get away with saying things to me that she can't." He got to his feet. "And she's right."

Her mouth dropped open. "So, what, I'm supposed to fix you or something?"

"Nope. You work on you and I'll work on me." He started walking away. "Speaking of work, I'd better get back to it." He disappeared into the house.

She stared blankly at the ocean and did a quick self-assessment.

New life on an island in the Caribbean. *Check.*

New house and B&B. *Check.*

Hot ex-boyfriend is now man-Friday. *Check.* Sanity. Checked out.

She dreamed of Adler dying and woke shaking in a cold sweat. A hot shower helped a little, but she felt sweaty before her coffee was ready. There was bacon and eggs in the fridge, but her stomach protested at the thought of food. Maybe some yard work would help calm her.

She stepped outside, glanced at the harbor, and realized why she was sweating already. There were deep, dark storm clouds rolling in, as if boiling up from the bottom of the ocean. The breeze was already stiff, but the question was how much worse was it going to get? There hadn't been anything worse than rain showers since she got here.

Should she board up the windows and cover the solar panels on the roof? Stock up on water and perishables? Send up a flare?

"Mark," she called out as she went back inside.

"Yeah?" His voice sounded sleep-rough from his room upstairs.

"Looks like a storm coming in," she told him. "I'm going to ask some of the locals how bad they think it might get, see if we have to batten down the hatches."

"Okay." She heard a thump on the floor above her. He'd gotten out of bed. "Coffee's hot," she said as she left, trotting down the stairs toward the shops at the bottom of the hill.

She didn't even have to ask anyone what they thought of the storm. Everyone was already closing and latching their storm shutters over windows and doors.

She stopped anyway to ask a few questions of Pirate Perry, a retired navy man who ran a gift shop/coffee bar. "Perry, how bad is it going to get? Should I worry about my solar panels? Buy extra water?"

"It's off season for a big one, but the clouds are telling a different story," he said, taking a look at them. "I'd plan for four or five days of water and food. Probably without power." He frowned at her. "Is your generator working yet?"

"Mark was sure he found the problem. Something about no maintenance and spark plugs."

"Come see me if yours isn't working. I have a backup to the backup generator I could loan you. Tell that army man of yours to knock on the back door."

Josie started back to her place. "He's a fireman, Perry, not military," she called out over her shoulder.

"I like him better already," Perry yelled back.

When she got back to The Pirate's Cay, Mark was nowhere in sight and didn't respond when she called his name, so she grabbed her purse and drove over to the grocery store. Lots of people were there stocking up on the same essentials she wanted: drinking water, canned food, bread, matches, candles, and beer. Thankfully, no one was being greedy—people weren't taking more than they could use. Obviously these people had weathered storms like this before. She threw beer in her cart because they had to have something to look forward to.

Then added a bottle of whiskey for good measure.

When she got home, Mark was just walking up to the back door with a gas can in one hand and a case of bottled water in the other.

"You got the generator going?" she asked.

"Yes, ma'am. I filled it with gas, which pretty much emptied the can, so I figured I'd better fill it. Grabbed some extra water, too."

"I've water and some other essentials in the trunk." She angled her thumb at it.

"Good job, Jo. I'll be back to help unload in a sec."

Josie started with the food, leaving it in the kitchen. By the time she got back to the car, Mark was there and had the rest in hand.

"I'm going to start closing shutters," she told him.

"I'm right behind you." His conspiratorial grin gave her an extra boost of energy.

She headed toward the front of the house, which was taking the brunt of the wind, excitement making her feel like she could run a marathon every day for the next week. She and Mark were working like a well-oiled team, anticipating what the other needed, jumping in to help without having to ask.

Just like when she and Adler…

Grief and guilt gutted her, and she came to a stumbling stop.

How could she be comparing her relationship with Mark to the one she'd had with Adler? Mark didn't love her. Still didn't, not in the way she wanted.

Guilt stabbed her again.

She couldn't breathe and didn't want to.

Didn't want to ever forget why she was here in the first place.

The wind rattled the windows.

She made herself move, continue the job she'd given herself. The first shutter weighed far more than it should have. The second wasn't quite as difficult and the third seemed almost easy. By that time Mark had joined her and they worked to finish closing all the shutters around the house.

He kept looking at her out of the corner of his eye, as if he knew something was wrong, but he didn't say anything, just kept working.

The wind was really picking up, throwing plant debris and garbage around.

"Why don't you go inside?" he said in a careful tone that told her he noticed her attitude had changed. "There's only two left."

"Okay." She didn't look at him, just walked into the house.

The kitchen was a disaster. She began putting the food and water away with all the enthusiasm of a zombie chowing down at a salad bar.

The moment Mark walked in the room the temperature went up until she felt like she was swimming through pea soup.

He grabbed half of the water and took it down to the cellar. Before he left to close the last of the shutters he asked, "This is going to sound like a dumb question, but do you have a first-aid kit?"

She had to think about it. "I brought my mission kit, so yeah."

"Mission kit?"

"It's…comprehensive. I'll show you when

you get back."

She heard him leave the room and sagged in relief. There was another storm blowing in, but this one wasn't outside.

Mark's heavier footsteps warned her he'd returned.

"It's a ghost town out there."

"Is it raining yet?" she asked, happy to have something as innocuous as the weather to talk about.

"Nope, but it's only a matter of time."

She filled her kettle with water and turned it on. "Tea?"

"No, thanks." He stood staring at her with one eyebrow raised, asking a question without asking a question.

"I'll show you my mission kit." She headed upstairs to one of the guest rooms then waved her hand at the pile of stuff in the middle of the room. "So, this is it."

He took in the collection of cases and bags on the floor. "Holy shit."

She winced. "Too much?"

"You could open your own ER with all this stuff."

That made her laugh, but it was a poor effort.

"What's what?" he asked.

"The big one with the wheels is a go-anywhere mass-casualty trauma station. The two backpacks are smaller, more portable versions of the trauma station. They even have flexible stretchers. The hard cases contain surgical supplies, bags of saline for IVs, a handheld blood analyzer, extra splints, bandages, and blah, blah, blah."

His gaze was steady on her face. "Blah, blah, blah, huh?"

"I know I brought too much, but where most women pack clothes and beauty products, I pack suture sets and splints."

"You're blaming this overkill of medical supplies on habit?"

"Hey." She punched him on the shoulder. "I was going to donate some of it to the local hospital or one of the clinics, but I haven't gotten around to it yet."

"Yeah, right." He danced out of range of her second punch while making a big show of rubbing his shoulder.

Ha. Like she hurt him at all. He was solid muscle. "I suppose you'd be happier if it were beer?"

"I'm a guy, that goes without saying." He was trying to be funny.

She'd lost all her funny a few minutes ago. "Time for tea," she said, leaving the room.

With the windows shuttered, the house seemed dark and smaller. She flipped on the overhead light in the kitchen and made tea. When she turned around, Mark was seated at the kitchen table with an open beer in front of him.

"Got any idea how long the storm is going to last?" he asked.

"Not a clue." She joined him at the table, shivering in the cool, damp air.

The silence was broken by the howl of the wind and lash of the rain echoing through the house. The air pressed down on her diaphragm like a too-heavy blanket and she had to force herself not to panic, to take in deep, even breaths.

"Can you imagine what it would have been like to be at sea in a storm like this?" Mark leaned forward as he asked the question, his face alight with curiosity.

"I get motion sickness," she said, focusing on his voice. "So I'm sure I know what I'd be doing."

Mark's expression turned thoughtful. "Those old sailing ships didn't have GPS or motors or radios."

"They also didn't have modern medicine, microwaves, or hot tubs."

"No hot tubs?" he asked with mock disdain. "That's it, no pirate's life for me."

She grinned. "Pansy."

"I'm a modern, fully evolved man, and I'm proud of it," he said with a nod.

"No man is fully evolved. As a gender you have a *lot* of evolving to do yet."

"Hey, I haven't once complained about breaking a nail."

She rolled her eyes.

He smiled at her, took a swig of beer then said, "It's good to have you back, Jo."

"Back? Where did I go?"

"I don't know. Back *there*. For me it was that damn apartment fire. I don't know where your personal hell is located."

A damp, cold frost settled over her, crawling down her body until it covered her entirely. Her stomach rolled and for a moment she thought she might throw up, but she took a sip of tea instead, and the warm liquid did a lot to calm her. She drank some more, small sips, with both hands wrapped around the mug.

"Syria. That's where my hell is."

Mark's jaw clenched. "I've wondered…"

He didn't finish his question, so she finished it for him. "Adler died? Yes."

"That much I knew." Mark was silent for a minute, then two. When he finally spoke again it was to ask, "Why did you go there in the first place?"

"A lot of noncombatants were being killed and injured. We were part of a large medical team to help the civilian population. We were supposed to be in a section of the country where there was no fighting, and there wasn't for the first two weeks. But that changed."

"Dangerous place," he said in a tone that was so even she knew he was bothered by it. "How did you get out?"

"American military. I have no idea what branch. I don't remember much after… Not the color of their uniforms or any of their faces." She swallowed hard, but her throat was so tight she thought she might choke. "Anyway, they got us out and home."

"How many people in your team?"

"Twenty-five."

There was another long silence.

Mark's voice was a rumble over the storm. "Benita said you quit your job. I had a hard time believing that."

"It was surprisingly easy."

"You were so passionate about working in the ER," he said, angling his head to one side as if he didn't understand her at all. "I've seen you face down drunks, drug addicts, and the damn near dead and not flinch. You have a gift for dealing with trauma cases, knowing when there was more wrong than what immediately presented."

"I *had* a gift." It still hurt her deep inside to admit she was terrified to step foot in a hospital again. "Watching violent death happen puts everything in a different perspective." She could hear the bitterness in her voice, but couldn't stop it, couldn't hide it.

"So this is your place of healing?"

She opened her mouth to tell him healing from the wound caused by Alder's death would never happen, but shut it before she could say anything.

Was coming here, fixing up The Pirate's Cay, and running a busy B&B her form of therapy? "I don't know," she finally said. "I didn't think about it like that. I just wanted something completely different from Boston."

"Well, if you've got to pick a place to do a little soul-searching and heart-healing, the Caribbean is easy on the eyes."

She gazed at his long legs stretched out in front of him as he leaned back, his T-shirt molded to his muscled arms and shoulders. He could say that again, especially since she was looking at him.

A few minutes later, Mark finished his beer then told her he was going to play with the plumbing.

Josie decided that the perfect job to keep her mind off Mark, Adler, and anything else confusing was cleaning bathrooms and got to work.

They took a break for supper—pasta and a salad. When she finished with the bathrooms, she started on the kitchen, determined to make the place shine. By the time she tumbled into bed, she was good and tired. Too tired to do more than wish Mark a mumbled good-night.

The screaming started two hours later.

Sleep didn't come quick. The sounds of the storm, howling wind, driving rain, and the rattle of trees hitting the side of the house reminded her of Syria, of the day Adler died. But after a while, she realized the storm had a pace that didn't match the hail of bullets that killed her husband. There was a rise and fall to the noise that transformed it into a full philharmonic performance.

There hadn't been music the day Adler died. It was hot and dry, the wind a sigh, until the gunfire started. Bullets pinged like hail against glass and metal all around. People yelled and shouted, some to warn, others because they'd been struck.

Someone shoved her to the ground. The cinder blocks behind her were better than armor. She called for Adler. Screamed his name over and over.

There.

He was running toward her, gesturing for her to stay where she was. Stay safe.

Another wave of bullets rained down, sending clots of dust into the air. Adler collapsed like a marionette whose strings had been cut mid-performance, his torso twisted, arms and legs splayed awkwardly.

She surged up, tried to run to him, but someone held her down, telling her she couldn't go. She watched his blood soak into the ground beneath him until there was nothing left.

Adler was dead. Dead.

She fought harder, screaming her rage and disbelief.

Hard arms wrapped around her. A man's voice called her name. Not Adler's voice, but it was a voice she trusted.

She stopped fighting to listen.

"—up. Josie, wake up!"

"Mark?" She wasn't in Syria. She was on an island in the Caribbean. There was a storm outside—rain, not bullets. Adler wasn't lying dead on the ground. He'd been buried for a year.

"God, Josie." He breathed out a huge breath. "You scared the shit out of me." He hugged her hard.

She wrapped her arms around him and breathed in his warm, musky scent. "I'm sorry."

He didn't relax a muscle. "Nightmare?"

"Yeah." Her hands clutched him tighter. "I was back there. Reliving the whole horrible—"

"We're lucky there's a storm outside or the neighbors would be calling the police."

"I wasn't just screaming in the dream?"

He rocked her back and forth. "You were yelling at the top of your lungs."

"What did I yell?"

"The only thing that made sense was your husband's name."

"Damn. I'm sorry."

"Hey." He pulled back to meet her gaze. "Don't apologize. You've got nothing to apologize for. It was the worst day of your life. Having a nightmare about it is *normal*."

She missed the warmth of his body and realized he was shirtless and wearing only a pair of boxers. "You sound like a therapist."

"I—" he intoned with great dignity, "—am the voice of reason."

A snort escaped her before she could grab it.

"Are you laughing at me?" His tone sounded incredulous.

"I would never," she replied, not quite able to keep the grin off her face.

He grinned back. "I believe you'd roll around on the floor laughing if you had only a sliver of a chance."

She shrugged.

The window rattling startled her and she pressed against him, her heart rate accelerating along with her fear.

"Whoa, I've got you," he said, smoothing one hand down her back.

"I'm so tired of being afraid," she whispered.

"Me, too. If I have to keep carrying barf bags with me when I go out on a call, I'm going to get some funny looks from the rest of the guys."

She tried to hide her smile, but wasn't too successful. Snuggling a bit closer, she put her head on his chest. His heartbeat thrummed, its tempo rising.

Then she realized that not only was he mostly naked, he was also very happy to see her. He would want to leave. She could tell by his tense muscles and hands that tried to slide her off him. She was hanging on to the here and now by the very tips of her fingers.

"Hey," Mark whispered into her hair. "I'd better get back to my own bed."

She had to convince him to stay. She took a deep breath and said, "Is there something wrong with mine?"

He cleared his throat. "No, but…shit." He squeezed her then pulled away.

She didn't even try to cooperate.

"Josie—" He tried to remove her arms from around him.

She gripped him tighter. "What?"

"I need to leave." He sounded like he was choking on the words.

The thought of being alone sent a shiver through her. "Why?"

"Because if I don't I'm probably going to do something I can't take back."

She buried her face in his neck. "I need…I need someone to hold me. Please, at least for a little while."

"Damn it." He groaned. "You're killing me, you know that, don't you?"

"Yes. No. Maybe this is payback for showing up at the airport instead of Benita."

"Hey, I had nothing to do with that stunt. I thought you knew I was coming." Mark lay down next to her and pulled her across his chest. "Come here."

Thank God. He was staying.

She snuggled close.

He petted her, running his hand over her hair. His voice was a deep rumble beneath her ear when he said, "I want to kiss you."

Every muscle in her body went on alert. No. Oh no. Bad idea. Very bad. "Why?"

"It's stupid."

Curiosity had her head off his chest and her

gaze searching his face.

He was ready for her. Palming the back of her head with one hand and tilting her chin up with the other.

His lips were on hers, and he was kissing her like a marauding pirate, giving no quarter, no respite, and no escape.

She didn't want to escape.

Fright transformed into a heat that fired up the pit of her belly and spread out to warm the rest of her body. For the first time in a year, she wanted someone. Wanted Mark.

She pulled away, and he let her. They stared at each other, panting.

"Did you..." She stuttered to a stop then tried again. "Did you find the *stupidity* you were searching for?"

"Oh yeah. I discovered I'm really, *really* stupid."

A surprised laugh bubbled out of her. She slapped a hand over her mouth. "That's not funny. It isn't. Not at all."

He groaned. "I'm a complete moron."

He was not making it easy to keep a straight face. "Why do you say that?"

"Because I want you. Bad, in case you hadn't noticed."

"I may have noticed, um, some evidence of that..." She glanced at his groin and the tent his erection was making under the blankets.

"Exactly. So what do I do? I kiss you to find out if it's as good as I remember." He stopped talking.

"And?"

"It's better."

"Oh." What was she supposed to say to that? She hadn't started things. Oh, wait, yes she had. She'd screamed and then begged him to stay with her. "Do you want to go?"

He snorted and adjusted himself. "No." Then he gathered her up so her head was over his heart. "Go to sleep."

She listened to his heart beating. Its lullaby was the most beautiful thing she'd heard in a very long time.

Josie woke slowly and found herself tucked into Mark's arms with him spooned behind her.

She let herself just be for a while. When was the last time she had done that? Years? Mark's scent filled her nose, his taste was on her tongue and his heat wrapped around her. She could have stayed there for hours.

"You awake?" His voice was a rumble she felt all over her body.

"Maybe."

He kissed the back of her neck. "I bet I could wake you up."

"I know you could, but I'm comfortable right now."

Her stomach growled. Then so did his.

They looked at each other and started laughing.

"I need to use the washroom," she said, propping herself up on her elbows. "Maybe a shower."

"I'll start breakfast." Mark bounded out of bed. He was about to leave the room when he stopped and turned to face her. "Are we…okay?"

She'd slept, really slept for the first time in forever. "Yeah, we're good."

He winked and went down the stairs.

She turned the bathroom light on, but nothing happened. She moved to the doorway to shout at Mark, but he beat her to it.

"Power's out," he hollered. "I'm going to start the generator. You might want to wait on that shower."

"Okay, thanks."

The lights came on a minute or two later and she gave herself a sponge bath with a soapy washcloth.

Josie chose a pair of khaki shorts and a short-sleeve top to wear. If the power was out, there could be damage to parts of the island or the surrounding islands, and the people on them. She might not have admitting privileges at the hospital, but she'd worked a few shifts here and there to cover for an absent doctor, seeing nothing worse than a broken bone or two.

Could be worse after this storm.

The storm blew out by late afternoon, but it had left its mark on the island.

Debris littered the veranda and pool. The power was still out and Mark reported a few people visible on the roads or walking around when he checked the roof. He'd gotten up there as soon as the rain started to taper off, and was very happy with himself when he discovered no damage.

Other people weren't as lucky.

As soon as the rain ended someone pounded

on her door. It was a neighbor who'd cut his hand while trying to repair his own roof.

Josie took a quick look at it. "This is going to need stitches, Larry. Come in."

"I went to the hospital first, but the lineup of people waiting to be seen is down the street."

"It's okay," she said as she led him to the kitchen table, then hollered in the general direction of the veranda, "Mark, we've got customers."

He came trotting in a few seconds later. "Customers?" As soon as he saw Larry, he came to a stop. "How much of that gear do you want down here?"

"Bring the mobile trauma unit and a couple of the backpacks."

"Gotcha."

He was back with it all in a minute or two.

Josie opened the trauma unit and pulled out a suture kit and some lidocaine. "This won't take long, Larry, but you're going to have to stay off your roof for a while." She turned to Mark. "Can you let the hospital know I'm on my way over in about fifteen minutes?"

He nodded and grabbed a cell phone, but glanced at her and shook his head a few moments later. "No reception. The storm must have damaged a cell tower or something."

"Damn it."

"It'll be faster if I go over and tell them," Mark said. "If you're willing to do this kind of stuff…" He nodded at Larry's hand. "…they might be fine with you staying and working out of The Pirate's Cay."

Did she want to work in a busy ER or her

own kitchen? "Yeah, I think I'd rather stay here. Having a satellite location might be useful."

Mark gave her a quick grin, and a kiss on the lips, then he was off.

Larry smirked. "I bet it would take him *two* weeks. I owe my brother some money."

Josie narrowed her eyes. "Larry, I'm a woman with a sharp needle in her hand. Now is not a good time to piss me off."

He wiped the smile off his face, but the humor was still in his voice as he said, "Yes, ma'am."

She finished with Larry and sent him on his way, then got things ready for her next patients. Either Larry or the hospital was going to send a few her way.

Four arrived at almost the same time.

One with Mark, an older lady Josie didn't know, who'd likely broken her arm.

"No power for the X-ray machine?" Josie asked when Mark explained that the triage nurse wasn't certain the woman had broken her arm.

"Yeah," he replied with a shrug.

Josie examined the woman's forearm. A pronounced bump rose from a spot about two inches up from her wrist. "Looks like a simple break to me. Let's get it splinted for now. You can have an X-ray to determine how bad or good it is when the power is back on." She glanced at Mark. "Can you triage people as they arrive?"

"Absolutely. I'm also a certified paramedic, so I'm at your disposal for whatever you need." He headed toward the front door where the three other walk-ins were waiting.

Silence from Josie's patient reigned for two

whole seconds, then she said, "I'll take him if you don't want him."

"He's my fireman," Josie told her, letting her declaration settle over her. It felt right. "Get your own."

Three lacerations, two broken arms, and a concussion later, Mark brought her a cup of hot coffee and a sandwich instead of another patient.

"Eat now while you have a chance."

"Anyone waiting to see me now?"

"Yes, but you won't do anyone any good if you pass out because your blood sugar bottomed out."

She rolled her eyes. "Yes, mother." She ate her sandwich quickly and gulped down the coffee.

A half dozen people were seated outside on the veranda, waiting to be seen. She asked names and problems and put them in order of need and was about to stitch up another deep laceration in a tourist's leg when the yelling started.

"Girlie! Doctor Girlie, are you here?" A handsome man who looked like he should have been recruiting for the navy tromped onto the veranda.

"I'm right here, Captain Jack," Josie said. "What do you need?"

"A doctor."

"For what?"

"We need some first-aid supplies and a pair of hands who know how to use them on the island."

"What kind of injuries?"

"A couple of people got cut up pretty bad and one guy broke his hand."

"I can go," Mark offered.

Did she want him to? People were injured. Could she say no?

Her stomach wound around itself until it hurt and her breathing became so painful it was all she could do to take one more breath.

"You can't have him for long," she told Jack. "Grab one of the backpacks and come back as soon as you can," she said to Mark.

He nodded. "Can I have a minute before I take off?"

She followed him into the house and up the stairs to one of the bedrooms. "Is something wrong?"

He turned to face her. "I'm coming back."

"You darn well better. I need you here."

He sighed. "That's not what I mean."

"I don't—"

He took her by the shoulders, interrupting her. "I'm coming back, not shot. Not hurt. Do you understand?"

"I never thought—"

"I can see it in your eyes." Mark's voice was a low rumble. "The worry, the fear. You've been having flashbacks since Larry showed up." Mark bent until he was nose to nose with her. "I'm fine and I'm going to stay that way."

She should have known he, of all people, would understand. "I can't stop it." She rubbed her forehead. "I can't shut it off, and I don't know how long I can keep it together before I break."

"I know something that will help, at least for a little while."

"What's that?"

"This." He kissed her, gently for the first two seconds, then he groaned, yanked her up against him, and plundered her mouth. Desire and need burned through the chill haze of memory that had her in its grasp, wiping it from her mind. All she knew was Mark's taste, scent, and the firmness of his muscles under her hands.

He pulled away to stare into her eyes. "When I get back, we're going to finish this *conversation*." He leaned down to whisper in her ear, "It might take a couple of days."

A shiver went through her. "You don't pull your punches, do you?"

"No." His gaze was as steady as the Rock of Gibraltar. "I know what I want."

She took in a deep, shaky breath. He hadn't known before, when he left her all those years ago. "Okay."

One of his eyebrows rose.

"Okay," she said, putting some steel into her voice.

"Don't forget," he said when she would have turned to leave.

She snorted. "I won't. That kiss damn near caused me to have a seizure. You should come with a warning label."

His grin was all kinds of bad. "Where would be the fun in that?"

Shaking her head, she led the way downstairs and watched as Mark grabbed one of the backpacks and followed Captain Jack out of the house.

Josie went back to work, but kept watching for his return.

He wasn't gone five minutes and she missed him already.

A steady stream of people needing medical

care flowed through the house, most of them locals, but a few were tourists who were staying at other B&Bs close by. Every single one of them asked why she was opening a B&B when she was an experienced trauma doctor.

She told them she got tired of seeing death.

Most of the locals also asked about Mark. The women wanted his cell phone number or wanted to leave their cell phone numbers. The men wanted to know if he was a full-time roofer and was he interested in a little work on the side.

She told them not until The Pirate's Cay was finished.

She closed the door on the last patient at about 10:00 p.m.

Cleaning up took a little while, maybe an hour, then the only thing she was left with for company was the wind and the sigh of palm trees.

The stack of first-aid cases she'd shoved to one side of the kitchen drew her attention despite her efforts to not look at them at all.

The memory of Adler laughing at something she'd said while packing those cases over a year ago taunted her. She caught her breath, bracing herself for the rest of the flashback, but the feel of Mark's lips on hers pushed it out of focus.

Trembling, she turned away, climbed the stairs, and went into her bathroom. Sweat had dried on her skin, but it felt like desert sand. Washing it off was the only way she had to break the cycle of memories trying to pull her under.

Mark's kiss was another, but he wasn't here. Not yet.

Water, steam, and soap washed her clean, but her stubborn mind wouldn't let go of the memory spiral.

Mark's voice calling her name gave her a lifeline. It took her a moment to realize it wasn't a figment of her imagination, but real, in the here and now.

She shut off the water and called out, "I'm in the shower."

Footfalls on the stairs had her stumbling out of the shower and drying herself off as fast as she could.

He was in her room now, his footsteps approaching the bathroom door. She wrapped a towel around her body. The door opened and she launched herself at him.

"Josie, are you— Oomph." He rocked back on his feet as she glommed on to him, burying her nose against his shirt to breathe in his scent and the scent of the sea.

His arms came around her, enveloping her in their warm strength. "Are you okay?"

"Yes. No." She leaned back and tried to pull his head down. "I need your kiss."

His lips were on hers and she dropped every shield, every barrier and took him inside where he could fight the desert demons of her own thoughts.

His groan mirrored her own as he kissed her like she was more necessary than breathing. One of his hands landed on her ass where the towel had rode up. Those fingers clenched on her, tugging her against him.

He pulled his head back. "Josie," he said, breathing heavily. "Slow down."

"Don't want to go slow."

"Babe, we need to talk for a minute."

She was breathing so hard she could barely talk. "Why?"

"Because you're dressed in almost nothing, you look like a wet dream, I'm hard as a rock, and we're about to do something neither of us can take back."

"I need you, your kiss. You promised."

"I did and I'm yours," he growled. "But I want all of you in return."

She looked up at him. The veneer of safe male was gone, leaving a pirate in his place with wild eyes and a wicked grin, and she made her decision. "Are you afraid of me?"

He swallowed hard. "You're the most dangerous woman I know."

"You're the most dangerous man I know, but I want you to stay."

His eyebrows went up. "Yeah?"

"Yeah." She stroked one index finger from his neck down his chest. "I'm tired of being afraid of myself, tired of feeling alone, tired of feeling sad."

"You're playing with fire." His voice rumbled out of his chest. "Be sure, Josie. I don't want you to regret this in the morning or any day after."

"I'm touch starved and you're the only man alive I trust enough to…" She caught her breath. Had she said too much? Would he run away if he realized how badly she needed him? He'd run before.

"To what?" he prompted as he took her hand and guided it down to the waistband of his jeans.

She undid the button and slid down the zipper. He wasn't running. At least not yet. "To burn away my tattered edges, to release the real me from the prison I put myself in. I've felt nothing but grief for the past year. I'll kill myself if I keep going on like this." She slung one hand around his neck and stretched up until she was almost kissing him. She hooked fingers into his underwear, pulled the top back, and slid her hand inside to stroke his cock. "Free me," she whispered against his lips.

Would he run now or take what she was offering?

He groaned and exploded into action, jerking her close and kissing her like she was his only source of oxygen.

Sensation washed over her, chasing the chill of despair away, heating her blood until she thought she might set them both on fire.

His hands held her close with a strength that should have frightened her, but made her feel safe instead. One of those big hands moved from her back to her torso to cup a breast and she moaned as he flicked his thumb over her nipple.

Hungry lips moved from her mouth, down her neck, to her collarbone and into the valley between her breasts. He pulled back long enough to snatch at the towel she was wearing and throw it aside.

He caught her, his hands spanning her rib cage just below her breasts. He stared at them for a long moment, then his gaze moved up to meet her own. "I love your breasts."

Breathing was optional, wasn't it? "I remember."

He laid her out on the bed very carefully. Then he looked her over, from her toes to the tips of her hair. "Fucking gorgeous." He ran his hands over her as if he were a blind man relearning her body all over again.

"Mark?"

"Darlin'?"

"You're going too slow."

He grinned and started taking his clothes off. "Really? Are you sure? 'Cause slow can be a lot of fun."

His shirt hit the floor. His muscles were more defined than she remembered. She licked her lips. "I've decided fast has its place."

"What place would that be?" His jeans and underwear were next.

His cock, as large as the rest of him, drew her hands like a magnet. "The one where I get to enjoy multiple orgasms."

Laughing, he joined her on the bed, grabbed her wrists, and planted them on either side of her head while he kissed and nipped at her bottom lip, her chin, neck, and breast. When he got to her nipple he paused to play, sucking, nipping, and sucking again, until she arched under him. Every touch drove her higher, wound her tighter, until all she could do was shake.

"I want to touch you," she managed to say, her voice quivering as he caught both wrists in one grip and sent his other hand down to stroke into her heated core.

"You can touch me...later. After the first three or four... God, you're slick. And hot." His breathing became erratic.

He leaned away to grab something out of his pants. A condom. He put it on then came back to her, his hands tormenting her again.

She twisted against him, trying to find what she needed, but what she needed was more. "Mark, stop teasing me. I need…" She paused, the words drying up in her throat as he pressed his cock at the entrance to her body and pushed inside. "That," she moaned. "That's what I need."

He paused after he'd seated himself inside her. "Fuck."

"Yes, please," she replied and deliberately tightened the muscles surrounding him.

"God damn, I like it when you talk dirty," he told her as he pulled out and stroked in, setting a relentless pace that had her orgasm hovering for what felt like forever.

"Please," she begged. "Faster."

He groaned. "You're killing me, Josie."

"I'm going to if you don't—" The words died in her throat as he stepped up the pace, giving her what she needed, and her orgasm rolled over her.

Gasping, tears rolling down her face and shaking, she held on to him. When his own orgasm overtook him, holding him rigid above her, his head thrown back, she found herself fascinated and hungry for him all over again.

He sank down to kiss her languidly, like he had all the time in the world.

She kissed him back, not knowing how long the calm inside her was going to last.

Morning arrived with pounding on the front door.

Josie cracked one eye open and glanced at her watch. 6:00 a.m. Nope, she wasn't getting up. If it was an emergency, the police could blare their siren. Then she'd get up.

The pounding continued.

Mark swore as he rolled out of bed and landed on the floor with a thump. Josie heard some scuffles, more swearing, then he stood up wearing only his jeans and stomped down the stairs.

A few seconds later she heard him yell, "What?"

Masculine voices rumbled, but not loud enough for her to make out individual words, but if Mark was actually talking to whoever was at the door, that someone was probably going to insist on her getting out of bed.

She went to the bathroom and brushed her teeth. When she came out, Mark was waiting for her.

"Who was that?" she asked.

"Someone from the hospital," he said in a cautious tone. "They're asking if you'll work in the ER today."

"They run out of doctors?"

"No. They have too many patients."

The worst medical case she'd seen on the two shifts she'd worked at the St. Thomas hospital was sunstroke in a two-year-old. Today would be more of yesterday, times ten.

"I barely held myself together yesterday. The only thing that kept me from falling apart was your…" She caught herself. Dare she finish the sentence? Confess how much she needed him?

"My…what?"

She stared into his eyes, watching for a reaction to her next word. "Kiss." She shrugged. "You were right. The tactile memory kept me from imploding."

"That was here, in your home," he said, meeting her gaze. "Where you feel relatively safe."

He was right again. She did feel safe here, and yet the PTSD almost knocked her to her knees yesterday.

"I can't do it. There are too many triggers at the hospital."

"That's what I told the guy waiting downstairs," Mark said with a short nod. "So I asked about the older people on the island. The ones who need a medical check, but aren't mobile enough to get to the hospital without assistance. He said they can't spare anyone to check on the homebound." Mark let that sink in for a second then asked, "What do you think, Jo, want to offer to do some house calls? I can be your man-Friday."

"You're already my man-Friday, and I think it's a brilliant idea. Let's do it."

Clothes. She needed clothes, something that said both professional and island. She settled on a pair of khaki pants with way too many pockets and another short-sleeved collared shirt, also with pockets.

"We've got to get the hospital on board with the idea first."

"Somehow I don't think it's going to take a lot of convincing to allow a doctor to take care of patients in their homes instead of those people overtaxing emergency responders who are already too busy. We've got all the medical supplies we should need downstairs. A quick restock and we can be ready to go." She pulled on socks and found her hiking shoes in the closet. Right about then, she realized Mark was still in his jeans and nothing else. "What?"

There was a small smile on his face. "I love you."

The shoe tumbled out of her hands.

Mark strode close and knelt in front of her. He took her hands in his and that's when she realized her hands were shaking. "It's okay," he said softly. "No pressure, I promise. I just want you to know where I stand."

"But you..." she began. "You've only been here a week, you can't possibly..."

"I never stopped."

"Stopped?"

"Loving you. I never stopped." He shook his head. "I was an idiot for telling you I wasn't ready to settle down five years ago. By the time I realized I loved you, really-deeply-for-the-rest-of-my-life loved you, it was too late. You'd met Adler and he'd given you the commitment you needed."

Her mouth was open, but she couldn't speak.

"I won't leave here without being completely convinced you don't love me back," he told her. "Captain Jack gave me a few pointers on how to be a good pirate yesterday." He leaned forward until his forehead rested against hers and whispered, "I plan on stealing your heart."

She freed one hand so she could cup his face and run her thumb over his bottom lip. "You already did, you damn pirate. I love you."

He kissed her, heaved a huge sigh then got to his feet and pulled her to hers. "All right then, girlie, time to get to work. This ain't no vacation."

"Excuse me, mate," Josie told him with her hands on her hips. "But I be captain of this ship. I'm the one giving orders."

"Right you are, sir," Mark said, slipping his arms around her. "And what would your orders be?"

"Kiss me *then* we'll get to work."

"Aye, sir. Vacation first it is then."

"It's a kiss," she said, laughing. "A minute or two is *not* a vacation."

He leaned down to whisper against her lips, "It is if you do it right."

About…

Julie Rowe's first career as a medical lab technologist in Canada took her to the Northwest Territories and northern Alberta, where she still resides. She loves to include medical details in her romance novels, but admits she'll never be able to write about all her medical experiences because, "No one would believe them!" In addition to writing contemporary and historical medical romance, and fun romantic suspense for Entangled Publishing and Carina Press, Julie has a short story in *The Mammoth Book of ER Romance* (September 2013). Her book *Saving the Rifleman* (book one of the War Girls series) won the novella category of the 2013 Gayle Wilson Award of Excellence. Her writing has also appeared in several magazines such as *Today's Parent, Reader's Digest* (Canada), *Canadian Living,* and *Romantic Times Magazine.*

For more information about Julie, please visit her online at www.julieroweauthor.com, on Twitter @julieroweauthor, or at her Facebook page: www.facebook.com/JulieRoweAuthor.

Interested in reading more medical romance and adventure? Check out Julie's published backlist of books!

❧

Julie's War Girls series is set in German-occupied Belgium during World War One. Discover danger, daring, and passion with three nurses who risk their lives to save the men they call their own.

Saving the Rifleman - John and Maria's story.
Enticing the Spymaster - Michael and Jude's story.
Aiding the Enemy - Herman and Rose's story.

❧

For contemporary stories of adventure and romance set at the top and the bottom of the world, look for *Icebound* and *North of Heartbreak* at your favorite ebook retailer.

Enjoy more Timeless Tales by

Ruth A. Casie ~ Lita Harris ~ Emma Kaye ~
Nicole S. Patrick ~ Julie Rowe

Available Now

Timeless Keepsakes
A Collection of Christmas Stories

*Join us on five remarkable journeys that heal old
wounds, remind us of days gone by, play
matchmaker, sweep us back in time and prove that
love can conquer all.*

Coming October 2014

Timeless Treasures
Stories of the Heart

*A special wish of hope, strength, and love brings
five couples what they treasure most in this
heartwarming collection of short stories.*

❧

To receive up-to-date information on future
Timeless Scribes publications, visit our website at
www.TimelessScribes.com and sign up for our
mailing list.

Timeless Scribes
Publishing

www.ingramcontent.com/pod-product-compliance
Lightning Source LLC
Chambersburg PA
CBHW071126200626
46817CB00018B/2322